To Mrs. Murphy

who always thought
I was a terrific
kid but never knew
I'd grow up to be
a writer!

Ratt Cos

5/4/10

ROBERT
COSMER

MUSSOLINI'S
MONEY

NEW CENTURY PUBLISHING

Library of Congress Cataloging-in-Publication Data
Cosmer, Robert
Mussolini's Money
by Robert Cosmer

ISBN   978-0-9824711-6-6

new century
PUBLISHING
1040 E. 86th Street, Suite 42A
Indianapolis, IN 46240

Dedication

Special thanks to all of those people that made this book possible. Thank you all for allowing me to live my dream.

Cynthia, thank you for saying "You really should." When I was walking through the bookstore saying I should write a novel.

Thank you Barbra Zimmermann Bogue, Associate Professor, Ball State University. I'm so happy you told me my writing was "crass" and to "just go" to Sicily. "That's what writers do. You are a writer."

Thank you Tracy Donhardt, Associate Professor, Indiana University Purdue University at Indianapolis. Doing the first reading of my novel and sorting through the train wreck was a monumental task.

Dan Fischer, New Century Publishing. Thank you for liking my manuscript and getting behind this project. You have good taste in writing.

David Caswell, New Century Publishing. Thank you for making my publishing experience pleasurable. I hope we can do this again soon.

Mom and Dad. Thanks for everything.

Table of Contents

Chapter One

Late May 1945, Italy–Switzerland border

The two young GIs were guarding some unknown road outside some unknown town in the heart of the Swiss Alps. Their orders were to disarm any German military personnel and allow them to pass. The war in Europe had been officially over for about a week. Hitler was dead, and the Nazis had surrendered.

"So where did you say you were for the last two years?" the younger replacement soldier asked.

"I was stationed in Palermo, Sicily. I was commanding a cannon unit that was hit by a tank round in the mountains outside the city. I was the only one injured. I took a piece of my own cannon to the back of my leg. No one else in my squad got a scratch. You should have seen the cannon. It was totally destroyed. With our gun disabled, we walked down the mountain to the access road to see if we could join up with the advancing forces. As we got to the road, guess who shows up?"

"Who was it?"

"General Patton."

"You're not serious. General Patton himself?"

"Old 'Blood and Guts' in the flesh, with his pearl handled .45s, took one look at my bloody bandaged leg and offered me a ride."

"Now you're pulling my leg."

"No, he ordered my squad into the back of a deuce and a half. We rode off in his jeep with the little flags that had the three stars on the front."

"Really?"

"Really. We talked all the way into town. Well, actually, he did most of the talking. He took the whole squad back to the palace where he was staying, inside the city of Palermo."

"You stayed in a palace with General Patton?"

"No, I went to the makeshift infirmary where they cut the shrapnel out of my leg. When I woke up the next day, the entire division had already moved out. General Patton was trying to beat Monty to Messina. Because I speak Italian, they ordered me to stay at the Villa Malfitano as a goodwill military liaison and assist the new Sicilian government any way that I could. I was the only U.S. military man in Palermo."

"What did you do all day?"

"I mostly dealt with the local government officials and the head of the dock workers. They just wanted to know when ships would be arriving and departing so they could get medical supplies and start trading fish and produce again."

"Were there many ships?"

"No. Only two in two years. There were still Kraut U-boats patrolling inside the Straits of Gibraltar all over the Mediterranean. The two ships that arrived, I didn't even know about them until they were in the harbor. The head of the dock workers let me know just before dawn both mornings. The ships sailed straight south out of Rome in the middle of the night when there was no moon…"

Just then an American military Jeep pulled up to the checkpoint carrying two soldiers. The G.I. that had been stationed in Sicily walked over to the Jeep. He immediately recognized the soldier driving the Jeep. It was one of the dock bosses from Palermo.

"What are you doing here in a soldier's uniform?" he asked in Italian. With that, the men in the Jeep both went for their guns.

"Open fire!" he yelled as he ducked and struggled to get his Thompson submachine gun off his shoulder. The man on the passenger side of the Jeep stood and fired at the soldier behind the sandbags. The young soldier standing behind the sandbags strafed the Jeep with rounds from his stationary 50-caliber machine gun.

It was all over in seconds. Both soldiers inside the Jeep were dead.

"All clear!" yelled the soldier now lying on the ground beside the Jeep looking down the barrel of his machine gun.

"What happened?" yelled the soldier behind the sandbags.

"I knew these men in Palermo. They're not soldiers. They're criminals from Sicily. They run the dock workers at the pier in Palermo."

"What are they doing all the way up here from southern Italy?"

"Let's find out."

The men walked around to the back of the Jeep to find two wooden ammunition crates in the back seat. The soldier who had been stationed in Sicily opened one of the crates.

"Holy shit," said the younger soldier. "Have you ever seen anything like that before?"

"No, I haven't."

Chapter Two

Oh, my God, was it awful. My head was pounding. I felt my pounding pulse in each of my temples. Each pulse felt like a sledgehammer to my brain. My hair follicles hollered in pain and I didn't even think there were any nerves in follicles. My eyelids hurt even though they were closed. I was a sweaty mess. My neck and back were twisted and contorted. The sun was beating down on my face and bare chest. I was thirsty and had the terrible taste of stale rum and cola in my mouth. As I licked my dry lips, I imagined how nice it would be to take my teeth and tongue out of my head and soak them in something. They needed a good cleaning. The sun was unseasonably hot and I must have been getting a very nice sunburn.

I could barely hear the sound of water lapping against my metal Jon boat. I had no recollection of what had happened; I had no memory of leaving the bar. But I knew what had happened: I had forgotten to charge the trolling motor battery in my boat as I forgot about once every summer, and this was that time. My face and chest itched terribly. I was covered in mosquito bites. Serves those little bastards right, I thought. I hope they all die from alcohol poisoning. I felt at that moment that I might die of alcohol poisoning. I was in bad shape.

I opened my eyes only to have my retinas burned by the hot and bright sun. I was struggling to focus. I wiped my face and eyes and knocked something warm and slimy off my face. Sitting upright only made the pain in my head worse. My legs were slung over the bench seat at the front of the boat and my shoulders were resting against the center bench seat.

I needed some water. I struggled to figure out where exactly I was. Obviously I was in my metal boat on Bear Lake in northwest Wisconsin. Where specifically on Bear Lake was unclear. My boat was up against a thick wall of tall reeds and cattails. There are no reeds or cattails near my home, or the bar for that matter.

I must have drifted to the south end of the lake. The wind must have been blowing from the northwest last night. That meant that there would be an arctic storm moving south very soon. It was Sunday in late September. Winter would be here shortly. That must have been one hell of a breeze last night. Bear Lake is more than five miles long. I would have an extremely long and painfully arduous hike back to my house.

I struggled to roll over and climb onto the center bench seat. I wondered if there were any pain killers on my boat. I looked around while rubbing my stiff neck and shoulder. No, there was nothing in my boat save a couple of orange life vests. I wonder what happened to my shirt? I really need to buy an oar or an extra battery.

I took off my shoes and rolled up the legs of my jeans past my knees. The warm slimy thing I had knocked off my face was a leech. There were leeches all over my chest and the bottom of the boat. It seems Barnacle Bill and Sam were up early fishing this morning. They are obviously using leeches for bait today. I would have covered them in live bait myself had I found them passed out somewhere first. That's what I get.

I set my sneakers and socks on the seat by the side of the hot metal boat. I squatted and stepped down into the very cold water of the lake. It was only about a foot deep where I stood. The coolness of the water was a little soothing at that moment. Just then a bull moose stuck its nose right through the cattails in front of my face. I let out a scream and shit my pants—literally. My bowels just let loose. I'd like to think it was because I hadn't taken my daily constitutional, but that moose scared the shit out of me.

The moose was so close that I could feel the warm stench of its breath on my face. It was huge. It towered over me. As I stepped backwards, my calf muscle caught the side of the boat at the gunwale and I fell back into the boat I'd struggled so hard to get out of, hitting my head on the opposite gunwale. That's all I remember.

Chapter Three

That's me unconscious, hung over, bleary-eyed and scared shitless by a moose. My name is Jim. I own this little bar called The Muskee, on Bear Lake, in northern Wisconsin. Yes, it is misspelled but there was already a bar called The Muskie in Kenosha.

My best friend Brad is the cook. He also sells drugs to the tourists and a few select locals. The select locals include anyone who asks and has money. He has a real talent for growing marijuana. After all, I don't pay very well.

Brad is one great friend to have. He's more loyal than a Labrador and crazier than a coked-up Chicago commodities broker on a snowmobile after four shots of Jagermeister and a seven-hour car ride with his wife and three kids. Those brokers have become my clientele, as well as Brad's. They are truly insane. Brad was a union plumber for twenty years, and he can get his hands on just about anything you might ever need, or want, down at the union hall. Twenty Percocet pain killers, no problem. Stolen stereo with surround sound, okay. Used backhoe, sure. Eight-foot tall bamboo tree with Christmas lights, no sweat.

That jewel of a tree has managed to stay alive in the back corner of The Muskee for six years in spite of many a man and woman's attempt to poison it with spilled liquor, vomit, urine, cigarette butts, and a nasty little fire bombing incident last Fourth of July. It was a good thing that Old Style pitchers were on special that day. It's also good they were handily close by to douse the flames, or we may have lost the whole bar. There are a few scorches on the trunk to remind us of the tragedy that almost was. In fact, there are a lot of reminders of tragedies that almost were and were not all around The Muskee.

You could say Brad just seems to have a knack for finding things. Last year for my birthday, he gave me a fully automatic pre-ban Uzi submachine gun with two thousand rounds. The only problem was that it was four months until my birthday. But he explained the early birthday gift.

"My friend, I mean a buddy, needs to lose this fast." To that I responded:

"I'm the only friend you've got, and that ain't mine. But since we are such good friends, I think I can help your friend, I mean buddy."

He knew I had always wanted an Uzi. It only took us about forty minutes to shoot the whole wad of rounds while cutting down two, 50-foot pine trees on the back half of my property. Okay, they were really on the saw mill's property that butts up against my property, but it was still fun as hell. We both managed to burn our hands on the blistering hot barrel.

Aside from owning The Muskee, I also have guest cottages on the lake. I bought all the land and The Muskee about ten years ago after my divorce. I turned the first floor of this turn-of-the-century cottage into the bar and lived upstairs for my first four years back up here in the great white north. The basement is what we affectionately refer to as the smoking lounge. It was great fun to wake up hung over every day and have a bunch of friends drinking in your living room and smoking in your basement. I felt like a thirty-year-old college student.

For the sake of my lungs, and my sanity, I had to move out. All the smoke from the patrons, Brad's cooking, and the basement seemed to end up in my bedroom. As a consequence, I always smelled like The Muskee. This wasn't a problem for me as much as it was for others, especially when I went to the hospital. That seems to happen more frequently than I'd like. Anyway, I always smelled like stale booze and smoke. Even when I wasn't drunk. That isn't all that often, but it does happen a couple of times each year.

There is always a game or car race on TV, so we're always betting drinks. The Muskee does have eight televisions. We only bet money on dice games and pool, unless you want action on the game. In that case you need to see the high drug-dealing cook in the kitchen. If that doesn't turn you on, there is always a fishing or hunting or boating or snowmobiling story to talk about. If that isn't the topic of conversation, it's an argument about the Packers and Bears or some great debate about whether Jim McMahon was a better Super Bowl quarterback than Brett Favre. I really love The Muskee.

In the winter, which in Northern Wisconsin starts some time in early October, my customers are nut job rich folks from Chicago. They drag their families up to snowmobile, ski, and ice fish. It's a beautiful place to visit, but you have got to love snow to survive up here. I didn't set foot outside The Muskee from December 2002 through March 2003. That won me $225 and a blow job.

One night after half a bottle of Courvoisier, which I got free from my local liquor rep, Brad promised to give me $25 for every week that I didn't leave the inside of The Muskee. After nine weeks, he just got tired of paying me. So, instead he paid Wendy, who dances down on the Indian reservation under the stage name Peaches, $50 to take me into the boathouse and give me head. Did I mention how much I love The Muskee?

I built all five cabins on the lake, as well as The Muskee's boathouse/hangar and the docks over the last several summer seasons. The Muskee is located at the easternmost edge of my fifty-two acre property. I own about 1,500 feet of waterfront that tapers off into wilderness the saw mill owns. The forest is pretty thick to our north, and that's where Brad and I hunt any small or large varmint that come into gun range.

After my divorce, I took all the money I had left and bought this little piece of property in the middle of nowhere, Wisconsin. I have managed to live here in a liquor-fueled stupor quite happily for the last ten years.

The Muskee is not all that big, but it comfortably holds about twenty-five patrons. It will hold fifty in the summer if you use the outdoor seating on the deck. The winter crowd is more rowdy, more local, and usually, more drunk. The summer crowd is much more mellow, thanks to Brad and his drug sales, and typically larger. They pretty much just want to hang out on the deck and check out the guys and gals that spend too much time at the gym.

Being half naked when you wipe out on a waverunner also seems to humble a mighty Chicago Bears fan. It's more painful than falling from a snowmobile in a padded suit with a crash helmet. Don't get me wrong, I love visiting Chicago. The people there are great when they are in Chicago. The problem arises when they cross the Illinois state line. People from Chicago don't realize that the universe doesn't revolve around Chicago. For crying out loud, the Midwest doesn't even revolve around Chicago.

The five guest cottages in the center section of the property are each about twenty yards apart. They sit about 100 yards from The Muskee along the lake. Each cottage has two bedrooms, two full bathrooms, a small kitchen, family room, and a loft with extra beds. Each cottage also features a wonderful view of Bear Lake. The cottages are booked solid through the summer and fill up on weekends and holidays for snowmobilers in the winter.

My house is the newest cottage at the western edge of the property. It sits half way around the cove. In the winter, I ride my snowmobile to the bar in the morning. My mornings start around 11:00 when The Muskee opens. I stagger home inebriated whenever. Brad usually drives my sled back over to pick me up the next morning.

In the summer I just commute in my little metal Jon boat. The one I'm currently unconscious aboard. Brad and I can then fish when we wake up early, at say 9:30 a.m. Navigating a boat to work is only an adventure when I forget to charge the trolling motor battery. I only forget about once a summer. You'll be able to tell when I've forgotten by the mosquito bites all over my face. Once again proving that I passed out after cussing profusely and furiously paddling with my hands for about ten minutes. After that, I lean back panting and sweating, and intoxication gets the better of me. Why does the battery only die halfway across the cove and not at the dock?

Thankfully, the prevailing winds blow my boat close enough to shore by morning. That way I can wade in and walk home. Brad and I will take the pontoon out later on that day to retrieve my Jon boat. Unless, of course, Barnacle Bill and Sam feel like towing me back to the docks.

They fish on the lake every day during the summer, as well as pretty much every day in the winter. They have been known to tow my boat back to The Muskee's docks more than once. Occasionally, I'll still be inside of it. Usually covered in worms or leaches or whatever bait fish they happen to be using that particular morning. They seem to find it amusing to wake me up by throwing live bait at my face. Today, I didn't even wake up.

Chapter Four

When I finally regained consciousness, Brad was towing me across the lake behind my pontoon. He shouted back to me,

"I'd have done more, but I hate leeches, and you smell like shit!"

Barnacle Bill and Sam just left me knocked out in my boat. They just laughed themselves silly and went to The Muskee and told Brad and whoever else would listen.

"Take me home!" I shouted with a pounding head. I had to get ready for the Packers game. No matter how hung over you are, you must drink at a bar when the Pack are on television. It's just a rule if you live in northwest Wisconsin. The only exception would be if you were going to the game or watching from your ice fishing house. Then your absence would be accepted, but not really permitted. The only things we take more serious than the Packers up here are fishing and hunting.

As kids, Brad and I camped, fished, and hunted everything together. When I say he was a good friend to have, I mean it. His older brother paid us (well, really, he just paid Brad) to grow pot for him. We started practicing growing weed at $1 per plant when we were five years old. We'd steal soil, fertilizer, plant food, or anything else we needed from local farms and grow plants in the woods all summer long.

It started somewhat innocently. We didn't know, care, or even understand what pot was. To us, it was just like running a lemonade stand. Hell, most people in our town knew what we were up to. They didn't care because Brad's brother was a great hockey player. Most of the money we made, we ended up giving back to Brad's brother for candy bars, car rides into town to get bait, or boat rides to good fishing and hunting spots around the lake. Brad's brother went on to play semi-pro hockey in San Jose while I was in college.

During college, I met my future ex-wife. I was married for five years in Tennessee before divorcing and moving back to the great white north. I was a decent, hard-working businessman while I was married. I was at the office every day at 7:00 a.m. managing a plastic injection molding company that made car mirrors. Like clockwork, from 4:20 p.m. to 5:00 p.m., I'd be at the gym before heading home for dinner with my wife. That all was great for the first three and a half years. Then somehow it all went south. My life is far different today. I bet half the people that knew me in that life wouldn't recognize me today. I'm nothing like that corporate guy I used to be. Not that anybody cares anyway. Well, maybe Brad cares. A little.

Aside from skills like growing crazy good pot, being able to acquire just about anything you'd ever need, and an uncanny ability to find me passed out in my Jon boat on the other side of the lake, Brad really isn't good at much else. He only gets about three out of ten burgers cooked correctly in my bar every day. That's alright, because The Muskee is dog-friendly and most dogs like their burgers well done or raw. Brad's cooking doesn't bother anyone because if you've ever been to Northern Wisconsin, you've probably heard of cannibal sandwiches. If you haven't, a cannibal sandwich is basically raw meat on a bun. No bullshitting. We really do eat them up here. Which is a good thing because that is how seven out of ten Muskee burgers are cooked.

I'd warn customers on the menus that they won't get a perfectly cooked burger, if I ever get around to getting menus. It's simple, Brad tells you what he's cooking today, and you either eat it, or you don't. Anyway, most people send their burger back, and they get cooked well done. Besides, people come to The Muskee for the atmosphere and beverages, not to eat. Or they come to see Brad. At any given time, on any given day, there are at least two dogs, two alcoholics, and a high cook at The Muskee. I'll generally fall into at least one, if not more, of the aforementioned categories.

The Muskee and the cottages provide me with a decent enough income that I don't actually work, as you may have already gathered. I'm not rich per se, but my whole life is a vacation unto itself. Brad and I do manage to scrape by. Believe me, I deserve a lifelong vacation after five years of marriage to my ex-wife. I do have all the toys I'll ever need between the snowmobiles, ATVs, boats, waverunners, and our float plane. After all, what good is living if you don't have a few toys to play with.

About three years ago, I stayed sober long enough to get my pilot's license. Basically, I learned to fly so Brad and I could hunt and fish and visit Brad's brother Tim in Canada. It's nice to take a vacation from my lifelong vacation. I split the expense of our float plane with Barnacle Bill, and that explains why it is our plane.

Barnacle Bill hasn't felt all that comfortable flying alone since he tried to land on a lake in Canada and ran out of water. He was going fishing for the day and had heard rumors of Giant Pike in a spring-fed lake shaped like a perfect right triangle, exactly 200 miles north by northwest of Pelican Lake, Minnesota. He tore up the floats on his plane pretty good when he slid up the gravel shoreline into the scrub brush, not to mention completely trashing the propeller. Since then, he rarely flies alone.

The expense I split with Bill was in transporting new floats and a new propeller to the middle of nowhere Manitoba,

Canada, and rebuilding the plane in the middle of scrub brush. Transporting those new parts was more of a military-style airlift because there are no roads 200 miles northwest of Pelican Lake. We had to saw the tops off of a dozen pine trees and wait for a fifteen-knot southeasterly wind to fly the plane out of that lake. It took us just over three weeks. I think it may have been cheaper to buy a new plane.

Bill said it was a severe case of wind shear, but we all know what a shitty pilot Bill is. He has destroyed more floats, wing tips, and propellers than any other pilot alive. When he used to fly a lot, he was always hitting sea walls, tree stumps, boats, docks, pilings, or just missing the ramp to get onto dry land and trashing his floats.

Chapter Five

After I cleaned my crap-filled pants and took two pain killers, I had to hurry to get showered and back over to The Muskee before kickoff. It was a typical Sunday in September. I got a standing ovation when I entered the bar. Everyone had heard Barnacle Bill and Sam talk about me screaming like a little girl after kissing a moose. They said that a bald eagle halfway around the lake jumped from its perch when I screamed. I cannot remember the last time I was this embarrassed. I had to listen to them talk about throwing leeches on my face and chest. They must have retold the entire story at least five times.

I was half wasted after watching the Packers beat the Redskins at Lambeau. We had Leinie's draft pitchers on special and Brad had been grilling bratz and frying cheese curds all afternoon. How anyone could fuck up hamburgers so badly and make the world's greatest bratz and curds is truly one of the mysteries of Brad. It's not that his cheese curds are that great. It's just that after living in Wisconsin and fishing his whole life, he has truly mastered the art of deep fat frying. That and his homemade ranch dressing are real crowd pleasers. We always have a good crowd for the Packers games. All the regulars started showing up as soon as Brad unlocked the door.

Dice games start a full two hours before kickoff. Ship-Captain-Crew is my favorite dice game, but a lot of people like high roll or low roll; there is also the shake-a-day, and a Yahtzee gets you half off your next pitcher. Of course, the Yahtzee must be witnessed by at least two other unbiased people. The regulars are always trying to con me into giving out free booze. Sometimes they succeed.

The football game wasn't very close so the local crowd got drunk early and left right after the game ended. There weren't any Chicago tourists staying in the cottages because it seemed to be that strange time of year known as "bad sledding weather." The fact that the Bears played at home didn't help since most of my Chicago clients have season tickets. Brad and I played pool alone and watched the first half of the late game until he was pretty smashed. Brad left before the second half kickoff, and I told him I'd take out the trash. He reminded me not to feed the bears or kiss the moose and headed off in his truck into the much cooler evening.

It must have been the fog of alcohol that kept me from hearing the approaching footsteps. I had just closed the lid on the dumpster when I heard and felt the thud hit the back of my head. I fell to my knees on the pavement of the parking lot. As I reached up to feel the wetness of my own blood through my hair, the second blow knocked me out cold.

Chapter Six

The wheels of the 747 wide-body touched down in Toronto, Canada, at eight Wednesday evening. The eight well-dressed Italian men sitting in first class collected their laptop computer bags and the few carry-on bags they had and headed for customs. They walked in pairs, making sure each stayed several groups of passengers apart. They chatted leisurely about soccer, the weather, or women in Italian as they strolled through customs. They were selling computers, visiting family, going skiing, and going to party in the strip clubs, respectively.

At least that was what they told the customs agents as their passports were stamped. They were met immediately outside of customs by two men who had a couple Chevy Suburbans waiting in the parking garage.

"I understand you don't have any checked bags," said one of the waiting men in Italian.

"Che e corretto," replied one of the men in suits.

"I was told you all speak fluent English," said one of the men.

"That's right, yeah buddy, uh-huh, true dat, fuck you, yes, we do, and sure," came the chorus of replies.

"Great, just great. Eight fucking dago comedians. I'm here to help you. You should all keep practicing your English.

It's the best way not to attract attention while you're here. Fuck you too."

Once inside the two Suburbans and safely outside of the airport, each man reached into his computer case or suit coat and removed 2,000 euros and passed them to the driver. The driver, in exchange, handed the man in the front passenger seat a paper bag containing 4,000 U.S. dollars. The man in the passenger seat then distributed the money, each of the Italians getting eight 100 dollar bills, two 50s and five 20s. Their next stop would be the border crossing in Detroit, Michigan.

The ride took about six hours, and most of the Italians slept the whole way. Like the other 20,000 vehicles that cross the border every day, the two SUVs crossed over into the United States with little more than a wave from the border agent. The two drivers went directly to a small Italian restaurant in downtown Detroit. The restaurant was closed, and there were three men dressed in custom suits waiting inside at the bar. There were three cooks chopping, baking, and working diligently in the kitchen.

Once inside, the Italian with long blonde hair and clear blue eyes immediately walked to the boss and shook his hand. He gave the man a big hug, kissed each of his cheeks, and said,

"Thank you so much for your help. How's your Italian my friend?"

The boss smiled widely and spoke in perfect Italian,

"It is not as sharp as my wit these days, but I will manage." Perusing the Sicilian crew that had arrived, he said, "The last real food you men will eat in America will be right here in this restaurant. You won't believe what passes for food over here." With that all seven remaining men chuckled. The men sat down at two tables with white tablecloths that had been specifically set with plates of cheese, bread, olives, cured meats, as well as bottles of wine and water.

The boss pointed to the kitchen and took the man with blonde hair through the empty restaurant and back into the kitchen. The two men walked past the food preparation area and into the large cooler, and the boss handed the blonde-haired man a heavy black backpack.

Still speaking in Italian, the boss said,

"There are four guns plus twelve clips each containing twelve rounds. There is a clean cargo van at your hotel. The keys for it and the two rooms are also in this bag. You said you would need the rooms for a week and that starts tonight." The Italian reached inside his suit coat pocket and handed the boss 5,000 euros.

"Grazie! You didn't need to bring me anything but your friendship," said the boss.

"You know I would never do business in your backyard without your blessings."

"Let's dine together before you leave my friend." With that, the two men strolled out of the cooler and back to the restaurant.

The men finished eating an hour or so later and headed to the back of the kitchen. They walked through the delivery doors and into the parking lot. Parked there were a large Cadillac sedan and an Escalade.

"Don't worry, they're clean, and they're legally registered to dead people," said the boss. "If you get pulled over, hand them the two papers in the glove box and your Italian passport and act like you own the road. It may take twenty minutes or so, but they'll let you go. There is no way a cop in this country wants to try and fill out that much paperwork. Just say, 'Auto Show,' and they'll think you're executives in town for the car show."

The Italians thanked their drivers and the boss and changed into their new cars. The Italians drove straight out of Detroit and headed to Port Huron, Michigan. Upon arrival, the men went to the SLEEP INN motel and surveyed their two rooms on the back side of the motel. The cargo van was right in front of their rooms on the first floor just as the boss said it would be. It was getting late, and the men needed to shower, check their equipment, and try to get accustomed to the new time zone. Jet leg is pretty bad when you fly east to west around the world.

The blonde-haired man and another left the motel at eight on Friday morning. They went directly to the Wal-Mart across from the motel and purchased the rest of the equipment they needed. The men returned to the motel about an hour later with four handheld radios, two rolls of duct tape, eight pocket knives, a bag of zip ties, two baseball bats, black rubber gloves, a case of bottled water, eight two-foot long sub sandwiches, two cartons of cigarettes, eight Zippo lighters, and two large emergency first-aid kits. Each pair of men had a laptop, a nine millimeter Berretta with 36 rounds, and 2,000 U.S. dollars. About 9:30 Friday morning, the men climbed into the two cars and headed out. It was a long drive to Northwest Wisconsin.

Chapter Seven

The pain was excruciating. My eyes were swollen. My head was throbbing. The taste of my own blood was warm in my mouth. The worst part was the dude in my face whose hands were squeezing my trachea. He had long blonde hair and blue eyes. He didn't look like the kind of guy who should be choking me to death. He let go of my throat, and my head fell back against the hard tile floor with a thud. I was lying behind the bar in The Muskee. Ouch, that hurt a whole lot.

I began coughing and choking and gasping for breath. I was desperately struggling to get oxygen into my airways. As hard as my body tried to breathe, I just couldn't get any air into my lungs. If I could have spoken, I would have explained to blonde-haired dude that I was having trouble breathing with his knee on my chest. Before I got the chance, he punched me in the nose with a gloved hand. What the fuck was going on? Is my ex-wife still pissed? This has got to have something to do with Brad. Just ask him what he wants, I thought to myself.

Now what most people fail to realize is that the worst part about being punched in the nose on a tile floor is the shock to the back of your skull. It's like being hit on both sides of the head at the same time. I didn't have time to fully appreciate this phenomenon because that shot to my nose was immediately followed by two punches to each of my eyes.

I'm not sure if he was aiming for each eye or just the whole side of my face, but he caught dead center of both of my eye sockets with at least one of his knuckles, hitting that space between my skull and eyeball right under my eyebrow. The pain blinds you if the punch itself doesn't. That is really painful, I thought.

Following those three quick blows, which felt like six because of the tile floor phenomenon, I immediately coughed up blood onto blonde-haired dude's shirt and gasped again for air. That's going to piss him off, I thought. Not so easy to get blood and snot and saliva out of a fancy starched yellow shirt and silk tie like the ones he was wearing. Yeah, right, he couldn't get more pissed off at me right now. At least I hope he can't.

The fact is, I don't know anyone I've ever been this pissed off at. Not even my ex-wife. I might be able to punch a guy in a bar fight in a fit of drunken anger, but I've never even been in a bar fight, and I'm in a bar a lot. I'm just saying that I could, if I had to, but I haven't. I got into a hockey fight or two growing up, but that was just part of the game.

Even then we had Brad's brother or Vince Mason. Vince Mason was the local defenseman goon whose job was to protect the rest of the team, or more specifically, Brad's brother Tim. Every hockey team has one. Ask anyone who ever played hockey what the name of their goon was, and they'll tell you straight away. I'd like to have Vince here now, I thought as I continued to gasp for breath. I mean this blonde-haired dude is really pissed off at me. He must have me mistaken with the guy that ax murdered his whole family or someone like that.

In all my pain I had failed to notice each of the large assholes wearing fancy suits and expensive shoes. The only reason to take note of their shoes was the fact that they were standing with their sleek wooden heels digging into the back of each of my hands. Their other shoes were standing on my wrists. I couldn't see who or what was holding my feet down, but I was definitely immobile.

It's strange how the mind works at times like these. As I was struggling to breathe, the next thought that popped into my head was that the blonde-haired dude had no suit coat on and that it was a little chilly not to be wearing a jacket. Or, maybe I was cold and delusional from the blood letting that the blonde-haired dude was performing on my face. It was simply a strange thing to think of at a time like this.

I barely saw the Everclear bottle label flash in front of my eyes. At least he's using the cheap stuff, I thought. Before I could see what was happening the blonde-haired dude poured the bottle into my eyes. Holy mother of Christ!

"Aaaaaaaauuuuuuughhhh!!!" That fucking burns. I arched my back and lifted the blonde-haired dude and my whole backside right off of the tile floor. I definitely did not scream like a little schoolgirl tonight. The scream that came from the fiery needles in my eyes was low and guttural and came from a very dark place in my soul—the kind of sound I didn't even know I could produce. The kind of scream you never want to hear yourself make.

I can't believe there was even enough air in my lungs to produce any sound at all. I think I shit myself. Again. Twice in one day has to be some sort of record. That really hurts. It burns, it burns, it burns! My God that burns my eyes. Unfortunately, the scream didn't help anything. The unimaginable pain and fire in my eyes continued to scorch all the way into my brain. I must be blind. It won't stop burning. With that, suddenly, the blonde-haired dude spoke.

"Where is the chest?" he asked in a thick accent. I couldn't open my eyes to even acknowledge his words. I was gasping, weeping, moaning, twisting my head in agony, choking, and coughing. The pain. My eyes, my nose, my hands, my head, my eyes, oh my God, the burning in my eyes.

Now he grabbed my whole face with one hand and slammed my head back against the tile floor. Again, only much louder he asked,

"Where is the war chest James?" Ouch, my eyes, my fucking eyes. What the fuck was he talking about? No one calls me James. Oh, my God, the pain.

"I think he's a gonna go into a shock," one of the other men said in a funny accent as he watched my eyes roll back into my head. Thankfully, mercifully, I lost consciousness once again.

Chapter Eight

I woke up with my eyes still burning. Only now it was more like a light sautéing. My head was still throbbing, but that wasn't so bad. I am sort of conditioned to this fact, seeing as I usually wake up hung over. As I turned my head, I noticed that one of the fancy-shoed sons of bitches that did this to me was still standing in the bar. I was happy to see that he was standing on the other side of the bar and not on my hand. All I could see was his pants legs to about his calves and his shoes.

Now about eight months ago, Brad and I started our own bowling tournament when The Muskee was empty. We played on Tuesday mornings about 9:30 or 10:00 before very many people showed up. As I said earlier, there are always people in The Muskee. Except, of course, when I'm getting the ever-living shit kicked out of me by men in suits. Then, of course, there is no one around.

Anyway, Brad had five old bowling pins and his brother's twenty-five-year-old twelve-pound bowling ball. So we started our own league with Barnacle Bill and Sam. It worked great, until I dropped the ball and chipped a big piece of resin out of it. After that, it just didn't roll in a consistent manner. I mean we could play the grout line bounces in the tiles, but with that chip in the ball, our scoring became unpredictable, and the action was just too erratic.

Brad took the chipped ball down to the bowling alley and swapped it out for a new sixteen-pound ball. This one was big enough for him to get his big fat thumb into. Which he claimed was the reason for his high handicap. We all know he sucks at everything except growing, procuring, and deep fat frying. We decided to try out the new ball when he got back to The Muskee late that night.

As it was late, we were all drunk. When Brad started the approach for his throw, he staggered and lost his balance, as he was not wearing regulation footwear. Which in fact, we had also each procured at the local bowling alley. This stagger caused Brad to fling that ball like a human catapult. Brad fell sprawling into our beverage table knocking all the glassware off of it. Let me tell you, that sixteen-pound ball looked like it got shot out of a cannon. I think there was actually smoke coming off the back of it. It flew through the air for ten feet before it hit the tile floor and went right through the whole bar. When I say the whole bar, I mean it. It went right through the foot rest, the trim piece, and the wood panel behind it. It left a big circular splintered hole in the bar and put a giant dent in our mop bucket sitting against the back wall on the other side of the bar.

Terry Hutch happened to be shooting pool with Big Jack Slade when all the commotion started. He and Jack came over to see what the noise was all about. This would not have been a problem; however, Terry owns the bowling alley, and he was not very happy to see his bowling ball fused to the side of my mop bucket. He also didn't like the fact that Barnacle Bill, Sam, and myself were lacing up our stolen bowling shoes. Oh, you better believe he was pissed off. If Big Jack hadn't held him back, Terry would have done some damage to us for sure. Thus, ended The Muskee Bowling League. And, no, I don't think Terry sent these assholes over as retaliation.

That hole in the bar allowed me to see Mr. stand on my hand with your fancy fucking shoes on the other side of the bar. As I lay there in pain, I tried to regain my wits and clear my head. What the hell just happened? I'm in far too much agony to be dreaming. I could feel my hands were now bound in front of my stomach, which was one of the few places on my body that didn't hurt. My head was really sore, and I could feel my upper lip swelling. I could feel dried blood on my face under my nose. Looking down with burning eyes and lifting my arms revealed my hands were bound with a little black plastic zip tie like you get at any hardware store.

I now realized that I had a bar rag tied around my head and shoved partially in my mouth. Maybe it's just the rag and my lip isn't so swollen, I thought. No, no, my lip is definitely swollen as well. And, if you think blood tastes bad, you should suck on a Muskee bar rag. I could feel something binding my feet together as well. My eyes were still burning, and I was having trouble focusing as I lay on my back staring up into the neon beer sign lights and disco ball.

These guys weren't local. If they were, I'm sure they would have known about the shotgun I keep behind the bar. Fortunately, they had failed to notice the sawed-off 12-gauge resting on hooks just above the glass washing sink behind the bar. After all, this is Northern Wisconsin.

I don't know why I have a loaded, sawed-off 12-gauge behind my bar. I'm just really happy I do. Especially today. It's not like anyone is going to rob this bar. You would have to be a fool to try and steal at The Muskee. Hell, all the locals who come in carry handguns. On any given Friday night, there have to be at least ten people all carrying pistols in The Muskee. In the summer, it's probably not as many because we usually wear bathing suits and keep our guns in our tackle boxes.

Believe me, if you reel in a pissed-off Northern Pike the size of a railroad tie and you're only in a small Jon boat, you shoot that fat bastard. When we're not arguing about the Packers with Bears fans, we're debating Smith and Wesson,

Browning, Colt, or Winchester. During deer season everyone has at least one shotgun and one hand gun for bears on them at all times. We're so deer-hunting crazy up here that if a car hits a deer, the meat will be cleaned, packaged, and re-sold before it even gets cold. And believe me, it gets really cold, really fast up here.

Chapter Nine

My eyes were watering badly by now and stinging even worse. All I could think of was getting to that shotgun. Mr. stand on my hands with his fancy shoes is staring out the side window looking intently toward the guest cottages. I could hear someone trashing the upstairs of The Muskee. Lots of knocking on the floor, glass breaking, and papers rustling. By the location of the noises, I could tell that whoever was upstairs was just finishing my office and moving into one of the spare rooms. They are obviously looking for something, a war chest, whatever the fuck that might be. Or is this some sort of fucked-up robbery? Maybe they're going to kill me and make it look like a robbery. Think, Jim; think quickly, Jim. I begin looking through my tears around the bar.

I could just barely see the black plastic handle of the knife we use to cut lemon and lime wedges on top of the beer cooler. I don't think I could reach it without making a lot of noise. Then I remember the bar darts are on top of the keg cooler just behind my head. Maybe I could use one of them to poke enough holes through this plastic tie to weaken it enough to break free. Maybe I could stab Mr. fancy shoes in his aorta.

Before I could decide how, if at all, I could use the dart, assuming I could even get to it, I heard an excited voice call down from upstairs.

"I a have it! Come a you see!" I see Mr. fancy shoes turn and step directly toward me and the bar. I close my eyes and lay motionless, frozen with fear. Please don't kill me, please don't kill me, I silently pray. I'm sure he can hear my heart pounding through my chest. Surely he could hear my heart pounding through my chest. Each thud was nearly deafening to my own ears. I then hear Mr. fancy shoes lean over the bar and take one quick look at me, and dash up the stairs. I hear him take the first nine steps, turn around on the landing and then stride up the other six steps to the second floor. I can also hear the man upstairs speaking in a foreign language. Then a radio squawk and someone responds in a foreign language. I can hear the voice on the radio respond, "OK."

I knew perhaps my only chance of escape was now. Sitting up quickly, I rolled forward onto my side and pulled myself up onto my knees, grabbing the beer cooler for support. As I do, the bottle of Everclear they tried to blind me with topples off the cooler and hits the tile floor with a loud clank—followed immediately by two more clanks and the sound of glass rolling across tile. Fuck! I watch the bottle roll along the tiles in absolute horror; the noise seems to be amplified at least a thousand times and echoes inside my head. The whole scene seems to take place in slow motion.

I grab the knife and hold it just long enough to realize THERE IS NO TIME! I drop the knife onto the floor. I quickly spin around on my knees and clutch the front of the sink basin to keep from falling over. Spreading my knees, I can feel my foot bindings dig into my ankles. I grab desperately for the shotgun. I snatch the pump-action stock and lift it off the hooks.

I then slide the butt end onto the tile floor between my knees as I pump a round into the chamber. I let go of the action and watch the barrel fall slightly to the right away from me.

It falls into the front of the stainless steel sink with a loud metal to metal tonk. I reach feverishly for the handle and switch the safety off. As I fumble about with the shotgun, I hear the distinct sounds of loud, heavy footsteps, of people running out of the spare bedroom, past the office, down the hall, and approaching the top of the stairs. I then swing the sawed-off 12-gauge up and struggle to point it accurately at the landing. I point it half way up the stairs while resting the stock on the bar. It is all I can do to keep the wooden stock from sliding down the bar rail and blowing a large gaping hole in the jukebox hanging on the wall. Just then, I see Mr. fancy shoes' shoes and legs come around the landing through the rungs of the banister. I realize just how bad things are about to get.

Being an experienced hunter, I know exactly what's going to happen when I squeeze the trigger of this modified Browning sawed-off 12-gauge shotgun with number nine buckshot. I'm totally fucked.

If you have never fired a forty-year-old 12-gauge shotgun, then you wouldn't know that it kicks like a mule. After firing all five shots, which is all the shells this particular model will hold, you'll have a pretty good-sized bruise on your shoulder. When the stock has been cut down to a pistol grip and the barrel sawed off, you better believe it kicks even harder.

After you have modified the gun, it has less mass; therefore the recoil, or kick, is much greater. The other thing that happens when you cut the stock down to make a pistol grip, you can no longer brace the gun with your shoulder. Thus, all the energy is transferred to your hand. When you shoot one with both hands tied together with a little black zip tie at the butt end, you're just a fucking idiot. Unfortunately, I don't see as I have any other choice. As I pulled the trigger, the shotgun blast made a deafeningly loud POP, echoing loudly throughout The Muskee.

Fire and thick blackish blue smoke burst out of the barrel. Mr. fancy shoes took pellets to the front of both his legs from just below his knees to just below his rib cage. I saw the material in his fancy suit pants, suit coat, shirt, and tie slap his body the very second I heard the shot. He fell, face first, arms swimming forward, from the top of the landing right through the smoke cloud of burning gun powder and hit the floor with a dull thud.

His gun slapped the cold tile floor and slid across the room, skipping over each grout line as it slid into the wall. He never made a sound, not a scream, not even a whimper—he was done. Two seconds of a calm, eerie silence followed as I tried to peer through the smoke floating above the bar at the base of the staircase. When the shotgun blast went off, his partner in crime froze solid. He stopped dead in his tracks. I couldn't see him around the landing or the back side of the stairs. Instead, I heard him clamber back up the stairs screaming into his radio. That old gun had a hell of a lot of kick. The force of the blast ripped a small slice in the back of my hand where the zip tie was pressed into my skin. It felt like it broke bones in my right wrist. That's going to be stiff for a couple of days, I thought. When I pulled the trigger, the gun jumped out of my hands and landed on the bar. I actually knocked myself on the point of my chin with my bound hands.

I quickly managed to grab the gun, shove the butt end into a half empty long neck beer case box, and pump a second round into the chamber. I set the gun stock back on the bar and aimed for the landing. I didn't hear the man upstairs moving. He seemed to be explaining, rather vigorously, that I had a gun and Mr. fancy shoes was down. Mr. fancy shoes was down hard, really hard. There was still no sound from over the bar.

I quietly set the gun on the rubber drink mats on the bar and listened intently for a moment. After hearing no sound from Mr. fancy shoes, I reached for the knife on the floor. Placing the knife between my knees, I was able to get the tip of the blade between my wrists and pull it out from between my knees. I stuck the handle against my stomach and the back of the blade on the sink and was able to half cut and half break through the zip tie. I then cut the zip ties around my ankles and stuck the knife into my back pocket. With my left hand I grabbed the pump action of the shotgun and began removing the bar rag from my mouth with my sore-wristed right hand.

Just then I heard someone speaking on the radio and car doors slam shut outside the bar. I stopped tugging at the bar rag now on my chin and put my right hand on the trigger. I stepped toward the end of the bar trying to get down into the basement as quickly as possible. As I turned to look back toward the small glass window in the side door, I saw the blonde-haired dude with a radio in his left hand next to his mouth. I could not see his right hand. Luckily I saw him first. As we made eye contact I pointed the shotgun at the window and fired at his face. Pop.

Damn this gun kicks! I saw him ducking away from the window as the crack of my shotgun filled the room with more smoke and noise. The window shattered; and the wooden door splintered as the buckshot blew it open about two inches, before the automatic closure spring on top caught it and slammed it shut again.

I didn't look back as I jumped down the whole flight of old wooden stairs into the basement. I sprang forward when I hit the concrete floor of the basement and tumbled like a helpless uncoordinated moron into the coffee table, slamming it into the couch against the wall in the smoking lounge. The wood and steel pump action of the shotgun acted like a crow bar, crushing my forehead and the left side of my face, preventing me from landing softly on the couch. Oh the pain, it just doesn't stop. Besides the shotgun hitting my face and forehead, I was pretty sure I had just sprained my left ankle.

I'm not sure if I hit the blonde-haired dude or not, but someone outside was now shooting into The Muskee. At first, the shots were more muffled coming from outside. But right now there were definitely guns shooting inside The Muskee. I quickly forgot about the pain in my body as the wood splinters started flying all around the smoking lounge and the gun shots continued and grew louder. I could hear shell casings hitting the floor like hail along with a whole lot of yelling in that cursed foreign language I didn't recognize.

Judging by the number of shots these guys fired, they had guns with large clips, or they had a lot of guns. Either way, it wasn't good for me, or The Muskee's wall paint. Just then the light bulbs from one of the fluorescent shop lights in the basement shattered, showering me with hot glass and dimming the room. I fired one more shot up at the basement door. Now there was smoke in the smoking lounge as well. I crawled, dragging my left leg, over to the gun safe where Brad and I kept our valuables.

The gun safe is in a separate room in the basement. I quickly pulled myself up, punched in the digital code and pulled open the door. I tried to make myself as small as possible by crouching partially inside and behind the relative safety of the two-inch-thick steel door. I could just see through the bottom corner of the basement door looking through the hinges of the gun safe.

The way the basement and bar are laid out, I was looking toward the kitchen and bathrooms. I couldn't see what was going on in the main part of the bar, which was located above and in front of me. They just kept shooting through the stairs and the door into the basement.

There were lots of footsteps upstairs as well as the screeching of wooden chairs and tables sliding across the floor. Everything now seemed to be moving very fast. The splintering wood, plaster, and glass were falling like rain over the card table and chairs and all across the couch. The shrill of the smoke detector upstairs made it impossible to hear what was happening up there. All at once, the shooting stopped and the outside door slammed shut. The only thing I could now hear was the smoke alarm.

Unfortunately, Brad and I had already spent all the rounds in the Uzi, because it would have been nice to have that thing fully loaded right now. I did, however, have two Magnum .44 Desert Eagles and two .38 Night Guard Smith and Wesson pistols. I always buy guns in pairs so Brad and I are shooting the same weapons, and he can't complain that his gun is less accurate. The fact is, I just don't mess around when it comes to buying guns. If I shoot something, I'm going to put a huge hole in it.

I slipped the .38's holster clips inside my jeans, one on each hip. I put the extra .44 clips, each holding ten rounds into my front pockets. I then stuck one Desert Eagle in the front of my pants, and one in the back. Reaching behind me, I noticed that I had managed to lose the bar knife. I slid two more shells into the shotgun and crouched motionless listening to the fire alarm and pointing the shotgun at the stairs.

After watching the second hand make a full sweep around on the wall clock and hearing nothing, I struggled to my feet. My ankle was swelling and sore. Not to mention the soreness in my forehead, nose, mouth, each of my hands, my right wrist, the back of my head, and of course, the burning in my swollen eyes. Just then I smelled the smoke. That isn't burnt gunpowder, I thought, that's a fire!

Chapter Ten

The blonde-haired dude and three others were busy ransacking my house, tearing through the closets and scouring the attic and basement.

"I have it! Come see!" the call came over the radio.

"Let's get out of here. They found the chest with the American in the bar." The blonde-haired dude yelled to the others. He pushed the talk button on his radio and said, "Okay." He grabbed some newspaper off the counter and wadded each section into balls and stuffed them under the cushions of the couch in the living room with the help of the other three men. When they were finished, the blonde haired dude lit them with his lighter sending the couch and then the drapes into flames. The four men ran to the SUV and headed toward the next cabin. About the time they got into the car, the man in the bar called over the radio.

"He's shot Antonio! The American has a gun! Antonio is shot! Come quickly! I have no gun! He will kill me!"

The other two Italians were outside the Cadillac Sedan about half way around the opposite cove on the road out of the resort. They were acting as lookouts for potential visitors to The Muskee. They were smoking cigarettes when the man upstairs started calling for help. The two men jumped into the car and raced toward The Muskee.

The passenger was calling the blonde-haired dude on the radio to say they were on their way to help. The blonde haired-dude was outside The Muskee, about to walk inside the bar, when the window in the door in front of him shattered from the gunshot blast within. The others from the sedan heard the blast and quickly raced toward the bar.

Two of the Italians began firing through the window into The Muskee as all four entered the bar and continued shooting at the wall where the stairs lead into the basement. The men in the sedan pulled up as the other two men were dragging Mr. Fancy shoes out of the bar. One of the men in the Cadillac sedan grabbed the first aid kit out of the trunk and helped to pull the injured man across the back seat into the car. He then began bandaging the man, who was bleeding profusely. He ripped the bleeding man's shirt open and saw the extent of the damage. Reaching into the first aid kit, he grabbed several cotton pads and began mopping the man's torso.

The man driving the car pulled the gun from inside his coat and ran toward the door into the bar. When he got inside, he looked down and saw another gun on the floor. He picked it up and saw his blonde-haired comrade lighting a table on fire and headed back outside. The Italian still upstairs ran into the spare bedroom and grabbed the ammunition crate. When he got to the top of the landing he started yelling in Italian, "Don't shoot me. I'm coming down."

As he ran past with the crate, the blonde-haired dude reached over the bar and began grabbing liquor bottles and poured them on the tables and chairs, covering the floor as well. He waved for the other man still shooting to leave and lit the alcohol as he walked backwards, still firing. The man who had brought the crate outside rushed quickly to the car and tossed the crate into the trunk. He closed the trunk and climbed into the front passenger side of the car as the other men climbed into their respective cars and sped away. The blonde-haired dude was on the radio as soon as the cars sped away from The Muskee.

"What happened in there, Giovanni?"

"The American shot Antonio, I think."

"We heard a noise downstairs and when we ran down to see, there was a gunshot. That's when I called you."

"When we get out away from the bar we need to stop and see what you have found. We must make sure it is inside the chest. We also need to help Antonio."

About another mile down the road, the blonde-haired dude said, "This is good, let's stop here." The two cars slowed to a stop on the dirt road.

Chapter Eleven

I limped silently toward the old wooden stairs leading from the smoking lounge back up to the main floor of The Muskee. I kept the barrel of my shotgun pointed at the open door. Holy shit, I thought, I'm a sitting duck. I stepped on the tread of the first step of the stairwell and only then realized how no one could have possibly heard my approach from the basement with the fire alarm screaming upstairs. Somehow, that didn't make the climb any less stressful. When I got to the third step from the top, I could see thick black smoke filling the top couple of feet of the ten-foot high ceiling in The Muskee.

Just then I saw Brad come running out of the kitchen with the forty-pound fire extinguisher. He's lucky I didn't shoot him. I startled him, and I know he scared the shit out of me. As he ran past the basement door he looked at me curiously and yelled,

"What the fuck, man?" He had quite a command of the English language. I climbed the last three steps and saw that the whole Muskee was on fire.

Those well-dressed men had splashed quite a bit of liquor around the bar and set it on fire. When I got there, the main room of the bar was one big fireball. There were tables and chairs on fire, and Brad was fighting a rather large blaze on the ceiling. I jumped behind the bar, reached the small twenty-pound extinguisher, and started spraying furiously.

It was surprising how fast we were able to get the fire under control and then extinguished. God bless the folks who make fire extinguishers. They really work. After the fire was out, Brad looked at me and said,

"What'd ya do?" He was now standing in the middle of one hell of a mess. There was smoke everywhere, white powder from the fire extinguishers, charred tables, liquor all over the floor, and Brad.

"Some guys that didn't speak English kicked my ass," I explained. "How many cars did you pass on your way here?"

"None," he said, followed by "what did they say?"

"They were speaking some foreign language, you idiot. They were looking for a war chest." I shouted over the fire alarm.

"I rode my quad back over when I saw the smoke."

The back trail is pretty much a straight shot to Brad's house over a couple of hills and through the Blue River at a shallow crossing. It only takes about ten minutes to get to his place from The Muskee by ATV. The only problem is that you always get wet at the Blue River crossing. I looked at him curiously and shouted,

"You could see that smoke from The Muskee fire all the way over at your place?" Brad just pointed out the shattered window of the side door, and I saw immediately what he meant. It seems that the blonde-haired dude had torched my cottage on the far end of the property.

"Oh, fuck me." I whined. He probably would have torched all the cottages had I not blasted Mr. fancy shoes. Hey, wait a minute. Where was Mr. fancy shoes? His body wasn't charred and laying where I left it.

Brad then yelled "What were you shooting?" and "Why did you start the fires?" He was truly fucking stupid.

There is only one road back to The Muskee. It winds all the way around the east side of the lake and wraps through a shallow valley along the Blue River. It's four miles long and takes about twenty minutes to drive because of all the sharp turns and switchbacks around the swampy ground. It intersects at a "T" into County Road 300 North. The county road isn't much; it's really just a farm and saw mill access road. Hell, if The Muskee weren't back up in here, saw mill employees, farmers, and hunters would be the only people who ever used it.

You have to take a two-mile snowmobile trail off the parks department trail system to get all the way back to my little resort. The two bridges that you have to cross are narrow and one lane. There is no way to get a boat trailer or recreational vehicle to the resort. It's really a pain in the ass because we have to launch all our boats and personal water craft on the other end of the lake six miles away at Johnson's boat ramp for twenty bucks each. Brad lets us keep the trailers on his lot just off County Road 300. We're planning to build a thirty-slip dry rack storage barn there for all of the guests' boats and personal water craft.

Chapter Twelve

"Stop here," said the man with blonde hair over the radio. The two cars pulled over. The man riding shotgun in the car walked to the trunk and opened it to reveal the old ammunition crate from WWII. The man with blonde hair opened it and saw all of my old junk inside. He picked it up and dumped all its contents into the trunk. He then turned it over and set it back in the trunk. He took his knife out and carefully shoved it behind the thin cedar lining. He removed all five interior panels of cedar and stared inside.

"We have it," he said and closed the trunk. The man driving the car had gotten out and helped bandage the shot and bleeding man in the back seat.

"How is he doing?" the man with blonde hair asked.

"His pulse is weak, but he's alive," the driver said looking back as he closed the door. He stepped to the back of the car, motioned to the man with blonde hair, and whispered, "He will not make it; he took several pellets to the liver and intestines. There may be one in his lungs as well; it's hard to say." Just then they heard sirens approaching in the distance.

"Quickly, let's prop him upright and get the blood wiped off!" exclaimed the man with blonde hair. They opened the car door and rapidly began working on him.

"Get the duct tape from the trunk and the bats!" he shouted. The men quickly taped the two bats together about eight inches apart. They heaved the shot man forward in the car and strapped the bats to his back by wrapping duct tape around his torso. The man with blonde hair finished by reaching into his pocket and placing his sunglasses onto the moaning, barely conscious man. They all returned to their respective cars and began to slowly pull away as the fire engine approached.

Chapter Thirteen

There is a lot about Brad that I've left out of this story to this point. Brad has been growing pot since we were kids. That you already knew. What I failed to mention was where Brad had been while I was in college and then married for five years.

Brad wasn't much of a student. Some people gave the standard reason for that and said "he never applied himself." Most people who know him personally know that roughly eight years of marijuana smoking before he turned age eighteen destroyed his short-, and pretty much all of his long-term memory. The truth however is different and I am one of the few people who know what the truth is. He's just plain old fucking stupid. I mean he's dumber than a tree stump and twice as thick. I love the guy.

We went through grade school and high school together, no problem. We were in most of the same classes together, except he was in slow math and slow English. I always let him cheat off me and let him think I was cheating off him. He never understood why I got As and Bs and he got Cs and Ds, but it was rare for him to flunk anything.

Anyway, second semester senior year I got accepted to the University of Wisconsin. Go Badgers! My mother was so excited that when I got the acceptance letter, she bought me a new suit and drove me down to Madison that very weekend and enrolled me in fall classes. I was a Badger, and I looked like a douche bag in my new suit with my mother on a college campus.

That same weekend in March, Brad's older brother Tim won San Jose's first playoff series. Tim scored the winning goal in overtime. So Brad loaded all, and I mean all, of his crops into his parent's old car and headed to Southern California. Well, of course, Brad got lost in Iowa, so he stopped to ask for directions. Two hours later when he pulled into the very same gas station and asked the same attendant for directions high as a kite, things went bad. Things went really, really bad.

An Iowa state trooper was using the bathroom when Brad arrived the second time. Brad failed to notice the squad car outside. That cop heard Brad's whole conversation with the attendant and suddenly appeared out of the bathroom to speak with Brad. I guess Brad just lost it and punched the cop. I told you he was fucking stupid. To make things even worse, he ran out the door. He jumped into his parent's car and took off!

Of course, the Iowa state troopers caught him almost immediately. Brad spent my whole college career in the Jolliet, Illinois correctional facility. He was booked on assaulting a police officer, making terrorist threats to an officer, speeding, reckless driving, attempted vehicular manslaughter, countless traffic violations, resisting arrest, fleeing capture, conspiracy to distribute narcotics, and felony possession of a controlled substance. To be a little more specific, it was just under twenty pounds of a controlled substance. Just under, because Brad smoked a big fat joint prior to the chase. Otherwise, it would have been a full twenty pounds. It really doesn't matter. Felony possession starts at like one quarter of one pound. Each additional pound just pisses off the judge.

The only job Brad could get after prison was as a cook at the local fast food restaurant. This also explains why Brad is such a shitty cook. That was until his brother sent him the photos Brad had taken of his brother back in junior high. The photos were of Big Jack Slade.

Big Jack Slade is the head of the local teamsters. He runs all the Wisconsin union halls, as well as every construction site north of Chippewa Falls. You better believe if you are building in Northwestern Wisconsin, or in the Twin Cities area, Big Jack is getting a piece of your job. He cut me a hell of a deal on my cottages thanks to Brad. He threw in my new boat docks for free. It seems Big Jack and Mr. Johnson, who owns the boat ramp on the far end of the lake, have a 'dispute.' I told you Brad is a good friend to have.

Big Jack is a regular at The Muskee on the first Tuesday of every month. Tuesday is Brad's night off, and Big Jack cooks a big Italian meal at The Muskee for all the union bigwigs. There isn't much business on Tuesdays so they are typically the only people in The Muskee. I usually go home to bed before they finish playing cards. Big Jack and the Union Local 184 also happen to be the team sponsor of the Northern Wisconsin Skating Bears, which, as everybody knows, is the regional high school traveling hockey team that won their division championship three years in a row before Tim went to San Jose. The Skating Bears just massacred the Minneapolis-area All Stars three years in a row.

After their third straight championship, Big Jack took the whole team to that Indian reservation tavern where my good friend Peaches works. Brad and I stowed away on the team bus because we weren't old enough to drive to the game. The fact that Brad's brother was the star allowed us certain privileges as well. Brad was designated team photographer, and he got to sit behind the bench and got some great photos of the team. Brad carried all the team's marijuana too, which helped a little.

Now I didn't actually see it, so I don't know if it's true. Supposedly, Brad got a picture of Tim and Big Jack doing some pretty naughty things to some of the 'talent' in that tavern's version of The Muskee's smoking lounge. Turns out the 'talent' was not eighteen years old at the time, nor was Tim. The whole thing really wouldn't be much of a problem at all. As a matter of fact, Big Jack would probably increase his social status down at the Local 184 if the photo ever surfaced.

However, Big Jack's wife, Louise, is a real high society type. She teaches Sunday school, runs the PTA, the Girl Scouts, the Rotary Club, and all that other stuff that Brad and I won't ever be allowed to be involved with. The fact is Big Jack dotes on her. They have been sweethearts since they were in grade school. Everyone knows about their fairy tale romance. When his wife is around, Big Jack's really a little pussy. But you didn't hear that from me.

That photo got Brad right through the fastest apprenticeship in union history. He was a full-on certified lead plumber union foreman two minutes after walking into Big Jack's office. Those twenty years as a union plumber only took him eight years to earn because after only eight years of work, he had fucked up so many jobs, it was cheaper to give Brad full retirement than keep him employed. He is that stupid.

After serving seven of twenty-five years in prison, Brad was released and had to stop growing locally. So he moved his operations north. His brother Tim had now retired and was coaching kids individually up in Ontario. His brother had purchased a small winter wheat farm up on Lake Nipigon in Canada. Tim would harvest Brad's crops from his greenhouse and sail his boat right down to the Upper Peninsula where Brad would pick them up and sell them directly to some of his old cell block buddies in Chicago.

Every year I'd fly him up for spring planting, and we'd hunt spring black bear together. I never transported plants in the plane. We just brought a little back for medicinal purposes and emergencies. We hid it in one of the floats below the water line. We got stopped by the Royal Canadian Mounties once and luckily didn't have any pot with us. They were very polite and didn't find the compartment in the float.

Chapter Fourteen

Brad and I had just finished putting out the fire in The Muskee. As we stood yelling at each other over the blaring smoke alarm, I explained to Brad that some foreigners had just tried to kill me. I explained how I had shot one of them on the stairs. I told him that they were looking for some sort of war chest or something and wanted it bad enough to torch me and my house.

"Do you mean that old WWII Howitzer shell box upstairs?" Brad asked.

"Yes. I think that's what they were looking for," I replied.

"Why would anyone want that?"

I had forgotten about my grandfather's chest. I hadn't been in the guest bedroom closet since I moved into my new cottage years ago. I put that old crate in the guest bedroom closet after my divorce. I had packed all the sentimental crap from college and my ex-wife into that old box and forgotten all about it.

"How did you know about the chest?" I asked Brad.

"I used to hide pot in it, but after about a week, all my dope started to taste like cedar," he explained. I should have known better than to ask a stupid question.

"Let's go kill the motherfuckers!" Brad exclaimed as he headed down into the basement. I limped back around the bar and shot water from the plastic bar drink gun into my eyes, hoping the cool water would flush some of the toxins and soothe my eyes. I grabbed another bar rag and wiped away the excess water and blew my bloody nose directly into the towel. It doesn't feel like the blonde-haired dude broke my nose. What a pussy, I thought. I then washed the blood and soot off of my hands. Just then Brad flipped off the fire alarm with the reset breaker in the basement.

I looked in the mirror and saw that the back of my clothes were filthy. As it turns out, I didn't shit myself again. That and the Packers victory were about the only good news of the day. As I cleaned my hands and face, I began to think about the unbelievable maelstrom I had just been through.

The blonde-haired dude called me James. How did he know my name? How did he know about my grandpa's WWII trunk? Why was that old crate important enough to torture or even kill me? Hell, if they would have come in and asked about it, I'm sure I would have given it to them. What kind of accent did they speak with? Why is that old crate so important?

I climbed the staircase, which now resembled a carpeted piece of Swiss cheese, to survey more of the damage. I was interested to see if they had the wherewithal to take the chest in the middle of the gun fight. Of course, I already knew the answer to that. As I walked down the hall and into the back bedroom, I looked into my office, which looked like someone had turned the entire room upside down and shaken it. The desk drawers were out, and all my papers and receipts were scattered about the room. The chair was overturned, and whatever clothing was in the old dresser and closet was now on the floor, as were the dresser drawers.

"What kind of fucking idiot looks for a trunk in a desk drawer?" I asked aloud. As I reached the back bedroom, I was immediately able to see the closet door was open and the trunk was gone. The trunk was simply a wooden shell crate that my grandfather brought back from Sicily after the war. He fought as part of a cannon unit in Italy in World War Two. As General Patton fought Operation Husky in his now famous push through the mountains of Sicily, my grandfather's unit provided fire support for the tanks and troops. My grandfather had simply packed his belongings and knick knacks in it to haul them home.

At some point he had stained the crate and added hinges to it. He had replaced the original rope handles with braided leather straps as well. It still had the U.S. ARMY brand burnt into it as well as some numbers painted on the side. He had taken the time to put thin cedar sheeting inside so whatever was inside would smell like cedar for a while after it was removed. Why would anyone want it? Why would anyone be willing to kill over it?

Just then Brad called up to me, "You better hurry up; those assholes are getting away!"

I rushed down the first section of stairs and around the landing. I slowed to see the view that must have been the last thing Mr. stand on my hand with his fancy shoes ever saw. I couldn't see the top of the bar where I had rested the shotgun. Mr. fancy shoes never had a chance. He simply turned the corner and went down. I'll bet he never even heard the shot.

I wondered what had happened to him. That was the only human being I had ever shot. I hoped it was the last. It was self defense. Would the police consider it self defense? I think it would be considered self defense. I was afraid for my life when I pulled the trigger. I thought I remembered seeing his gun fall when he fell. I felt a sick and uneasy feeling take over my senses. I would need a bottle of antacid very soon.

As I continued down the stairs I saw Brad holding the gun I had given him in return for the Uzi. I mean how do you really say thank you for a fully automatic illegal machine gun? I did it with a 50-caliber Special Forces sniper rifle with a ten-shot magazine. It fires a three quarter ounce copper-coated lead slug that is just over one-inch long accurately out to about 1,500 yards. That's fifteen football fields. I fitted it with a Leupold 25 x 50 mm 8.5 scope with laser range finder. We spent hours shooting that thing from the top of the hills around the lake. You can cut down trees as big around as beer cans from 2,000 yards away with only one shot. Needless to say there aren't many beer-can sized trees within three quarters of a mile of the hills we climb to practice. You should see what it does to a one-gallon paint can from 500 yards. It's awesome!

Of course, I did have to get a special permit from the ATF to buy it. I'm now on the list of psycho nut militia types the FBI keeps track of who would actually buy a weapon like this. It seems the government wants to know who has operational cannons, machine guns, bazookas, rocket launchers, and heavy guns like the 50-caliber I bought for Brad. My lawyer said I really didn't want to be on that list. However, that is the only way they will let you buy one of these guns legally. They even ask you what you intend to do with the gun. Like you could really do anything with a 50-caliber semi-automatic weapon! It totally destroys anything it shoots. It cuts down trees half a mile away. My attorney filled out my paperwork for me because he said they wouldn't find "squirrel hunting" as my intended use very amusing.

Brad was also holding my hunting rifle. He told me he probably should have a handgun as well, but they weren't in the safe. I gave Brad one of each of the extra pistols I had, and we headed for his four wheeler.

"How did you see the smoke?" I asked. He told me he had taken a shower when he got home to sober up and get The Muskee smell out of his hair. When he got out of the shower he looked out his window and saw the smoke from my burning house.

"I figured you were up to something pretty cool with that much smoke," he said. "Then when I saw your house on fire, I guessed you must be extremely pissed off and drunk in The Muskee," he explained. "When I turned off the quad and heard the smoke alarm in the bar, I just grabbed the fire extinguisher." We strapped the rifles to the front of the quad. I rode bitch, and we sped toward my burning cottage to take the snowmobile trail. I guessed the blonde-haired dude and his friends would be long gone. I didn't think we had any chance to get in front of the blonde-haired dude before they got to County Road 300.

Chapter Fifteen

When we got to the top of the hill that overlooks the saw mill and the road to The Muskee, we could just see the tail lights of a dark SUV in the distance. We couldn't believe how slowly they were driving. The tail lights seemed to be crawling along at less than twenty miles an hour I'd guess. They disappeared around the side of the next hill down the valley. I knew we could get ahead of them and have time to set up for taking a few pot shots at them. We would be ahead of them long before they got anywhere close to the county road.

I then realized why they were moving so slowly. The flashing red lights lit up the evening sky. It seems someone had called the fire department. The flashing lights preceded the pumper truck rounding the corner followed by the fire chief's SUV, an ambulance, and a sheriff's cruiser. It seems a lot of people were interested in my fire.

"We're gonna nail those motherfuckers!" Brad yelled at me as we jumped over the crest of the next hill.

"I can't wait!" I shouted back as I bounced around holding onto the rack on the back of the quad for dear life. Brad was usually an overly cautious driver when in the woods on a quad. We tease him all the time about how a little old lady in her electric scooter could pass him on his quad. I don't know if it was booze or adrenalin, but he never drove this fast. We were flying through the woods. Brad didn't even let off the gas when we went through the stream.

The water seemed extra cold as we swamped the quad almost bringing it to a complete stop.

"Don't get us killed!" I screamed as I shook the water off of my face.

"Fuck off!" he shouted back. We raced down one last hill and up the other side before Brad slid the four-wheeler to a complete stop. We jumped off and laid down next to a tree stump that we regularly used as a shooting stand to shoot small trees with the 50-caliber.

Just then a large dark Cadillac sedan followed by an Escalade pulled around the hill about 1,000 yards away. I could read the emblems on the front of the cars through the scope on my hunting rifle.

"I think you should shoot the tire of the car in front after it crosses the bridge," I said to Brad.

"Good idea," he responded. The bridge that crossed the creek was one of the old steel erector set types. Every year the local graduating high school class painted their year on the bridge, as well as countless other graffiti sayings. The bridge was known as 'the haunted bridge' by everyone in town. There were the usual rumors of Satan worshippers hanging dead goats from it and suicide attempts on the bridge as well. None of it was true, of course, but everyone has a haunted house, or barn, or cave or whatever with the same sort of stories in their home town.

It was an ideal site for our little ambush. The cars would have to slow down almost to a stop to make the 90-degree turn after crossing the narrow old bridge. The other good thing about the bridge was that we were only about 200 yards away looking down at it. We could kill them all if we wanted to. I believe that was Brad's plan.

As the cars approached the bridge, I could clearly see into the lead car through my scope. There were two men in suits in the front seat, one man sitting upright behind the driver and another man lying in his lap across the back seat. I could see him working on the man laying in back. I assumed it was Mr. fancy shoes that I had shot. In the SUV behind them there were two more men in front and two in the back. I couldn't see the blonde-haired dude.

As the car turned onto the bridge, I heard the click as Brad released the safety on the fifty. I did the same on my rifle. I took two more deep calming breaths and tried to feel my pulse before having to decide who, if anyone, I was going to shoot.

Suddenly a horrible feeling washed over me. I don't know if I can do this, I thought to myself. Up until this point it had just been another one of our stupid little adventures. It's one thing to shoot a man in front of you who intends to do you harm. It is an all-together different thing to sit on a hillside and ambush people like some sort of military sniper. We were about to take the law way, way into our own hands. No trial, no due process, just a death sentence. I was terrified, more afraid than I had ever been in my life. I hadn't been this afraid when they were beating me up. I didn't feel any fear whatsoever while we were shooting at each other inside The Muskee. I don't know if it was a survival instinct, or adrenalin, or if I was just reacting to a bad situation. Right now, right here on the side of this cold hilltop, I was terrified. I began to shake violently.

If it were a deer or moose, I'd kill it and eat it for days. I'd be proud to tell everyone the story again and again. But these were human beings in those cars. I could see the color of their hair through my scope. Even if they did burn down my house and try to kill me, they were still people.

"We should go get the cops," I said to Brad.

"Fuck that. These bastards burned down your house," he replied. This was a line that I wasn't sure I could cross. Sure, I've broken the law with Brad on numerous occasions, but this was a total disregard of the founding principles of society. I lifted my head and opened my left eye and looked down on the car turning off the bridge. I turned to my right just in time to see Brad squeeze the trigger on the fifty.

The muzzle flash was especially bright in the twilight of the evening. I closed my left eye and pressed my cheek against the wooden stock to take aim with my hunting rifle. As I refocused on the lead car, it rolled to a stop in the grass on the left side of the road. I could see the passenger in the front seat talking into his radio and pointing at us. The driver had already opened his door, and I could see the muzzle flashes coming from his pistol. I heard a bullet whiz over our heads and crack a tree branch behind me. Brad squeezed off another round.

I saw the driver of the car's head explode.

"One down," Brad said with no expression in his voice. I looked at the SUV that had now stopped alongside of the car. All four doors were open, and I could hear gunfire and see muzzles flashing. It sounded like a string of firecrackers.

"Two down," I heard Brad say as if ticking off items on a grocery list. Just as I placed my crosshairs on the blonde-haired dude stepping out of the driver's side rear door, dirt erupted all around me. Dirt flew up onto my scope; it was in my hair and spraying my face. I realized that these guys could see us and were good shooters. Bullets whizzed all around us as I rolled over behind the quad and looked back at Brad. He was laying face down on top of the fifty.

"Brad!" I screamed. "Brad!" I screamed again. He didn't move.

Just then one of the tires on the quad exploded and sprayed me with a burst of air. It blew dust and debris right into my eyes and all over my face. I began rolling down the hill away from the crest taking cover from the incoming rounds.

I crawled to my left, scrambling behind the ridge about twenty yards from my original position before standing up to a tree to shoot. I placed the side of my rifle against the tree and looked through the dust-clouded scope. Two men in suits were firing from behind the front doors of the SUV at Brad and the quad. The guy standing outside the rear passenger door was speaking into his radio. The blonde-haired dude was tossing my grandfather's war chest into the open door of the back driver's side door of the SUV. I placed my crosshairs on the guy on the passenger side front door and squeezed the trigger.

I saw the blood spurting from his neck as he fell to his knees and then flat to the ground. The Escalade started to speed away with the rear side passenger jumping over the man I shot in the neck and holding on to the top of the door trying not to be left behind. My next shot shattered the front passenger side window of the SUV. I took aim at the rear window of the truck and fired a shot shattering it as I watched the truck speed away around some trees.

The silence was absolute. I looked down on the dark sedan and the carnage we had caused. There was a man in a bloody suit lying in the back seat of the car. Another man was lying behind the open lid of the trunk splayed straight out. The man I had shot in the neck was on his knees bleeding profusely in the dirt. His hands were pressed against his neck trying in vain to stop his hemorrhaging.

"Fuck you," I said angrily aloud.

My shoulders sagged as I turned and began walking, holding my gun across the front of my body with both hands. It only took two paces before I could clearly see the blood and part of the back of Brad's head missing. He hadn't moved from where I had last seen him. There was blood in the dirt and steam rising from the hole in the back of his skull. I turned away and began to dry heave. I began throwing up and coughing.

"I'm so sorry, Brad. I'm so sorry." I began sobbing.

Chapter Sixteen

I walked down the hillside to where the Cadillac was stopped alongside of the road. As I approached, I saw the man I had shot in the neck several yards behind the car lying face down in the dirt. The car doors were all open except for the rear one on the driver's side. I could hear the beeping of the alarm from the keys being left in the ignition. The man I had shot inside The Muskee was slumped over a computer bag sideways in the back seat with blood smeared all over the tan leather.

Another body was lying straight out behind the car. The man just looked like he was asleep. No pool of blood, no real noticeable damage. When I got closer to the car, I could see a hole in the trunk lid. This had to be the second man Brad shot. I looked inside of the trunk of the car to see my old photos and plastic beer mugs and t-shirts from college. There was no crate, just another laptop computer case next to it. What am I going to do now? What the hell were we thinking?

I decided it wasn't a good idea to leave all these dead guys in the road with the fire and sheriff's departments at my house. They were probably getting the fire under control and would soon find the mess inside The Muskee. They'll be looking for me and Brad soon enough I thought. I set my rifle down in the trunk of the car and searched the body of the dead guy at the back of the car lying in the dirt. Nice shot, Brad, I thought. He put a bullet right through the back of the trunk lid and dead center of this guy's chest.

There were only a couple of drops of blood on the front of his shirt, but he was lying in a large pool of blood that seemed to be growing. I opened his coat and checked the inside pockets. I found a lighter, cigarettes, pocket knife, and his passport with some other form of picture identification. *Italia* was on the front cover of his passport. It was Italian they had been speaking inside the bar. I checked his front pants pockets and found a large wad of cash.

"Thank you very much," I said as I tucked the cash into my pocket. There was also a hotel check-in envelope. It said, "Sleep Inn Port Huron, MI," and had two plastic card keys and a handwritten *#115* inside. I shoved the envelope with the keys into my back pocket.

I dragged his body around to the back seat of the car. My lord, a dead body is heavy and awkward to move. Fuck this, I thought as I got him to the back door. I was sweating and panting and now had his blood on my shirt and pants. I decided just to drag his body off the road and stash it in the woods. Forget putting it into the car—that would be way too much work. Multiplied by three bodies, and it was more work than I had accomplished in the last few years.

The other two bodies had the same wads of cash, same cigarettes, same lighters, same knives, and same forms of picture identification. I left all three in the weeds in the woods just off the road, only dragging them far enough not to be noticed. I kicked dirt and gravel over the blood in the road to cover it. This was a lot more work than I had first imagined. It took as long to cover the blood in the road with dirt as it did to move the bodies. There was a lot of blood in the road. I decided to drive the car, flat tire and all, to Brad's old house as it was only a couple more miles away.

By the time I stashed the car in Brad's barn, it was 9:45 p.m. It was dark, and I was tired and sore. I needed to get back and get Brad's body. I needed to get back there before anyone left my house fire. It would not be good for me to be seen on Brad's snowmobile right now by anyone. People would definitely wonder why I was driving Brad's snowmobile down a gravel road towing a rescue sled when there is no snow on the ground. I had been formulating a plan while hauling bodies into the woods and driving over here. I didn't think I could go to the police at this point.

"Yes, officer, I killed two Italian guys and Brad got two before they shot him. We did it sniper style with a 50-caliber from 200 yards. Well, really, the first guy I killed with an illegal sawed-off 12-gauge in my bar. It was self-defense because they spilled booze in my eyes and tried to burn me alive. They stole my grandfather's war chest and torched my house." I didn't even know how I would explain it to my lawyer, let alone the police. Hell, I didn't believe my story, and I was there. My plan wasn't great, but it was a plan, sort of.

First, I needed to stash the car and the bodies so they wouldn't be found for a few days. That I had already accomplished. Then I had to get back and get Brad's body and wait for the police to leave my house and The Muskee. I couldn't just leave my friend on that cold lonely hillside.

I figured the authorities would be leaving pretty soon. They must have the fire under control by now. I could then call Brad's brother Tim to start funeral arrangements and leave Brad's body in the cooler until we could have a proper burial. I wouldn't feel right leaving his body on the hillside for a bear to eat. He was, after all, my lifelong best friend. I could then get my things and try to beat these assholes to the Sleep Inn and get my grandfather's war chest.

I wondered, why were they staying in Port Huron? Would they even go back to the Sleep Inn? They had the war chest; maybe they'd just go back to Italy. The war chest was the key to everything. Why was it so valuable? What was it? What was inside it? How did they even know about it? How did they know my name? Why did eight men travel halfway around the world to kill me for a wooden box from WWII? All are good questions, but I have to keep moving. I sure hope they are going back to Port Huron. Maybe I should go to the police right now. No, I just can't go to the cops.

Brad and I keep all of the keys to all of our toys in their respective ignitions. Most of the time, you'll even find our car keys in our cars. We live in the middle of nowhere Wisconsin; who would steal our stuff? With the exception of tonight, there's always somebody around. The only vehicle left in Brad's barn was his snowmobile. That would be the way I got back to Brad and to The Muskee. I didn't want to try to hoist his body into his pickup truck. Besides, I can't take the truck on the snowmobile trails.

Brad has this sled we use when we camp or ice fish in the winter. It is the kind of sled mountain rescuers use to take injured skiers off the mountains. We use it to haul gear when we ice fish. We also use it when some crazy Chicago client wrecks a snowmobile. Then we have to haul their dumb ass off the trails to safety. I never thought I'd need to use it to haul Brad's dead body. I can't believe what I let happen.

As I hooked up the sled to Brad's snowmobile, I began sobbing uncontrollably. That quickly led to just plain old crying. I grabbed a plastic tarp and strapped it to the sled. My tears rained onto the tarp like a spring shower. I drove back to the top of the hill where Brad had been killed. My sleeves were wet from wiping away my own tears. Driving the snowmobile down the old gravel road, I could hardly see because of the tears in my eyes. It had grown cold, and the tears blew out of my eyes and ran all the way back into my ears. I haven't cried like this since I was a child.

I scraped along all the way down the gravel road and bounced up the hill on the snowmobile to where the quad and Brad's body were resting. I laid the tarp next to his lifeless body and rolled him into it. I carefully wrapped him up like a big blue human burrito. Once he was wrapped, I said a prayer as I knelt over his body and cried my eyes out.

This was undoubtedly the most difficult task I had ever performed. I struggled to treat my best friend's body with respect while folding him into a cold plastic tarp on the side of some stupid little hill just over a mile from his home. Why was I looking at him instead of shooting those Italian bastards when the fighting started? I kept asking myself that question. Why did we even come to this hillside?

If we'd only told the police what happened when they arrived with the fire department, we'd both be drunk and roasting bratz on my still smoldering house right now. It would all be just another stupid happening at The Muskee. Instead, there were three dead dagos in the weeds, one in Brad's barn, and my best friend was dead in a blue plastic tarp. I'm sure I'll be arrested. Oh, shit, I'll be arrested! I'll be jail bait. I'll be forcibly sodomized in prison.

My mind shifted from mourning to panic. I'm going to be arrested. I could blame it all on Brad. Sorry, pal, but you are a dead ex-con. Everyone knows you're a drug-dealing alcoholic. I sure as hell don't think any less of you because of that, but you do make a great scapegoat. Shit, why did I shoot that guy in the neck? They'll know that the bullet that went through his neck didn't come from the 50-caliber rifle. It will be quite obvious because his head is still connected to his torso. A shot from the 50-caliber would take his head clean off. He'd look like his headless friend that Brad shot. They'll trace that round to my rifle. They'll trace the pellets in Mr. stand on my hand with your fancy shoes back to the 12-gauge in the bar.

Try and think, Jim. Can I go to the cops now? Right now, can I just go tell the cops what happened? I'm sure I'll need to call my attorney first. I'll definitely need a lawyer. I'll undoubtedly need a whole legal team. No, I can't go to the cops right now. I'll have to get back to the bar and call my lawyer. If they don't find any of the bodies, I'll have some time. I wonder if they found the mess inside The Muskee. I think I left the 12-gauge on one of the tables inside the bar. Of course, they'll go into The Muskee. That's always the first place people look for me. Oh no, if the cops go into the basement and look inside the gun safe, I'm in real trouble.

The two safes in the basement of The Muskee are used for secure storage for Brad and me. Most of the cash in the safe was from Brad's drug sales. Besides, we need to have cash on hand to pay off big gambling losses. Let's say one of my clients from Chicago would bet on the Bears on Monday Night Football. That client would usually call up a friend, or two, or eight, and see if they wanted a piece of the action. If that client lost, we would only charge him the vig on his initial bet. That way he was able to charge his friends the vig and recoup some of his initial loss.

Most of the time my client didn't end up owing Brad any of his own money if he lost his initial bet. He only had to cover the total loss of his friends' bets. One of my clients actually gave Brad his gold Rolex to cover his loss because he didn't have enough cash with him, and we don't take personal checks. When he got home and collected the cash from his friends, he just went out and bought the newest Rolex model. So, now we have one gold Rolex in the gun safe as well. Having cash on hand also makes it easy to get in 'our' plane and fly to Canada. We'd just grab some cash and go hunt.

I'm sure I left the safe open. If Brad left it open as well, the cops would find an open safe with an illegal Uzi submachine gun, a gold Rolex wristwatch, and probably 20,000 dollars. All of that on top of an illegal sawed-off shotgun, a torched house, a bullet-riddled bar, and three dead Italian hit men in the woods. Not to mention a Cadillac with a bullet hole, flat tire, bloody seats, a dead body, and Brad's head blown apart. Yeah, I don't think that going to the cops right now is a good idea. I think it probably best to wake my lawyer when I get back to the bar.

Chapter Seventeen

I needed to get to The Muskee without being stopped by the police or the fire department. I shoved my arms under the tarp and heaved Brad's body into the rescue sled. It was quite a bit heavier than any of the dead Italians. As I finished strapping it down, a pair of headlights pierced through the darkness on the road below. It was the fire engine followed by the ambulance. They must have gotten the fire put out. That meant I only had to wait out the fire chief and the sheriff.

They were undoubtedly drinking in The Muskee waiting on me or Brad to show up. Knowing both of them as I do, they're probably filling their back seats with cases of my beer from the cooler. I wouldn't be surprised if they had already filled the entire fire truck and ambulance with my booze. The fire truck passed over the bridge, turned and headed down the dirt road past my position on top of the hill. As the ambulance turned off of the bridge it slowed and turned to point its bright headlights into the woods where I had stashed the Italians' bodies. My heart sank, and a sickening feeling came over me. The ambulance rolled to a stop just before its tires went into the weeds on the side of the road. The driver turned on his flashing lights. The EMT riding in the front passenger side opened his door and climbed out. He stepped over the tall weeds and walked straight toward the spot where I had dragged the three dead Italians. He appeared to be looking down at the blood trail the bodies left. He quickly ran back to the ambulance and grabbed a medical kit. He said something to the driver who was now speaking into a radio and ran back to the bodies. Now I'm totally fucked.

It seems my plan might have a few holes in it. I could hear the sirens of the fire engine that had already passed crank up. A few seconds later more sirens came from over the hill back at The Muskee. Everyone who had been at my house and bar was now on their way to the three dead men. I couldn't start the snowmobile for fear they would hear it and see the lights. At this point I had no clear thoughts. I just started running for the relative safety of The Muskee.

I dashed down the hill, running as hard as I could and trying not to tumble down the hill. I got to the bottom and ran into the freezing water of the river, falling forward but catching myself with outstretched arms. I stumbled and struggled to get back to my feet but just as I did, I stepped into a hole and fell backwards to my left. The current pushed me downstream on my backside. I struggled to flip myself over but that was almost worse; I was now being pushed by the current with the front of my body facing down so my knees bashed against every rock and boulder I passed. I grabbed a large rock, stopping my forward motion, but as I dug my feet into the rocky soil, the rocks gave way. It took several failed attempts for me to get enough of a foothold to allow me to crawl to the opposite bank and stand up.

I splashed my way onto the bank and gasped for breath. Slumped over on dry land, I placed my hands on my knees and tried to catch my breath. I watched the water pour off of my body and onto the ground while my clothes clung tightly to me. I stood upright and began shaking uncontrollably from the frigid water and 40-degree air temperature as I tried to regain my wind, panting like a dog. I'd never felt so cold in my life. There was steam rising off of my soggy clothes.

Keep moving, I thought to myself as I watched my frosted breath pour out of my mouth. I peeled off my outer collared shirt and threw it to the ground. It made a soggy squishing sound as it slapped the dirt. I watched the steam rise from my arms. No time to stop I said to myself as I began running up the last hill before reaching my property. As I crested the top of the hill that looks down on the cabins and The Muskee, I stopped to see if anyone was there and to listen to the sirens. I was gasping for breath and my body was shaking harder than I thought imaginable. I placed my left hand on a tree for support and lifted my right hand to look at it. My right hand was trembling so violently it actually looked blurry. Just then the sirens stopped.

I guessed they must all be at the ambulance and would soon begin looking for me and Brad. I sloppily stomped heavily down to The Muskee, making sure all the emergency vehicles were gone. They were. As I approached the kitchen door to The Muskee, I noticed the yellow crime scene tape placed across the door by the police. There was also a white sticker placed over the door and the molding. Well, they can just add this to the list of multiple felonies I've committed today, I thought as I ripped through the seal.

As I walked past the ovens, I could almost feel Brad's presence in the kitchen. The warm stink of The Muskee never smelled so inviting. I paused briefly to listen and make sure no one was inside. After hearing nothing, I ran upstairs and into the bathroom. My first priority was to get out of my soaking wet cold clothes. I must be hypothermic. I stripped naked and jumped under the hot water of the shower head. I stood under the warm water trembling.

You don't have much time Jim, I thought. I had only been under the shower for about a minute and then toweled off quickly. I was still shaking but wasn't nearly as cold as I had been. I had to keep moving. The sheriff would definitely come looking for me right away. They'll probably begin searching the woods and the lake at first light. It will only be a matter of hours before they find Brad's body. I went into my trashed guest room and found clothes I hadn't worn in years.

When I looked into the closet where my grandfather's war chest had been, I found my two old suits. They were still in the dry cleaning bags with their shirts and ties. Perfect, I thought. If suits were good enough for Italian hit men, they would be good enough for me. I hadn't worn either of these things in years. It seemed to be the perfect disguise. Aside from the waist being a little snug, and my gut hanging over the belt a little, they still fit fine. Well, I couldn't button the coat, but I felt pretty good that it fit at all. I grabbed one of my old suitcases and a duffle bag from the back of the closet. I stuffed my second suit in it and grabbed my trench coat.

I was now in the midst of a mad dash around The Muskee to get everything I needed. I had to get the hell out before the sheriff or someone else showed up. I went back into the bathroom and picked up my cold soggy jeans, reached into the pockets and got my wallet, the large wads of money each of the Italians were carrying, and my .38 revolver and holster. I'd lost my Desert Eagle somewhere along the way.

I pulled the soggy envelope containing the plastic key cards from the Sleep Inn out of my back pocket. The water had caused the ink to run and I struggled to recall the room number. Was it #113 or #123, maybe #115 or #125? Shit! I just didn't remember what had been written on the envelope. Right now it didn't matter. I had to get the fuck out of The Muskee. I stuffed everything into the duffle bag and ran down to the basement. Leaving the suitcase at the top of the steps, I went down to find both safes closed and locked. That's great news, subtract a few extra years of jail time from my sentence.

I opened the gun safe first and began grabbing all the cash and flinging it into the duffle bag along with my passport. It just made sense to keep my passport in the gun safe because this was the first place Brad and I came before departing to

Canada in 'our' plane. I grabbed the box of shells for my .38 and slid them off of the shelf into the bag. I figured I should ditch the Uzi at some point, and somehow it seemed like a good thing to bring along. I decided to throw the Rolex in just to clean out the whole safe. I slammed the door and moved on to the next safe. This is the one that I could do time for. This was Brad's safe. I had a pretty good idea of what was in it, but I never actually opened it before.

I had bought it for him years ago when I was helping him look for his wallet. He had just moved into the vacated upstairs of The Muskee when I finished my new house. He had misplaced his wallet, and we began going through dresser drawers and dirty clothes looking for it. I kept finding piles of cash and drugs all around the upstairs of The Muskee. That was enough. I went out that day and bought this heavy as hell antique cast iron safe for him to stash things in. We agreed that with all the people that stay at The Muskee or use the upstairs rooms during bachelor parties, we just couldn't have all his cash and drugs sitting about not locked up tight someplace. Because I bought it, I knew the combination. That and the fact Brad couldn't remember the combination. There really is something about short-term memory loss and habitual drug use, and alcoholism, and stupidity. I was curious to find out what was inside the safe when I heard a car pull up outside.

Oh, shit! I was in a panic. I heard the car door shut as I got to the base of the stairwell. I just had time to dash up the stairs, grab my suitcase, and get around the corner into the kitchen before hearing the hinges squeak as the front door of The Muskee opened. I could hear a man's voice speaking quite clearly.

"Yes, honey, I don't know how late I'm going to be. It doesn't matter. He said I would get overtime. I'm supposed to stay here until Scott starts his shift tomorrow morning. Right now, it's only a triple homicide. I'm supposed to question and detain anyone who shows up here. I guess I'll just have a beer and watch highlights of all today's games."

How am I going to get out now I thought? Surely he'll hear the door if I open it now. I still hadn't thawed out completely from my dunk in the river but I was sweating. I could hear the man still speaking on the phone and pacing around the bar.

"You should see the inside of this bar," he said. "There was a fire and some sort of a gun fight. I'm not even supposed to be in here. No, this place is trashed. I'm just going to grab a couple of beers and go sit in my squad car."

I crouched in the corner of the kitchen behind the dishwasher. The kitchen of The Muskee is laid out in the shape of the letter L. The vertical part of the L is where the ovens and deep fryer are located. You can just see the last oven at the top of the L from inside the bar. Past the ovens along the same wall are the salad and condiment cooler station and then the dish rack. Across from the dish rack in the horizontal part of the L is a large sink with a garbage disposal and adjacent to it is the commercial dishwasher. There is about a two-foot space between the sink and the dishwasher in the corner. This is where I was crouching with my suitcase and duffle bag sitting in the aisle in front of the dishwasher. Between the dish rack and the dishwasher is the kitchen door, which is in the heel of the L.

The cop was still chatting on his phone as he strolled past the restrooms and entered the tiny kitchen of The Muskee. I could hear his shoes approaching past the ovens. My heart was pounding so hard I could feel each pulse in my forearms. His voice was getting louder. I could now see his left shoe and the back of his left pants leg. He was looking at the dish rack with his back to me. Don't freak out! Don't freak out! I kept saying silently to myself. Brad punched a cop and went to jail, whatever you do, don't punch the cop.

Just then the officer's police radio broke his conversation.

"Hey Phil, I need you to come sit on these bodies; there's a Cadillac with Michigan plates out at Brad's on 300. It's got another dead guy in it," the voice on the radio said.

"Ten-four" the officer replied. He turned away from me and trotted out of the kitchen.

"Did you hear that? I don't know what's going on. I'll be gone kind..." then the front door slammed behind him and the bar was silent. Looking down at my hand, my whole body was trembling again. Now I really did have to take a shit. Fortunately, I guessed I had time.

After finishing in the bathroom in about two seconds, I looked carefully out of the kitchen door window to make sure there were no police or sheriff's cars in the parking lot. I could see for a ways around the lake and didn't see any headlights. I gave one last look back into the bar of The Muskee to try and remember if there was anything else I needed. 'WaMPaGG' was the acronym Brad and I used to make sure we had everything before we left the bar. 'Wallet, Money, Passport, Gun, Go' was what we always said to each other before heading to Canada to hunt. I stared blankly into the dish rack and remembered one thing I had forgotten. I ran back into the bar and grabbed a bottle of scotch. It was one of the few bottles that the blonde-haired dude had not used to torch my bar.

Hurrying across the side yard and parking lot, I arrived at the boathouse. I kept all of my toys inside. Barnacle Bill and Sam called it my toy box. It is much larger than I need, but I am trying hard to fill it up. It has everything. My four wheeler, Harley, Rhino, backhoe, bush hog tractor, waverunners, boats, and cars are all inside. I also have quite a tool shop as well. I didn't come for any of that tonight. I flipped on the lights and strode over to The Mallard.

'Our' plane actually has a name, she is called The Mallard. It's a 1981 Cessna 206 turbine turboprop with green and black stripes. It comfortably seats four and has the capacity to carry all of our luggage as well. I have never flown at night before, so this was not only dangerous; it was completely stupid, but necessary. I threw my bags onto the front seat and opened the cargo door. The Mallard has an extra wide rear cargo door, which came in handy when we needed to haul a lot of gear. We could take out the rear seat and fit short kayaks for fishing trips. We could roll in scooters if we were going to a Packers game.

We could fit tons of camping equipment easily through the large door. I hooked the loading ramp to the floor of the plane and pushed one of the scooters into the back of The Mallard. I quickly half-ass strapped the scooter down and secured the ramp and cargo door. I then reached onto the front seat and grabbed my log book.

Step one, pre-flight inspection and walk around. I stopped to steady myself. You have time to do this, and you must do this, Jim. I took a couple of deep breaths. You never fly without going through the step by step pre-flight. Well, if I'm going to die in a plane tonight, at least it will be a safely inspected aircraft. My pre-flight routine usually takes about forty minutes. Tonight, I did it in ten. As soon as I finished the pre-flight, I ran to the side of the boathouse and hit the automatic door openers and the outside lights. The whole resort was suddenly flooded with light. If anyone on the lake was awake, they now knew where I was. I cranked the turbine, and it whirred to life.

I taxied out of the boathouse down the boat ramp into the waters of Bear Lake. I didn't waste any time at all, as soon as I felt the plane floating in the lake I pointed the nose southwest into the prevailing winds and increased the pitch of the propeller. You're supposed to wait for the oil temperature to come up, but I just didn't have time. The plane surged forward and began picking up speed. I took one last look back at The Muskee and didn't see any sirens.

The Mallard lifted skyward, and I tried to relax a little. Sure I did. The last thing I could do was relax. I was now a fugitive flying illegally at night. I was beginning to get comfortable as simply a fugitive of justice; it was the flying at night thing that had me worried. Just stick to the basics, Jim, I told myself. Wings level smooth turns. Check altitude, check speed, wing tips level. Trust The Mallard. She'll take care of you.

I turned northeast after getting above the tree line. The last thing I wanted was to get picked up in the Minneapolis/St. Paul air traffic. If the tower called, I would answer, of course, but if I could avoid any air traffic controllers right now, I would. Brad and I used to bet on how long it would take before we would get seen on radar and called by the FAA. We started with a stopwatch and quit after we managed to get back and forth to Canada and Tim's house twice without anyone ever calling us.

After flying at 200 feet for about five miles I turned east and headed for Port Huron. This was not a short flight. I figured it must be about a two- to three-hour flight. I would have to fly over Lake Michigan, the state of Michigan itself, and land on Lake Huron. I guessed it was probably somewhere in the neighborhood of 400 miles and would take me about two and a half to three hours.

That should give me about four extra hours to find the Sleep Inn before the Italians arrived, assuming they were returning to Port Huron. If they didn't show up at the Sleep Inn… well, I didn't even want to think about them not showing up. What would I do if they didn't show up? Worse than that, what the fuck do I do when they do show up?

My plan had worked so far. That is to say I'm not in jail, at least not yet. I reached over and grabbed the bottle of scotch. It was time to take a little nip. Screw that, it was time to take a big gulp. My hands weren't shaking anymore, and I didn't feel like I was going to shit myself. This seemed to be a large improvement over the past five or so hours.

The heater of the plane was now blasting warm air on me, and I was beginning to thaw. The scotch helped and tasted great. I thought I should feel tired, but there was no way I could sleep right now. My senses were on high alert. I started planning what to do once I landed. Of course, my plan assumed that I could find Lake Huron at night. That sounds quite a bit simpler than it really is. The horizon is pretty dark up here.

I would then have to land safely on water at night. Right now, that was the most concerning part of my plan. Just land safely Jim. Nothing else will matter if I crash The Mallard. I better get another shot of that scotch. Once I land, I'll have to unload a scooter, on a dock, by myself, at three o'clock in the morning. Sure, that seems nice and safe. What could possibly go wrong during that goat fuck of a procedure? First, I had to find the right great lake. Keep checking that your wingtips are level Jim.

Chapter Eighteen

Coming in for a landing in Lake Huron was intense. I hoped this was Lake Huron…? By intense, I mean cold and windy and spraying two foot tall white caps intense. Like I can't seem to keep my wing tips level intense. Like I hope I don't crash The Mallard intense. Like…

"HOLY MOTHER OF GOD!" The entire plane jumped up and to the left, and my bottle of scotch hit the dashboard as I was about twenty feet above the tops of the white caps on the waves. Hang on, Jim. Wingtips level, Jim. Calm down, Jim. Stop screaming, Jim. I could read those headlines. "Mass murderer dies in cold watery plane crash. Police suspect alcohol involved."

There were lights on both banks so I could tell where the horizon was, sort of, but I couldn't see all that well. There was a misty fog on the water because the temperature had dropped several degrees that day. I certainly couldn't see directly ahead of my plane. Now, I understand why Barnacle Bill had trashed so many sets of floats. If there were something in the water in front of me, I was going to hit it. Hard. I was praying it wouldn't be a coal ship or an oil tanker.

The Mallard did a belly flop into the water and skipped across the tops of the waves, bouncing along roughly as water cascaded across the windshield obscuring everything in my sight. I sighed and made the sign of the cross and thanked God I was alive. The prop wash continued to spray the windshield, and as I turned out of the wind, the chop on the water rocked the plane with a rolling motion. If I were susceptible to motion sickness, I'd be getting ill right now. The plane was rolling so violently the wing tips on both sides of The Mallard were almost touching the water as I taxied into Port Huron. I hope I'm in Port Huron. It's not like there is a big neon sign or anything.

I managed to find an out-of-the-way concrete commercial boat dock with a separate wooden dock. The commercial loading dock was empty of any ships, and the wooden dock was perfect to tie off against. As loud as The Mallard is, I didn't seem to wake anybody. Of course, no one is awake at this hour of the night anyway. I pulled the plane to the windward side of the dock. I reached into the back seat and pulled the rubber bumpers into my lap. Now I had to attach them to the landing gear without falling into the lake.

As I opened the door of the plane, I was blasted with sea spray. The wind immediately blew the light door of The Mallard shut. This was going to be a ridiculously difficult chore. I decided to turn the plane into the wind and make another lap of the harbor. I idled the engine and grabbed the bumper for the rear vertical landing support. I had to cling to the side of the plane bouncing around and not fall into Lake Huron. I managed to get both bumpers securely attached and climb back into the plane. That really sucked. I was cold, wet and shaking once again. What the hell am I doing?

I've been asking myself that question since I left Bear Lake. That question has consumed me for the past two hours. I can't go home. I hate the fact that I seem to have no real choices right now. I'm not in control of my own life at this moment. I'm a murderer. I killed two men. I don't know anything about the legal system. I don't know if what I did would be considered self-defense. All I know for sure is that I shot two men and then fled the scene. I know my best friend is dead from my direct actions. I don't know what I'll do when I find the Italians. I don't even know if I'll ever see the Italians again.

I throttled up and pulled The Mallard alongside the dock. The bumpers I put out banged between the dock and the landing gear float as I tied up the plane. I pulled the long awkward loading ramp down and attached it to the frame of the cargo door, all the while struggling to keep my balance and not fall into the frigid water of Lake Huron. The blowing sea spray made everything cold and slippery. I rolled the scooter down onto the dock without seeing anyone or being seen myself. This was quite a balancing act I was performing. This wooden floating dock is not very stable. There was a strong wind and the water was splashing over the floats on the plane and up onto the slick wooden dock. I started the scooter and rode onto dry land and went back for anything else I needed.

It took me all of five seconds to come up with a plan. It was more of a scheme than a plan. I would leave all of my cash locked in the plane and spend only the 4,000 dollars the Italian hit men had so generously donated to my cause. I would keep the pistol inside my coat pocket and the Uzi on the floor of the plane. I set the duffle bag full of money on top of the machine gun and slid it as far back in the cargo bay as it would go, where it wouldn't easily be seen.

My wallet was still damp and cold from my swim in the Blue River back home. I figured it was better to keep my left tit wet than my left butt cheek, so I put my wallet and my passport in my left inside coat pocket. I had laid all my belongings out on the copilot's seat during my two and a half hour flight, but that still wasn't enough to get them all dry. My first stop had to be a phone book to find the address of the Sleep Inn. I would check into a room at the motel, hopefully close to the Italians. When they showed up, if they decided to show up at all, I would have to make a new plan.

I found the Sleep Inn at about four o'clock that morning and scootered up under the portico and parked in front of the glass doors. As I walked in, the lady at the desk was talking on her cell phone. She looked rather strangely at me and asked if she could help me. Look at me, lady, I thought. I look like shit. Of course I need helping.

"I have some friends staying here from out of town," I announced as I looked around. It was after all, 4:00 a.m. and I needed to be in control for a moment. I had been completely out of control all evening and just needed to take charge for a moment. Before I could say anything else, she said rather authoritatively,

"They're staying in 113 and 115 on the back side of the motel. Their cargo van is parked in front of their rooms, but I haven't seen them since Friday morning."

She certainly has it together, I thought to myself. So much for taking control, Jim.

"They must be enjoying the trip," I replied politely.

"Whatever … what can I do for you?" she asked.

"I'm riding that scooter over there because my car isn't ready yet, and I noticed the gate in the block wall out back."

"Uh-huh," she said with a suspicious look.

"It would be easier for me to exit the parking lot through that gate into the alley," I continued. "This looks like a busy street out front, and I don't want to embarrass any Ferrari drivers," I joked.

"You might hurt your face," she said sarcastically looking at my swollen head, split lips, and blackening eyes.

"You should see what's left of my helmet, from my last wreck that guy caused. I think his name was Enzo," I said while pointing to my face and smiling as cute as is possible for me.

"No problem sir, the maintenance man gets in at seven, and I'll leave a note for him. Is there anything else? A room perhaps? One hundred eleven is available next to your friends around back? Is that good enough?"

"That would be fine," I replied. I paid in cash and took the envelope with my plastic key cards and walked back out to my scooter. I pulled in both brakes and revved that son of bitch up to 4000 rpm's. I honked the pathetic little horn at the clerk and tore into the parking lot. I think I hit a blistering 15 mph—right around the corner of the building to my room.

I arrived around the back of the Sleep Inn and saw the large white cargo van. The parking lot at the motel was mostly empty, and it was obvious why. The place was a dump. As a member of the lodging and overnight rental industry, I am often insulted and amazed by what passes as a livable room.

I decided that it was best that I disable the cargo van. At least with the cargo van at the motel, it seemed reasonable to assume the Italians would return. I parked the scooter next to the van and let all the air out of the van's right front tire.

"That's what you get!" I said with a sneer. It was fun. I hadn't let the air out of someone's tire since I was a kid. I think it was Mike Wilson's ten-speed at the drug store buying candy when we were kids. I hoped they wouldn't notice. I know it's not totally disabled, but this would at least slow them down.

I retrieved the keys I had taken from the dead Italian and tried them in room #113 first. They opened room #115. Big surprise, I had a fifty-fifty chance, and I got it wrong. I went inside and flipped on the lights. How stupid am I, I thought. If there had been any more Italians staying here I'd have gotten myself shot when I opened the door. I need some sleep. I took one quick look around the room and could see they hadn't left anything behind. The room was either unused or freshly cleaned. I left and walked two doors down to my room. I set the alarm clock for seven o'clock, knowing the Italians were in for at least a ten-hour drive if they were coming directly here and made no extra stops. I called the front desk and left a wake up call, just to be safe. I ended up pulling the scooter into my room so no one would know I was here.

I jumped out of a deep sleep as soon as the phone rang. It scared the hell out of me. I had stripped and climbed under the covers after making my wake-up call request. It felt great to lie down and take a break. I think I fell asleep as soon as my head touched the pillow. My face and head were sore.

My ankle and wrist were sore. As I hung up the phone from the wake-up call, the alarm clock began beeping. I sat up and turned on the lights. Walking over to the mirror I was finally able to take a good look at my face. I was a mess. My whole head seemed to be swollen. My eyes had black circles under them, but weren't blackened yet. My upper lip was split but not swollen. I filled the sink with cold water and stuck my face into it. The cold water felt wonderful and shocked me awake. I think I could have easily slept until next week. I began re-doing the drive time calculations in my head. If they had left for Port Huron and not stopped since I shot the window out of their Escalade, they should arrive roughly ten hours later. That would put them in town right about now. They would have stopped for gas and probably food at least once. I guessed they would arrive in another hour or two. I better get moving. I took a quick shower and got dressed. I collected all of my belongings and walked toward the front door.

A sudden panic attack gripped my whole body. It was hard to breathe, and the hair on the back of my neck stood up. As I approached the front door, I reached into my suit coat pocket and pulled out the revolver. My heart was pounding, and I was beginning to perspire. I quietly stepped to the door and cocked the hammer back on the pistol. I placed my shaking left hand on the door to steady myself and pointed the gun at the back center of the door. My heart was racing, and I could feel my whole body start to shake. I slowly and deliberately looked through the peep hole and saw nothing but an empty parking lot. I eased the hammer up on the pistol and stuck it back in my pocket. I fell back against the wall and looked up at the ceiling breathing deeply.

"You have got to be nuts, Jim," I said aloud. Placing my face into my hands and then pulling my hair straight up, I asked, "What the fuck am I doing?"

I opened the door and looked in both directions. The van was to my right parked in front of one of the Italian's rooms, and their other room was down a little further. A six-foot-tall concrete block wall surrounded the parking lot with the gate still locked. So I decided to go find the maintenance guy myself. I walked through a break in the two hotel buildings and headed to the office on the front side of the hotel grounds. I strode into the lobby and asked the new clerk for the maintenance man.

"You need the back gate opened, right?" said the clerk.

"Yes, I would, please," I replied.

"I'm not supposed to do this, but here is my key. Just bring it back when you're finished, and I'll lock it up after you check out."

"Thanks a lot." I turned and walked toward the glass front door just as a black Escalade passed the motel on the main street out front. I jumped behind a large potted plant. I nearly pissed myself. It was not the same Escalade. The one the Italians were using was green and had two windows shot out. I am definitely not cut out to be a secret agent. There was no chance of being cool after that. I was sweating and shaking again. My nerves were frayed. I looked back to see the clerk looking worried that he had entrusted me with his key.

"I'll just a…that is to say…a…be right back," I said as I pointed with my thumb over my shoulder and walked out. I paused to look carefully both ways before exiting through the glass door. The clerk was obviously disturbed and baffled by my behavior.

I walked around the buildings and unlocked the gate. It swung open into the alley, and I propped a brick in front of it to keep it open. I figured if I had to flee on my scooter I could escape into the alley and at least the Italians would have to drive around the block. Down the alley to my left about twenty yards was a street. Across that street, another twenty yards through two way traffic, sat a Denny's. Down the alley to my right it was about fifty yards to another alley that intersected the alley I was standing in. That alley gave access to the main street in front of the motel. I returned the key to the hotel clerk in the lobby and drove down the alley to Denny's for some breakfast.

I pulled the scooter up to Denny's and went in to begin my stake-out. The waitress came over and said,

"Nice watch; can I get you anything?"

"I'd like a pot of coffee and a menu. I won this watch on a bet over a Chicago Bears game," I said.

"I can tell it's real because the second hand sweeps smoothly and doesn't tick like it does on the fake Rolexes. I'll be right back with your coffee." I had forgotten how good I looked in a suit with a 5,000 dollar watch, even if I was riding a scooter. I finished eating breakfast and reading the paper and sat there waiting. I asked for my check just as the Escalade pulled into the parking lot of the Sleep Inn.

"Our Father, who art in heaven…" I started to pray as I began sweating. I then walked carefully out of the restaurant.

Chapter Nineteen

I pulled the scooter out of Denny's, across the road, and into the alley. I cut the engine off and coasted past the back gate. I needed a clear view of both hotel rooms. I could see the cargo van all the way from Denny's, and the Escalade was parked next to it. I did not see any of the Italian men. I stepped off the scooter and peered cautiously over the wall. The Escalade's shot-out windows had been covered with plastic and duct tape. I had seen the men get out and go into one of the rooms together. The ammo box must still be in the car, I hoped. I had lost sight of the Italians as they passed behind the cargo van and then disappeared into the room. I didn't think I would get a better chance than this. I pulled the gun out of my pocket and made a mad dash for the car. Crazy as hell! I got my gun, and I'm running across the parking lot as fast as I can. I believe I've lost my mind. I arrived panting at the back of the SUV and ripped through the plastic. Sure enough, the ammo crate was sitting there. I pulled the crate over and opened it. It was empty, and they had ripped the cedar lining out. I quietly slid the crate to me and tilted it to look inside. There was writing carved into the wood on the bottom. Just then the door to room #113 opened and out walked the blonde-haired dude who had tried to choke me back at the Muskee the day before.

He had a look of shock and disbelief on his face as he started yelling. I didn't hesitate. I dropped the crate and raised my .38. I shot at him through the front windshield. The windshield shattered and fell into the car. As the windshield exploded, I was running. I pointed my gun back over my shoulder and shot again. That was one of the dumbest things I've ever done. The pop of the gun deafened my right ear. Looking back I saw that my second shot blew out the large picture window in room #215 up on the second floor. Nice shot dickhead. You're deaf and can't shoot for shit.

I was looking and sprinting as hard as I could at the gate. I think I may have scared the shit out of myself again. Fortunately, the gate was located directly behind the SUV so they couldn't get a clear shot at me. It certainly wasn't from lack of trying. Someone was shooting. The concrete around the gate exploded and splashed over the right side of my face as I passed through. I kept my head down as low as possible as I tried to start the scooter. I pulled in the brake, pushed the start button, and twisted the throttle of the scooter wide open. I started running alongside it to gain speed. I jumped on and swung my feet onto the small foot platform of the scooter. Looking back at the gate under my right arm, I saw someone speaking into a radio and pointing at me. A muzzle flash was followed by smoke. He's shooting at me! I instinctively turned hard left into the small alley to get out of the line of fire. As I made the turn, I looked back to my left and saw another flash from his gun. No sooner had I rounded the corner than I immediately looked to see where I was headed. I slammed into the side of a steel dumpster which propelled me over the handlebars smashing my nuts squarely into the speedometer. My knees, my chest, and my face hit the blue metal dumpster. The tops of my thighs caught under the handlebars. I fell sideways to my right and struggled not to fall over completely. It was futile. I fell awkwardly to the ground and into a concrete block building stunned. Oh, my God, my nuts hurt. That was horribly painful. I quickly untangled myself from the scooter, which was now revving and spewing blue exhaust into the air. The back wheel was spinning at full throttle.

I struggled to stand and stepped to the corner of the nearest building between the shooter and myself. I blinked, shook my head and spun around the corner of the building, firing at the man with the radio who was rounding the same corner in my direction I barely had time to pull the trigger before he ran into me. My right wrist rolled over as his body smacked into the gun.

He fell into the front of my legs as I flopped over backward hitting my head on the asphalt. I barely felt the pain. Adrenaline and terror had taken over my senses. I looked down to see him clutching my coat and spitting up blood. I ripped my hand out from between our bodies and began pistol whipping him in the head and face. I was kicking my feet and hitting him with the base and side of my gun. I was slapping at him with my free hand.

"Get the fuck off me!" I yelled as I pummeled the man. I was scared out of my mind. He was dead. His limp body was like sandbags piled on top of me. I was able to get loose by sliding on my back and kicking as hard as I could at his head. I rolled over and struggled to get to my feet just in time to see the Escalade round the corner and begin bearing down on me, its tires screeching. It was just the blonde-haired dude driving the SUV with no windshield, a look of murderous rage consuming his face.

Man, did he look pissed off. I ran over to my scooter and grabbed the handlebars. It skipped along the ground slamming into the dumpster with the tire screeching as I struggled to regain control of it. I grabbed the back brake, got the scooter under control and headed in the right direction. I ran about two steps alongside it before jumping onto the seat—not looking back but still feeling that the SUV would run me down in another second or two.

I saw a narrow sidewalk between two brick buildings and grabbed the back brake as hard as I could without letting off of the throttle. The rear tire screeched loudly, and I turned the handlebars to the right. Putting my foot down, I was able to shove the scooter down the sidewalk. I pushed so hard with my leg that I nearly fell off the scooter. My foot flopped backward, and I bashed my ankle on the muffler. The scooter hooked up and gained speed. I swung my feet onto the platform and managed to once again get seated correctly.

I glanced back as my body got past the corner of the building. The bumper brush guard of the SUV crashed into the back of the scooter. I heard the crack of snapping plastic as I saw the passenger side mirror of the Escalade explode against the building as the back end of my scooter came apart. The scooter shot diagonally into the building on my right. My right handlebar caught the building, and I was again stopped by the scooter's center column. Once more my groin took the brunt of the impact. I immediately puked up Denny's. It looked like coffee and grits. I think my eyes stretched about two inches out of my skull when my balls hit the speedometer.

Again my thighs caught the underside of the handlebars as both legs and my arms flew forward. The scooter didn't move. After the initial impact I was flung backward and down with my spine hitting the point of the seat about mid-way down my back. My chin landed on the handlebars, and I was on one knee helplessly in a heap on the foot platform. I was in unimaginable pain as I pulled myself back up onto the seat. I was coughing violently and seeing spots. I first got to my hands and knees and was able to stand. I pulled the scooter upright and started to try to climb back aboard. Sputtering down the narrow sidewalk between the buildings, the scooter began to gain speed. I started spitting the awful taste of vomit out of my mouth. My eyes were watering so badly I could hardly see. My back, oh the pain in my back. Oh, the pain in my nuts.

I raced to the end of the sidewalk and shot straight across a busy street. I nearly ran into the front of a moving car. It scared the hell out of me. The car locked up its brakes and honked its horn as I passed. I shot directly across the street past a row of parked cars and hit the curb with my front wheel. I bounced the scooter onto the sidewalk and barely managed to get turned to the left before hitting another building. I was millimeters from scraping the brownstone with my right elbow and crashing again.

I struggled to maintain control and accelerated on the sidewalk just in time to see the blonde-haired dude in his Escalade screeching around the corner and coming toward me on the other side of the parked cars. I was now speeding toward him. He locked up his brakes and smashed into the rear quarter panel of a pickup truck. I couldn't get any closer to the building on my right to put more distance between the two of us. The shrapnel of exploding glass flew over my head and showered the building. I couldn't believe there was enough room for me and the scooter to fit behind the back bumper of the truck as it spun toward me and the building.

The blonde-haired dude wasn't trying to turn and chase me; he was trying to crush me against the parked truck. The back side of the truck might have hit me had it not been for a tree growing through a sidewalk planter. When the truck spun, its tail end came to an abrupt stop against the tree. There were too many cars on the street for the blonde-haired dude to turn around. It was a big mistake on his part. He had just caused a large traffic snafu, and there were about four cars honking at him. I turned right down the next alley and sped away as fast as the heavily damaged scooter could go.

The scooter had picked up a terrible vibration when the SUV ran into the back of it. It might have happened when I hit the dumpster. It could have possibly happened when I hit the brick wall on the sidewalk between buildings. It didn't matter; my scooter had seen better days. It was shaking so violently I almost hit the building when I turned down the alley. I made another quick turn down an alley to my left and followed it for about six blocks. I then turned onto an empty street and followed it for about a mile, wobbling and bouncing on the scooter's bent rear wheel. Oh, my balls. Pulling into another alley, I laid the scooter against a building and knelt down in the alley. I puked all the rest of my breakfast up. It was a horrifically violent and very painful upchuck. This wasn't like throwing up after drinking ten shots of tequila, where after you relieve yourself, you feel better. No, this was a projectile vomit that hurt my gonads. My whole body ached. I continued spitting up.

What a fucking dumb ass I am. To hell with this. No more. I quit. I'm going back to The Mallard and flying the fuck away. Oh, my God, my balls ache. I'm so lucky to be alive. Again. I'm in so much pain. I sat back gingerly against the building in the alley for a couple of more minutes trying to catch my breath before driving back to The Mallard.

A sudden wave of terror washed over me. I could now hear sirens approaching. I have got to keep moving. The sounds of sirens grew louder and closer. I can't slouch next to my scooter in some dirty alley sobbing from the pain any more. It took all the fortitude and strength I could muster to slide gently back onto the scooter and head for the relative safety of the plane. It took me another ten minutes to get back to the dock where I had parked The Mallard.

I pushed the scooter into the lake.

"You piece of shit." I yelled at it as it bubbled to its watery grave at the end of the wooden dock. I never want to ride one of those testicle wreckers again. I piled myself into the back of the plane. Reaching over the seat I grabbed the bottle of scotch and took a huge swig. I pulled the duffle bag under my head and lay there in pain with my eyes closed until I finally fell asleep.

Suddenly I was startled awake by a pounding on the door of the plane. I struggled to sit up and look out the cargo door window. I was in pain and groaned audibly while struggling to lift my body. As I rose and looked out the window, I found myself staring straight into the eyes of a police officer tapping his flashlight on the door of The Mallard. My stomach rose into my throat.

"Open the door, buddy!" the officer shouted. I reached for the handle with a shaking hand. I opened the door and stared blankly at the cop. I'm in so much pain and so mentally spent I can't even speak.

"What are you doing here?" asks the officer as he tries to see around me into the plane. I try to make myself as wide as possible in the cargo door to prevent him from seeing the Uzi lying behind me. "These guys got a boat waiting to dock here, and you're in the way," he explains.

"Sorry," I reply about an octave higher than my normal voice. "I was feeling a little drowsy and decided to stop for a nap."

"Well, move on, buddy, these guys got work to do," says the cop as he turns and walks down the dock. My nerves are so frayed at this point I feel as though I'm totally numb. With the exception of the unimaginable pain I'm feeling, I am totally numb. I consider asking the cop to just take me to jail; instead I slide forward, stepping onto the float while hanging onto The Mallard's cargo door. It is all I can do to not fall into Lake Huron. Man that water looks cold. I slide up into the front seat to grab my log book and begin my pre-flight. About half an hour later, mercifully, I point The Mallard into the wind and race across the water. There is a fueling station about ten miles away in Grand Bend, Ontario. I decide to head over there to gas up and figure out what the hell I'm going to do next. I know without even thinking about it, there is only one place I can go. As the floats on The Mallard rise out of the water, I grimace and say, "Fuck Port Huron!"

Chapter Twenty

After a brief stop in Grand Bend for fuel and lunch, I am beginning my three-hour flight. I purchased some frozen peas and am now sitting on them. The Mallard is pointed northwest and cruising on autopilot. Scratch number five bad guy, I think to myself. The blonde-haired dude must hate me with a passion. He and his boys flew all the way from Italy, drove for twenty-some hours in two cars just to get a wooden box, and I had to go and kill five of them. I know I had help, but this guy with blonde hair is going to kill me. He knew my name; he knew where I lived; he even knew about my grandfather's ammo crate. My whole body aches. I wonder what the cops are doing back in Wisconsin? I wonder what the cops are doing back in Port Huron? How am I going to get out of all this trouble? I need to call my attorney. I really need a drink. I reach over and rip open the aspirin bottle I had purchased at the fueling station and throw a couple of them into my mouth. I pull the cork out of the scotch bottle and take a nice big gulp. What have I gotten into? I'm in so much trouble. I'm in so much pain.

The Mallard touched down in Lake Nipigon about 1:00 p.m. local time. Before I got to the shore, Brad's brother Tim was running down the dock to meet me. He caught the float and had the plane tied up before I got the engine shut off and the door open.

"Look at you in that monkey suit man!" he said as I climbed backward out of the plane. I had forgotten about my bold fashion makeover. Before I had time to speak, he said, "You must be in it deep to fly all the way up here without Brad looking like that." He smiled. "Big Jack got here about an hour ago and said he'd wait for you. He's up in the house right now." I didn't know how to tell Tim about Brad so I just started talking. I looked right at him and said,

"There's been a lot of trouble. Brad got shot. Brad is dead." Tim stared at me, and his whole demeanor changed.

"What?… When?… How?" he asked. I looked at him and said,

"These Italian guys came into The Muskee and were trying to kill me. I managed to shoot one of them, and they left. Brad and I went after them and we killed five all together. One of them shot Brad in the head. He's dead."

Tim reached forward and grabbed me. I threw my arms around him and he gave me a huge bear hug.

"He's really gone?" Tim asked.

"Yes, Tim, Brad is dead."

We stood there crying on each other's shoulders for at least another five minutes. I walked in the back door of Tim's house and heard Big Jack Slade say,

"You're in one hell of a fucked up mess this time, Jimmy." He was sitting in the dining room around the corner reading a couple of hunting magazines.

I managed a smile and said, "How are you doing Uncle Jackie?"

"A lot better than you," he said sharply. I handed him what was left of the bottle of scotch. He gave me a big hug as he shook my hand. "I'm really happy to see you're alive, Jimmy." He said, "I'm surprised there's anything left in this bottle with the trouble you're in. Four dead zips with Michigan plates?

What did you do to our friends in Detroit? Somebody is trying to send you a pretty serious message. They only send zips for serious jobs. These guys are so fresh off the boat, they stink like tuna. You're fucking lucky to be breathing." That's right, Big Jack Slade is my Uncle Jackie Salvatore. He and my father were business partners in Chicago before my dad died in 1974.

"I didn't do anything; these guys came for grandpa's old ammo crate," I said. Uncle Jackie got very serious.

"You didn't give it to them!" he said raising his voice.

"I didn't have a choice. They killed Brad, and I've been shot at about a hundred times in the last fifteen hours," I whined.

"Where is the ammo box now?" Jackie asked abrasively.

"It's in an Escalade in Port Huron," I replied.

"What the fuck? You've got to get it back!" he was now shouting.

"I don't even know what it all means. Besides, I know why they wanted it. It had something carved into the wood under the cedar lining," I explained.

"What was it? What did it say?" he asked.

"It was a location followed by my father's birthday. Does that mean something to you?" I asked.

"Tell me the location!" Jackie was now shouting excitedly, but still shouting.

"You tell me why these guys want me dead and what's at that location!" I said pounding my hand on the table. "I've been shot at. Run over. I got the shit kicked out of me. My house got torched, and my best friend got his brains blown out!" Big Jack stared at me and pointed discretely. I turned around to see Tim standing behind me.

"I'm going to check my trot line and the traps; I'll be on the radio if you need me," he said.

"Sure, Tim," said Uncle Jackie. "Let us know if we can do anything at all, okay?"

"No sweat. I'll be an hour or so. I won't go across the creek to the north, and I'll stay north of the house and east of the access road," he said with a somber tone. Tim looked at me and said, "Thanks for telling me straight up, Jim. I do appreciate that. And thanks for taking care of Brad."

"It was truly a pleasure to have spent time with him," I replied. Tim cracked a smile and walked out the back door.

"Do you think he'll be okay?" Big Jack asked.

"He'll be alright. He's strong," I answered. "I want to know why they tried to kill me."

Jackie was pouring the scotch into two glasses he grabbed off of a buffet next to the dining table.

"It goes back to World War Two. It's just a rumor, and no one believed your grandfather. He didn't speak about it until he was old and half senile. My papa, your grandfather, had a saying. He always used to say, if we only had Mussolini's money."

"I remember him saying that a couple of different times," I interrupted.

"He said it a lot," Uncle Jackie continued. "He used to tell us stories about the war. He was sent to Italy as part of a cannon squadron. They shelled the Italian and German armies as a part of Operation Husky before General Patton's tank forces pushed through the mountains of Sicily all the way to Messina. After Sicily was won, your grandfather stayed on the island as some sort of liaison because he spoke fluent Italian. He stayed in Palermo. I think there may have been a few forces with him just in case the Germans tried to retake the island.

"He was there for a couple of years before he got moved to the northern border of Italy as the Germans were surrendering, and the war was winding down. He told us a lot of stories about Sicily, Northern Italy, Austria, and Switzerland. He said that by the time he left Sicily, he knew everyone on the island. He said he ended up seeing a lot of the Sicilian men crossing into Switzerland after the Germans surrendered."

"What about when Italy surrendered?" I asked.

"I'm not sure how the Italians surrendered exactly," Jackie continued. "Mussolini relinquished power long before the Krauts or Japs surrendered. I think he was removed in the summer of 1943."

I interrupted suddenly,

"If the mob put Mussolini in power, I wonder what they stole from him as it was all falling apart. Or even after he was gone? If the Mafia was tight with Mussolini, they may have had a license to steal while he was in power. It sounds like the ammo crate may have some of those answers in it. How do you like that? We had no idea that grandpa knew where Mussolini's money was hidden all along!"

"You don't know that for sure," Jack interjected. "Mussolini wasn't even a Sicilian. He may not have had close ties with the Mafia."

I rolled my eyes at Uncle Jackie and said,

"Come on, you are going to sit there and tell me Mussolini wasn't connected?"

"The only thing I do know is that whatever is in that ammo crate is reason enough to kill you, me, Brad, or whoever else gets in their way. Those Italian hit men are the real deal. The professionals you killed were probably the best Mafia hit men in the world. They wouldn't have sent zips like them if that case weren't worth its weight in solid gold," Jackie said forcefully.

"Well, they are long gone by now," I said.

"Why's that?" asked Jackie.

"I shot and killed one in the alley behind their motel in Port Huron. One caused a traffic accident as I was getting away. If they're not under arrest, they are not hanging out in Port Huron."

"What did it say inside the ammo crate?" Jack asked.

"It was a location carved into the wood. Under the location was my father's birthday," I responded.

"Where did it say?" Jack asked with a gleam in his eye.

"I'm not saying," I stated firmly.

"What, are you going after them on your own? You don't know what you've gotten into. These guys aren't going to make another mistake. They will be ready for you now. They will not underestimate you again. You killed five of them and found them four hundred miles away. They're going to wherever it says in the box, or they've already called ahead, and someone else is there waiting for them to arrive. Either way, you can't get anywhere near that place, or you'll be killed." Big Jack sat back and took a long sip of scotch.

I stood up, walked into the kitchen, and picked up one of the radios charging on the window sill.

"Hey, Tim, how do I access the Internet out here?" I asked. Tim's muffled voice called back,

"Just turn on the tower in my office."

"Thanks," I said.

Chapter Twenty-One

"Good luck!" Big Jack said as he slammed the door of The Mallard. I had given him the Uzi, and he stood with it next to Tim on the dock. I cranked up the engine and taxied away from the dock.

Big Jack looked at Tim and said, "You lost your brother, and I'm never going to see my nephew again." Tim had filled the plane's gas tank while I showered and shaved. I was going after the Italians. I figured that if I didn't, Brad and my grandfather would never rest in peace. Besides, I couldn't go home right now. The authorities would be calling Tim looking for me soon enough. I told Tim where Brad's body could be found, and he said he and Uncle Jackie would straighten things out at The Muskee. They both wanted to come with me, but I was able to talk each of them out of it.

I told Tim he had to lay his brother to rest. I told Uncle Jackie that he had to think about Aunt Louise and his twin daughters. They both reluctantly agreed with me. The Mallard lifted out of the water, and I pointed it southwest and headed for Thunder Bay. I absolutely, positively needed to get to Thunder Bay before four o'clock. It was the one stop I had to make before I flew to the Toronto International Airport. The Toronto airport had the fastest and last flight to Rome that evening.

I needed to get to an international airport and didn't want to try and enter and then leave the United States. I wasn't sure if there was an arrest warrant outstanding for me, but I didn't want to take any chances. I had eight hours to catch my flight out of Toronto. There were closer international airports in Canada, but they didn't have direct flights. I needed a direct flight to Sicily. The best I could do was, wait two days for a direct flight to Sicily, or fly directly to Rome in eight hours out of Toronto. At least that would get me on the correct continent fairly quickly.

I landed on Lake Superior at 2:15 p.m. local time. I took the box Uncle Jackie had prepared for me to the nearest Federal Express Store. It contained my .38 revolver and about twenty rounds. They were accommodating, even though I lied when they asked if there were any explosives in my package. What the hell, mailing firearms wasn't the dumbest thing I had done in the last twenty-four hours. Uncle Jackie bet Tim 500 dollars that the package wouldn't make it. They also bet that I would be arrested and thrown in jail when I tried to pick it up in Rome. Uncle Jackie was betting against me on both counts. I hoped he hadn't sabotaged my package just to win the bet. I didn't believe he would, but Uncle Jackie had done some pretty shady things for a lot less than 500 dollars.

I saw him steal an entire rib roast from a restaurant because he wasn't wearing a sport coat. We were in Chicago, and he wanted to take me to some famous steak house where Frank Sinatra used to eat. The maitre d' wouldn't let us in because Uncle Jackie wasn't wearing a coat. Uncle Jackie started cussing out the maitre d', right in the front door. When he picked up the phone to call the police, we left. Uncle Jackie told me to wait in the car, and he walked around to the back door. About a minute later he came running around the side of the building with half a cow! It was slung over his shoulder, and he was moving a hell of a lot faster than he looks.

He was yelling for me to start the car as the dishwasher and a couple of busboys chased him around the corner. I slid over into the driver's seat, and we took off. Uncle Jackie threw the side of beef into the back seat and jumped on top of it. We laughed all the way back to The Muskee. We ate steaks all week. We even let Brad cook a few. He screwed them up, of course. That was the last time I visited Chicago. Honestly, I haven't been back to Chicago since.

I touched down at night in the chilly waters of Lake Ontario on the east side of Toronto. This was the second time I had to fly at night, and I didn't enjoy it at all. Fortunately, the winds had died down, so the water was relatively calm, and landing was far easier this time. I taxied to the seaport and rolled out of the water and onto the tarmac. I tied the plane down and rented a car. I pulled my duffle bag and suitcase out of the plane and tossed them into the trunk. I had another stop to make before my British Airways flight left in four hours.

My stop was to Wal-Mart for a whole new mini wardrobe. I could use extra underwear given my proclivity to soil myself. My favorite new piece of clothing was a hat. What the hell I figured, no one knew me where I was headed, and I always wanted one. It was a black Kangol-type cap. I also bought a large backpack and some new shades to complete my disguise. I tried to get casual clothes that didn't look too American. Everything was black or beige. The last thing I needed to look like was a tourist. I wanted to not attract attention. I paid for everything in cash and walked out to my car. My car was parked under a light out away from the building.

I started stuffing cash into different places in my new clothes and my suit. I had 28,000-plus dollars on me and had to figure out how much I would need for my trip. I managed to get 15,000 of it into various shoes, pockets, and my new shaving kit. Thirteen thousand seemed like an awful lot of cash to carry through customs, but what the fuck. I was, after all, wearing a 5,000 dollar watch.

I arrived at the airport two and a half hours before my flight. I went to the British Airways terminal and checked in. I sailed through security and grabbed a book and a pair of magazines. I then went right to the bar. I had a first-class ticket to Rome. I would need to get a train ticket south to Naples and then take a ferry or some such over to the island of Sicily. I wasn't sure if I would even glance at either magazine as I was tiring fast. Tim had given me two pain killers and warned me to only take one at a time. I took both.

I walked up to the bar and began with a scotch. I have to say that before about twenty-four hours ago, I had never really cared for scotch all that much. I prefer rum or vodka. Gin and tonic with fresh lime. Margaritas, always on the rocks, lightly salted. Frangelico and Baileys on the rocks. I also drink beer and wine regularly. But, tonight I'm having scotch. Everyone knows why. You drink a scotch, and there's no going back. Just like this fucked up journey I'm on. There's no going back.

After two more scotches, they announced my flight would begin boarding first-class passengers. I picked up my backpack, fumble mumbling about a little bit, and went fumble mumbling to my gate. I sat next to the window in the back row of first class. Now this was the way to fly. I reclined and ordered another scotch on the rocks. I figured that if I were to sell The Mallard, I could afford to fly in first class for the rest of my life. That scotch should put me to sleep for the duration of the flight. The flight attendant brought me my drink, and I took half of it in one large gulp. I pulled my new cap down over my eyes and covered myself with the blanket. I was sound asleep when the captain came over the loudspeaker.

"We're clear to push back as soon as the last few passengers get on board," he said. Just then the female flight attendant announced to first class,

"And here they are."

I pushed my cap up to see the blonde-haired dude and his two friends walk onto the plane and head in my direction.

They sat in the three empty seats in front of me. They didn't recognize me, or maybe they didn't see me.

I tried to shrink into my seat. I pulled my cap over my face and began to pray. What am I going to do now? What if they see me? I think I'm safe on the plane. At least they won't be shooting at me for about eight hours or so. I just have to make sure they don't spot me during the flight. It looked like they were as tired as I was. Unless I give them a reason to notice me, they probably won't. I'll just sit here and not get up I think. From where I was sitting, I couldn't see any of them. They would have to stand and turn around to see me. Yes, if I stay seated with my hat over my face, they'll never see me.

The flight attendant came by and asked for my glass, telling me that we were getting ready for takeoff. I slugged back the remainder of my scotch and handed the glass to her. My hand was shaking so much I almost spilled the ice on the poor gentleman sitting next to me. The flight attendant sensed my nervousness and said,

"I'll bring you another once we're at cruising altitude."

"That would be great," I sort of whisper slurred at her. I couldn't keep my eyes open.

The plane angled skyward and went up like an escalator. We were on our way to Rome. Just me and two-hundred-and-fifty-or-so other people and the guys that killed my best friend. The guys that came to my bar and tried to kill me. The guys that torched my house and tried to blind me. Calm down, Jim. Stop grinding your teeth, Jim. Only 7:58.39 left before we land, Jim.

I wanted some sleep but seemed to be having a little trouble at the moment as you might imagine. Only 7:57.54 before we land now, Jim. Stop grinding your teeth, Jim. I kept my cap over my face only lifting it to drink my scotch. I fell asleep shortly after the blonde-haired dude began snoring. I think it was about 7:52.21 until we were to land. I didn't wake up until the plane touched down with a thud. It startled me. I didn't move. I hadn't moved. I had been in a pain pill-and-scotch induced coma for just under eight hours. I was trying not to freak out. The guy sitting right in front of me killed my best friend. The guy sitting right in front of me torched my house. That fucking dude with blonde hair sitting in front of me ruined my life!

The plane came to a stop at the gate, and everyone in first class stood except me. I unbuckled my seat belt and pushed back my new cap. The blonde-haired dude's eyes almost came out of his head! He was standing and looking back over his chair around the cabin of the plane. The look of disbelief on his face was priceless.

I leapt out of my chair and punched that son of a bitch in the nose. The point of his nose went between my second and third knuckles, and he stumbled into the back of the chair in front of him. I reached over the back of his seat and tried to grab the back of his shirt and pull it over his head like we did in hockey fights as kids. All I got was a left hand full of his long blonde hair. He screamed like a piglet squeals. I dragged him by the hair over the back of his first-class seat and socked him in the face with a massive right uppercut. It wasn't a perfectly clean shot, but I caught the left side of his face with a slapping blow that crossed his entire face. I pushed my hand back into his face as I recoiled for my next punch. I saw blood dripping onto the airplane's grey carpet as I cocked my right hand back and lined up to hit him again. I was going to drill him this time. I never saw which one of the other Italians decked me.

Chapter Twenty-Two

I woke up with bright lights shining in my face. I was strapped to some sort of miniature wheelchair with a woman shining a light in my eyes. Wow, did my jaw and neck hurt. This woman with the light was wiping blood off of my face. I can definitely taste blood. I am getting very familiar with its taste, and I don't enjoy it. It's a good thing I'm not mobile as I may have spinal damage. I'm not sure if I'm bleeding from my face, but it hurts a lot. I can only see a bright light and anything that would pass directly in front of my line of sight. My head and entire body are immobile. My shoulder and ribs hurt quite a bit as well. Just then the cargo lift they were using to remove me from the plane bottomed out with a loud clunk. They rolled me into a waiting ambulance and it peeled away with those weird European sirens blaring.

"Mr. Salvatore, can you hear me, Mr. Salvatore? I need you to tell me what happened, Mr. Salvatore," said a man's voice seated to my left. I strained to move my eyes to my left, but all I saw was the inside of the ambulance.

"What's going on?" I mumbled.

"You are on your way to the hospital to get checked out. Can you identify the man that did this to you?" he asked impatiently.

"Sure," I said matter-of-factly, "It was that blonde-haired son of bitch sitting in front of me."

The man to my left sighed audibly and held up his police badge so I could see it and said,

"The man with blonde hair who was sitting in front of you is a very dangerous criminal. Mr. Salvatore, don't speak again of this to anyone. My boss will come and see you in your room at the hospital. You will need to speak to a lawyer right away. Might I suggest we go to the American Embassy immediately?"

"No!" I shouted. "My neck, oh, my neck, I need to go to the nearest hospital and get my neck looked at. Quickly."

"Okay, Mr. Salvatore. We will take you to the nearest hospital," the policeman said.

Fuck me, now that was a close call. Don't take me to the embassy. I can't go home. I don't know how much jail time I'll get for a fist fight on a plane in Italy, but they'll lock my ass up for murder back in the States.

"Oh, my neck!" I yelled out again. I think I'll yell it at anyone who passes in front of my strapped down head from now on. Just don't make me go home. Please, don't take me home.

I arrived in the hospital, and they were all speaking Italian, of course. They tilted me onto my back and began unstrapping me from the wheelchair and restrapping me to a flat board.

"Oh, my neck!" I yelled again, smirking to myself.

They wheeled me on a gurney flat on my back into an x-ray room and took my pictures. I threw in some more neck hurting crap as I got wheeled around in the hospital. I must be in trouble here in Italy to have the policeman offer to take me to the embassy 'immediately.' Clearly it has something to do with the blonde-haired dude. Or, it could be that there would be less paperwork if I would go home right now. If they put me on a plane back to the States, I would simply vanish. No mess for anyone. Sorry, cop, I can't go home right now. You will just have to suffer through the paperwork. They pushed me into a room and left me alone for a moment. The silence was beginning to freak me out. All I can see is the ceiling tile right above me and a fluorescent light.

"Hey," I yell out. "Hello, anybody." I hear the door open, and the same cop says, "Mr. Salvatore, are you alright?"

"I just want to know, what's going on?" I reply.

"The men who attacked you were not just ordinary men," he began. "Each of them has been in and out of prison many times. They hang out with a lot of other very bad men that disappeared from our surveillance a little less than a week ago. They are all Sicilian, and they should not have been allowed to leave that island, let alone this country. We believe it is in your best interest to leave Italy and fly back to America as soon as you feel you are ready again to travel."

"I feel alright now; I'm just a little sore," I reply.

"Great, should we make your flight arrangements right now?" he asks.

"No," I state firmly, "I'm not leaving Italy right now."

"Do you understand what I have just told you, Mr. Salvatore? These men, they will find you and kill you. Why they attacked you on the plane is what we are trying to find out. These men are much more discrete. They usually just shoot you in the back of the head. Sometimes, they blow up your car. They might even slit your throat. Why do you suppose they would attack you on an airplane? They would have known they would be arrested. They have all been arrested before and they would not want to be arrested again. Why do you suppose they attacked you? I think it is in your best interest to take care of your business in Rome and leave quickly."

"I understand this," I replied. "I will be fine. I wore a Packers jersey to a Raiders game once, I'll be okay."

"American football, yes, this I understand," said the policeman. "I went to a New York Giants game in New York City once," the officer explained. "You Americans, you watch your sports games, and you eat your popcorns. You take your children to the game. When I go to watch football in Rome,

I bring my pipe, I got a gun. You are an idiot. You will not leave Italy alive. Then I will have to phone United States and tell your wife you are dead."

"You don't like me very much. Do you?" I said half asking and half stating the obvious.

The other policeman interrupted quickly saying, "The men that assaulted you will have lawyers on the way to both the airport and the police station right away. Only one of them has an outstanding arrest warrant. Even with that warrant, he will be free tomorrow. The others will walk free as soon as their lawyers get to the station in less than one hour. Their lawyers will walk into my boss's office with the prosecutor very soon; twenty minutes after that they will be free men. You have to leave now. You will not be safe anywhere in Italy. Please reconsider going to your embassy. We will be just outside the door in the hallway. Let me reassure you that these men will be looking for you, and they are very dangerous." With that, both policemen left my hospital room.

Nice, Jim. You couldn't just sit in your big cushy leather first-class seat and let them alone on the plane. No, you had to go all Hong Kong Phooey on the blonde-haired dude.

The cops were beginning to worry me with their advice. Hey, wait a minute. A wave of rage suddenly filled my soul. Screw the cops. Like I didn't know these guys were dangerous? I've had at least two gunfights with them and almost been run over with a truck. I crashed a scooter twice and almost crashed my plane into Lake Huron. Like I really need some Italian cop to tell me these guys are killers. These guys have to be worried about me. I've killed five of them, and I keep showing up shooting at them every time they turn around. They might not even know that I know exactly where they are going. Piss on these cops and piss on the Mafia. I'm on the offensive here. Oh, man, my left side sure hurts. Maybe I should just curse the mob and go home and take a hot bath.

The cops said I have about a one-hour head start. I need to get to Sicily before these guys do. That seems like my only option. I can't go home, and if I can get to Sicily before they do, I might be able to find whatever it is they're looking for. If I hurry, I might be able to get out before they even know I was there. Sure, Jim, that'll happen. If my aunt had balls, she'd be my uncle.

It didn't matter that my plan was insane. I didn't have any other practical options at this point. Sure, I could hide somewhere in Europe, but to what end. Someday, I had to go home. I do have a lot of cash, for now, but that isn't going to get me very far. I can't go back to Wisconsin right now with Sheriff Colson waiting to ask me questions about dead guys, without any reasonable answers. There is only one place I can go. Unfortunately, it happens to be the same place the Mafia is going. It is right in the town where the Mafia got its start. I should have gone to the police back at The Muskee.

Just then the door opened, and the doctor came in with a large x-ray envelope.

"I have good news. You don't have any skeletal damage. The x-rays are negative."

"You speak English very well," I said to him as he unstrapped my head and body from the board.

"I went to medical school in Indianapolis, Indiana. I'm a Hoosier," he said with a smile.

"I'm a Badger," I replied.

"You guys have had some good basketball teams over the years."

"You guys had some great ones, before they ran your coach out of town." The doctor stopped suddenly and asked,

"Is it true what they say? Did you really attack Luigi Servietto on a plane?"

"Does he have blonde hair?" I asked. The doctor laughed aloud.

"You have to be crazy! How are you going to leave this hospital without getting killed? You know he has connections everywhere. His nickname is 'Angelo della Morte.' It means the 'Angel of Death'."

"That's just fucking wonderful," I said sarcastically. "I guess that would be the 'good news, bad news,' thing, right Doc?"

"He is a very famous Sicilian killer. He is a top member of the Mafia. His uncle is the boss of bosses. His uncle has been hiding for the last twenty years. The authorities have no idea where he is, but they say he still runs the Mafia all over the world. I am Paulo Ferrara." He rose sharply.

"From Sicily, and my cousin still lives there. She told me he blew up a judge and his family in their car on a Saturday morning before his trial was to begin. She said there was nothing left of the car. Boom! They were gone. The man that was supposed to testify against him died in a skiing accident in Macugnaga two months later. He was found dead in the snow 3,000 meters up on the mountain. I heard he was wearing a suit like you would wear to church on Sunday. He had no skis, no gloves, no boots. I spoke to the Italian doctor who did the autopsy. He said the man had to have been dropped from a great height. They had to dig him out of the ice, and he had been dead for only a couple of hours. He guessed they had thrown him out of the cable car.

"The government didn't want the resort to get a bad reputation, so they covered it up. As much as we want it not to be true, the Italian government is still controlled by money. They also didn't want people to ask questions about how a man who was testifying against the Mafia in Sicily, fell from a cable car in Northern Italy while wearing a suit and tie. He was supposed to be protected. It was easier to call it a skiing accident."

"You're not serious. How could the government call it a skiing accident?" I asked.

"You are not in the United States any more my Badger friend," he continued as he finished removing my neck brace. "The wheels of justice in Italy do not always run true. Do you need a ride to the airport?" he asked.

"No, thank you, I need a ride to Sicily," I said. The doctor turned serious.

"No, my friend, you must leave this country now, or you will be found after a skiing accident as well."

"I need to get to Sicily before this 'Angel of Death' gets there," I replied sharply. "If you had to get to Sicily before 'Angelo della Morte' could get there, how would you do that? He is going to be at the police station a little while longer. I do not have time to tell you the whole story; I just need to get to Sicily as fast as possible."

The doctor cocked his head to one side, handed me an ice pack, and said,

"I would get on a plane to Wisconsin, or the South Pole, or anywhere but Sicily. If I were you, I would hope that 'Angelo della Morte' would not follow me. You must get out of Italy as fast as possible," he said with conviction. "You must NOT GO TO SICILY."

"I have to go to Sicily," I said. "There is truly no place I would rather go than Wisconsin. I cannot go home before I go to Palermo."

"You understand that you should simply jump in front of a train and save yourself the pain that will come with a journey to Palermo. You do know that the Mafia controls that island, especially Palermo. You know that is where the Mafia comes from. The Mafia was born there. This is not a movie. The Mafia really does exist in Palermo. The Mafia controls Palermo. You will see them at the shipyard eating watermelon on the dock. You will find them in fancy loud restaurants meeting with each other. You will find them watching all the air cargo at the warehouses. There is not a truck in all of Sicily they don't know about. They will spot an American tourist long before you will see them. They will know what time your plane or train or bus or ship arrives."

"So how can I get to Sicily without the mob knowing I'm there?" I asked frustrated. I then raised my voice. "I know, I know, I know. You and everyone else on planet Earth have told me that I'm committing suicide. The bottom line is that the mob killed my best friend for what is hidden in Palermo. I'm going to Palermo. I'm going to kill the Angel of Death because he is trying to kill me. Can you help me? Will you help me? Please, HELP ME." The doctor sat back and looked me over carefully. He was sizing me up.

"The best way to get to Sicily without anyone knowing you are there is to take a train from Rome to Messina and then on to Palermo. They transfer the entire train to a ship and cross the Straits of Messina. There are several different trains leaving at various times during the day, but it is a long journey. It will take about eight hours to get onto the island. There are also commercial flights daily. I believe there is a morning flight and there's an evening flight. You do not want the police to know what you are doing. Luigi has friends in the police as well. These men outside in the hallway, they are here to protect you. Not all police will be as trustworthy. I hope you speak fluent Italian. There are not so many English-speaking Sicilians. Sicily is very poor, and its people are less educated. You should also change your clothes. You look like an American."

"I have a pilot's license, and I am capable of flying myself, if there were a plane at my disposal," I said. "I have brought a lot of cash with me."

The doctor's eyes lit up. He turned away and said,

"That will not be the cheapest way to go, but that would be what I would do. Assuming I were crazy and was trying to get killed in Sicily. I know I have said this, a couple of times already, but you don't want to do whatever it is you are doing. I have a friend here at the hospital. He is a surgeon, and he has a plane. He is not working this week. We fly to Palermo once a month together. I am ten hours away from getting my own pilot's license. This will be expensive. Gasoline costs three euros per liter right now. Airplane fuel is more expensive than that. If he will help you, and I don't know that he will, it will probably cost you about 5,000 euros."

"Five thousand euros?" I exclaimed with a look of disbelief.

"You could fly commercial much cheaper. But you attacked the Angel of Death, and now you want to fly to his home. You will pay what is required or you could take a train."

"So do I get a meal on this flight?" I asked. The doctor was right. I was in no position to even attempt to negotiate a better price. I am wanted for murder in the United States. I just told him that I was basically a hit man coming to kill some mob guy in a mob town. It might be a bargain at 5,000 euros. The doctor walked across the room and picked up the phone between the other two beds. After a moment he began speaking in Italian. He spoke for about five minutes and hung up. I don't speak Italian, but I think he is getting a cut of my 5,000 euros. After hanging up the phone the doctor came back and sat on the stool beside my examination table. He spoke softly and deliberately.

"I can help you. You do not know me. You will never speak of what we are discussing here today. The Mafia is the scourge of my country. My family is from Sicily, and I have known this scourge my whole life. It was difficult for me to leave my home on the island. I had no chance of becoming a doctor had I stayed in Sicily. I had to leave my home, and it took me several years to get most of my family out of Sicily. I could not live under their black cloud any more. I would not raise my children there. I would not allow my family to live there. My younger brother is on his way here. You will need to pay him as well, but he will drive you to the airport. He will help you. My brother should be here in less than a half an hour. His name is Giorgio. I have other patients to attend to, and I will not come back before he arrives."

I stood up and stuck my hand out to shake his. A sharp pain shot through my left shoulder as I stood. As we shook hands I said,

"I really can't thank you enough for your help."

"Just take care of my little brother, he could use the money. Besides, I took the Hippocratic Oath in America, and it doesn't omit helping suicidal fools. Arrivederci my friend." With that he walked out of the room and the door closed behind him. I shuffled over to the door behind him, wincing in pain. I opened the door and asked the police if they knew where my luggage was. They said that they had picked it up at the airport, and it would be arriving any moment. I closed the door and smiled and said,

"I have got to fly first class more often."

Chapter Twenty-Three

As soon as my luggage arrived a police officer brought it into my hospital room. The officer brought in my suitcase and backpack, set the suitcase on the floor, and my backpack he tossed onto a sofa along the wall. I wasn't sure if I should tip him or not. With that funny hat and uniform, he looked like a bell hop with a pistol to me.

"Am I supposed to tip you?" I asked with a big grin. He said nothing. He gave me a dirty look and left the room, slamming the door behind him.

My room was not private. There were four beds in the room. There were two beds on each of the opposite walls. There were telephones hanging between each of the two beds. Each bed had a sofa along the wall next to it. There was a lot of room to walk around each of the beds. There were curtains that could be drawn around each bed so the room could be divided into four separate chambers with wide aisles between each chamber. Next to the sofas there were metal storage cabinets. The door that the police and doctor had used was on my left. To my right was another door. Both doors had long skinny windows with wire mesh inside the glass and were located directly across the room from one another.

I picked up my backpack, trying not to aggravate any of my multiple injuries, and walked over to my suitcase. After falling to my knees with shooting pains throughout my whole body, I started to unzip my luggage. I might not have any skeletal damage, but I think they bruised my spleen. Wow, while dropping to my knees, I let the biggest fart I have ever let in my life.

"Oh, man, that stinks," I said aloud. I might have to drag my luggage over to the other side of the room to unpack. I was a foul mess.

I began retrieving the cash I had hidden inside my clothes and started consolidating it into the backpack when the back door to the room opened suddenly. It startled me when the doctor's brother flung it open. If he had opened the door ten seconds earlier that fart might have turned my colon inside out. I quickly stuffed the last of my cash into my backpack thinking there might be weight issues on a small private airplane. According to the doctor, my version of an Italian disguise wasn't working. It looked as though I wouldn't need any of my new clothes or old suits for that matter.

"You are crazy America cowboy?" the young man asked.

"Yes, I am," I replied.

"We a go now, yes? This room smells a like a sewer."

"Yes," I said. "I'm not impressed with what passes for clean air in this country." I pushed the bed I had been strapped into only a few minutes earlier in front of the door so the police would find it difficult to pursue me if they noticed I had gone. Just as I finished moving the gurney, I saw a police officer peer through the window right at me. I smiled big and waved. He turned and said something to the other officer and began pushing at the door. It made an awful racket. Everyone on the first floor had to hear the noise. I just turned and ran. Each stride was painful. I popped through the back door of my room and looked to the right. About fifty feet in front of me was Giorgio walking nonchalantly past a set of double doors on his left. I looked back and heard the police banging the door against the gurney. I spun around and saw a fire alarm on the wall.

"Oh, what the fuck!" I said aloud. I pulled the plastic lever to the fire alarm. It made a large popping sound, and I felt something wet in my hand. The alarm started blaring and lights along the ceiling started flashing instantaneously. That may not have been such a smooth move, Jim. Hanging on to my backpack, I started sprinting toward Giorgio who had looked back to see me pull the alarm and was now running himself. Running rather quickly I might add. He's fast. I think I heard him yell,

"No!" as I popped the lever.

I held up my wet hand and realized I had just been marked with indelible blue ink. The entire palm of my right hand was a light bright bluish purple. That's just wonderful, I thought to myself as I began accelerating. I continued running as hard as I could. I was breathing heavily now. I saw Giorgio turn the corner to the left another seventy-five feet ahead of me. When I got to the corner, I collided into a security guard. He hit me on my left shoulder, and went sprawling into the wall catching himself with his arms. We hit each other hard, right in the middle of the corner of the two hallways.

I grabbed the handrail along the wall with my right hand and left a big blue and purple smear on it as I spun around hitting my back on the wall. The dull pain that was in my shoulder from Luigi's buddies kicking my ass was now a sharp stabbing pain. The guard was stunned and struggling to get back to his feet. I was gone. I tugged on the handrail and started sprinting again. I saw Giorgio hit the outside door just before my tears of pain blurred my vision. By the time I got to the door, he was in the car with the door open and the engine running. I jumped into the front seat of the small blue car and he popped the clutch as we tore off down an alley behind the hospital.

"Man, that was painful," I said breathing heavily as we turned left onto a busy street and darted away from the hospital. "Are you aware this vehicle has no seat belts and is smaller than the suitcase I left in the hospital?" I gasped for air and took a look back to see if anyone was following us. I saw no one. Not even the security guard I knocked down.

"You a crazy American!" He shouted at me. "Why a you start alarm?"

"I just figured that if the police were looking for me in Rome, then the Mafia would be looking for me in Rome as well." I responded rather proud of myself.

"Crazy American cowboy, yes!" He weaved out of traffic and nearly side-swiped another car. "Yes, policia look for you. Policia now look for a me. Policia now look for a my brother. You no good. You a bad man." A man on a scooter darted around on my side of the car. He then crossed in front of us and passed the bus we were behind on the wrong side of the street. It seemed everyone was in a hurry to get away from the hospital. After a couple more turns and hearing no sirens, Giorgio caught his breath and began to calm down. I was still panting.

"I take you to airplane now," Giorgio stated with conviction as he scowled at me.

"No, first I need to go here," I said as I handed him a small piece of paper with the FedEx address on it.

"No, this far to airport," he said with an unhappy expression.

"I have to go there first," I said pleading my case. "Your brother said you would help drive me anywhere I wanted to go, and that is where I want to go."

"No. We need to go to airport now. You a miss you plane."

"I will pay you extra. I have to go to FedEx. There is a package there for me. I will pay you more."

"Okay, America cowboy. We a gonna be a real late to a plane. You a crazy! You should not a pull alarm. You get everyone in big a trouble. You get my brother in big a trouble. You a gonna pay a me a lot."

"I need your help, and I really need to go there first," I said sincerely pointing at the paper I had given him.

It took us about fifteen minutes to reach the address I had given Giorgio. I had heard that traffic in Rome was some of the worst in the world, but it didn't seem so bad to me. There were a lot more scooters and motorcycles than I had expected, but aside from that it seemed like any other city I'd been in. Giorgio's car was a real piece of shit. It was by far the smallest car I had ever seen. There was barely enough room for the two of us in the front seats. There was no way this thing would be allowed on the road in the United States. Any SUV or pickup truck could drive over it like a speed bump. My little backpack took up the whole back seat.

The tires on the car were about half the size of a car tire in the States. The car looked like it was the pre-teen child of a couple of Mini Coopers. If I had a running start, I could almost hurdle the whole car in stride. As I looked out the window, I was at thigh height with passing scooter riders. Looking around it seemed that all the cars were miniature. The only exceptions were a Mercedes and the occasional Range Rover; all the other cars were tiny. Never had I seen so many scooters and motorcycles. A bus looked huge compared to Giorgio's tin coffin. The fucking engine is in the back of the car.

At every red light groups of scooters and motorcycles would weave between the stopped cars and move to the front of traffic. Some were even out in the oncoming traffic lanes and on the sidewalk. About a second before the light turned green, they would all rev their engines and take off as the light changed. Then it was like they were racing through traffic to get to the next light. The whole group reminded me of salmon swimming around rocks in a stream. There were scooters everywhere. It wasn't like back in the States where only teenagers and Brad and I rode scooters. There were men in suits, women in dresses, old ladies and old men, and teenagers zipping around on scooters everywhere.

We pulled up to the FedEx store. Oddly enough, FedEx store translates to FedEx store in Italian. Giorgio said,

"You a go, I a go round and pick a you up chinqua" pointing to his watch and raising five fingers. In the meantime he had caused a major traffic jam, and there were horns and scooters and people yelling and flailing their arms all about. I walked across the sidewalk and into the store. I asked the attractive Italian woman behind the counter if she spoke English.

"A little," she said with a smile. I told her my name and asked if she had a package from Canada addressed to me. I showed her my passport. She said, "Yes," and disappeared rather quickly into the back room.

I figured the police were going to come out and arrest me right away. My heartbeat was deafening as I waited for her to return. I don't know what the law is in Italy for shipping a handgun that had been used in a homicide into the country with about twenty hollow point bullets, but I am reasonably sure that I could, and really should, be arrested for it. I began to perspire as the seconds she was away seemed like hours. It was hard to stay calm knowing that I could be arrested as an international arms smuggler. I was just sure the police were going to pop out and beat me senseless with their batons any second. The lady came out a moment later with my package. That was way too easy, I thought. I was trying to hide my hand, which had now turned a deep shade of purple from the ink. I smiled and said,

"Grazie!"

I don't know how I knew to say 'thank you' in Italian; I just did. I strolled out to the curb just as Giorgio pulled up causing another traffic snarl. I had to let a scooter pass to get around the car. I jumped into the front seat, and we drove into traffic with Giorgio sticking his head out his now open window and screaming at other cars while shaking his fist out the window. He was pretty cool. It was something else to see him drive a stick shift through traffic with no hands. I tore open the box and removed my Series .38 Smith and Wesson six-shot revolver. It brought a large smile to my face. It had made the journey in better shape than I had. I was grinning as I held it up to show it to Giorgio.

Giorgio pulled his head back inside the window, still yelling Italian profanities. He looked right at me and stopped yelling mid-word. He looked mortified. He turned ghost white instantly. He paused for just a second with his mouth wide open.

"Oh! They a gonna kill you America cowboy! You a crazy!" he said with an upset look of disbelief and fear on his face. He reached into the center console and spilled two cigarettes onto the floorboard of the car. His hand was shaking, and his demeanor had changed from uneasy to flat, scared, shitless. He stuck a cigarette backward into his mouth. Without noticing, he lit the filter. He took two large nervous drags before throwing it out the window coughing. He looked over at me cautiously. The gun had changed everything. He was no longer just driving some crazy American to the airport. He was driving some sort of killer. He reached down and grabbed another cigarette. This time he lit it correctly.

As I loaded the six hollow-point bullets into the cylinder of my gun, I realized that this gun in my hand was a murder weapon. Not in the sense that you can kill someone with a gun but in the sense that this particular handgun had actually been used to commit murder. This was the gun that had taken a Sicilian man's life in an alley in the United States. I was holding a cold piece of stainless steel that was used for murder. For the first time that fact washed over me. The fact that it was in self defense didn't matter to me. The fact that it was in self defense sure as hell didn't matter to the dead guy. I felt as sad as I had ever felt in my life. I thought about my best friend lying face down in the cold dirt back on a lonely hill on my property. At the same moment, a fire of rage began to well up inside of me. The silence and my thoughts were interrupted by Giorgio.

"Can you a put that away?" he timidly asked.

"Sure, no sweat," I said as I reached back and shoved the gun and the bullet box into my backpack in the back seat.

"You know the policia here in Italy will kill you for that?" he said.

"How is that?" I asked.

"If the policia here see this gun, they a gonna shoot you. Criminal with a gun a dead. Man with gun a criminal. Policia kill man a with a gun. Nobody care. You a dead," he stated very seriously.

"I won't be taking that out again. I promise."

I think Giorgio finished his whole pack of cigarettes by the time we pulled up in front of the small airport. He didn't seem to be my friend anymore. I guess he was a little upset about the fire alarm and the gun. We pulled right up onto the runway alongside a beautiful sleek red and white plane. It was a Storm RG. At least that was what it said on the aircraft. I had heard of the plane but had never seen one. It was a low wing two-seater with a little storage space behind the front seats.

"Nice plane," I said to the man standing next to it.

"You were supposed to be here an hour ago. We must get going. The tower will cancel our flight permission soon if we do not leave right away," he barked at me as he climbed into his seat in the plane. I reached into my backpack and handed Giorgio ten, one hundred dollar bills.

"Thank you very much for your help, Giorgio," I said with a wide smile as I stuck out my hand to shake his. Giorgio took the money. He looked down at my purple hand, rolled his eyes, and walked away toward his car. He didn't say anything. He just sped away from the airplane as fast as possible. I turned around and smiled at the pilot. I tossed my pack into the space between the back wall of the plane and the back of the seats and climbed into my seat. It had been a while since I had someone fly me in a small plane. Whenever I'm in a small plane, I'm always the one who is flying.

"So how long of a flight is this?" I asked the pilot.

"We will be landing in Palermo in one and a half hours," he responded abrasively.

"I'm Jim," I said with a smile. He nodded and began firing up the engine. We taxied down the runway where he made his final checks of the control surfaces and said something in Italian into his headset. He slid the throttle forward, and the plane raced down the runway and into the sky. After about five minutes we passed over the coast and out over the Mediterranean Sea. I reached into my backpack and pulled out the two magazines I had purchased in Toronto. The one on top was *Playboy*. I smiled at the pilot and said, "If I'm going to die, I'm going to die with a cheery mental picture." He looked at me and frowned again.

"You should have gone to the Vatican and repented your sins if you are going to die."

"Well, I would have gone to church this morning," I said sarcastically, "but I was busy pulling the fire alarm at the hospital." I opened to the centerfold and held it up with my left hand so he could see Ms. September in all her spectacular naked glory. Grinning widely I showed him the palm of my right hand that was stained with blue dye and asked,

"Does this stuff rub off?"

He turned his attention back to flying the plane and said,

"I will pray for you."

Chapter Twenty-Four

The wheels screeched and thudded as we landed in Palermo one hour and twenty two minutes later. The flight was smooth and relatively easy. I sat quietly and thumbed through both of the magazines and a book I had purchased. It was pretty obvious that the pilot didn't care to chat with me and he was all business. I can appreciate that because I don't enjoy flying over water. I enjoy it even less when our plane doesn't have floats to land safely on the water in case of an emergency. As we rolled to a stop he cut the engine and asked for his 5,000 euros.

"I don't have euros, I have dollars," I said.

"Well that will be 10,000 dollars," he said arrogantly. "You know, with the exchange rate and all." He was back peddling. I reached into my backpack and handed him 8,000 dollars.

"I'll give you another 7,000 dollars to take me back tomorrow," I stated authoritatively.

"I'm leaving at one o'clock tomorrow afternoon. You better no be late. One o'clock," he repeated. I had already started getting out of the plane and walking away as he was yelling about one o'clock. What a prick. I mean, really, the guy's a fucking surgeon. It's not like he has any trouble buying a sandwich. Why would he try to take extra cash from me? As if 8,000 dollars wasn't enough for his time? Maybe I should show him my gun.

I walked over to the terminal, about a football field away. Being a pilot, I loved walking by all the private as well as military and commercial planes. It was interesting to see what people in Europe were flying into Sicily. Unlike the cars they drive, the planes are all about the same as the planes in the States. It was strange to see military aircraft with the Italian flag instead of Old Glory. Aside from that, the airport was pretty much the same as you would find in larger cities around the States.

The weather was simply beautiful. It felt about 80-degrees, and the sun was shining brightly. A breeze was blowing and a huge rock of a mountain was visible beyond the airport. I stopped to look around. Man, was it a beautiful day. I could smell fresh flowers. I walked into the terminal and looked around to see if there was an information desk. On my way to the information desk I stopped and changed 2,000 dollars into 1,200 euros. Ouch, the exchange rate hurt as much as the scooter wreck. My nuts are still sore. The clerk at the information desk was rather rude and didn't speak much English. I just walked away and went out front to find a taxi. What's up with his attitude? I'm a Sicilian myself. My grandfather fought here to free your country's sorry ass, douche bags.

There were several white cabs out front, and I decided to talk to the guy with the largest taxi. I felt like riding in something bigger than the glorified go-kart Giorgio had shuttled me around Rome in. The surgeon's plane was not very large either. Funny, that the taxis are white over here instead of yellow. While I was buying magazines in Toronto, I also picked up an Italian guidebook that has hotel and restaurant suggestions along with other useful information about Italy. I had looked up a reasonably priced hotel located in an old palace close to the train station after I had finished checking out Ms. September. The cab driver indicated that he was familiar with the hotel. I figured I didn't need a five-star hotel, and the proximity of this one to the train station gave me easy options for leaving. I was hoping there might be a direct train to the airport.

I thought it best to get some sort of base on land to operate from. At the very least the hotel room would give me a place to shave and shower as soon as possible. It would also provide me with a place to store my bag. The guidebook said that Mussolini had once given a speech from the hotel's balcony and that it used to be some sort of palace. I told the cab driver the name, and he pointed for me to sit in the front seat. We took off through traffic and if my pilot was a serious man, this cabbie was a statue. He didn't seem to want me in his car or my bag in the back seat. If he only knew about my gun, he really wouldn't want me in his cab. I guess he doesn't like me for some reason. I seem to be getting that a lot lately. We arrived about fifteen minutes later outside the hotel, and the cab driver told me he needed fifty euros.

"Fuck you," I told him. This little bit of English he seemed to understand, and it didn't make him happy. He began yelling and waving his hands about and demanding I pay him. I repeatedly told him no, and he continued yelling at me. Finally I said, "OK, policia," and I began to get out and call for the police. At that point we came to a quick agreement and settled on twenty euros. Apparently the cab driver didn't want to see the cops any more than I did. I was still getting ripped off, but that seemed to be an Italian tradition. I stepped out of the taxi and was surprised to see that the "palace" was a big piece of crap. Maybe it's nicer on the inside I thought. It wasn't.

The palace had fallen into disrepair. It was an imposing four-story building with balconies and large windows. Several flags flew off the center balcony and included both the Italian and American flags, as well as three or four others I didn't recognize. They were all as worn as the building as if they'd been there since Mussolini's speech and never brought inside. Two massive wooden doors filled the archway entry behind tall round columns that stretched to the second floor. I walked to the side and buzzed the doorbell labeled 'HOTEL.' A couple of seconds later I heard an electric sounding click and a smaller wooden door set inside one of the larger wooden doors cracked open. I pushed it open and stepped over the bottom of the larger door.

Inside was a massive courtyard full of cars and scooters that had once been the showpiece of this palace. It was evident the courtyard had once been beautifully gardened with horse stables around the outside of the first floor and a fountain in its center. The sun was beaming onto the crumbling fountain and its former glory was long gone. I closed the inset door behind me making sure my perimeter was secure. The hotel manager was standing on a balcony on the second floor waving me up the staircase across the courtyard. There was a fat pregnant cat walking toward me; I was standing beside a palm tree in the center of the courtyard. The whole courtyard smelled like cat piss.

I could tell that at one time this had been a spectacular palace. The staircase on the other side of the yard was wide and had deep orange marble treads highlighted with white marble patterns at each of the landings. I continued up the lengthy stairs to the second floor. There was no door leading up the stairs. The hallway off the staircase was wide open as well. The ceilings in the palace had to be at least twenty feet high and all had marble busts above each doorway. All the ceilings were arched and had wooden moldings crossing over in their centers.

The once opulent courtyard was now used as a parking lot, and the entire palace was subdivided into several tenements. The stench of cat urine permeated the center courtyard and most of the hallway. I guess that's the best way to control mice around this place. It was like some sort of interspecies biological warfare. The smell of cat piss would certainly keep me out if I were a mouse. Hell, it almost keeps me out as a human being.

I checked in and asked the manager if he knew where I could rent a vehicle. He spoke no English and handed me a brochure. I pointed to the scooter on the front, and he immediately called the phone number, spoke a lot of Italian, and then handed the phone to me.

"Hello," the man's voice came on the other end of the phone.

"You speak English," I said relieved.

"A little."

"I want to rent a scooter."

"Great, can you be out in front of your hotel in five minutes?" The man on the other end asked. "I will send someone to pick you up right now."

"That will be just fine," I replied.

About five minutes later a kid on a scooter pulled up out front. He stepped off his scooter and pulled up the seat. Underneath was a black helmet which he handed to me. I climbed on the scooter behind him. He stepped on, and we sped into traffic.

I believe the exact words of the doctor in Rome had been that I was a 'suicidal fool.' Compared to the guy that picked me up on the scooter and drove me to the rental office, I was a life-loving genius. This psychotic freak was zipping through traffic like a deranged maniac with a death wish. We were on the sidewalk at least half a dozen times passing stopped traffic. We played chicken with an oncoming bus, a large orange bus, and almost clipped two other scooters on separate occasions. This guy wasn't riding a scooter; he was angrily racing against every other driver on the road.

Each time my nervous apprehensions subsided, he jumped the scooter onto the sidewalk, or sideswiped two teenage girls that flicked us off, or raced around a dump truck. I went from relaxed to absolute terror about every ninety seconds. It was right at every minute and a half that we came close to death in a collision. I was happy to climb off the scooter when we arrived at the rental agency.

They were nice enough to give me a map before turning me loose on the streets of foreign country with my two-hundred-and-fifty cubic centimeter engine motorized scooter. This bad boy was much nicer than the ones I owned back home. It went from zero to 85km/h in under four seconds. No clutch to mess with. Just two hand brakes and full throttle. I understood quickly why the guy who had delivered me to the rental shop had driven the way he did. The answer is quite simple. It is because you can. I have never been someplace where driving was as intense and scary and fun as it is driving a scooter in Palermo.

The key to driving a scooter in Italy is to continuously check in your mirrors. Other scooters will be passing you on both sides any chance they can. Many times I was passed by another scooter that had to be going twenty miles an hour faster than I was. Because all the car drivers grew up on scooters, they are vigilant of them. Chances are good that the driver of the car next to you will be on a scooter in the next day or so. With gas costing three euros per liter, I couldn't afford to drive a car here myself. Although the drivers of cars seem to be diligent in looking out for scooters, the drivers of buses are not. The bus driver seems to be the nemesis of the scooter driver. I totally understand why. It has to be difficult enough driving a bus in this city traffic, but throw twenty million scooters weaving ahead and all around, and you can see why the bus drivers hate scooters with a passion.

As I was filling out the paperwork for the rental agreement, I could hear my testicles telling me not to do it. I know that I swore off scooters only yesterday, or was it two days ago? This is just not the same. This scooter is much larger than what I had been riding in Port Huron. It looks a whole lot more like a motorcycle. I only rented it for one night. I felt, or hoped, that I would be able to get what I came for and get the hell out of here in one day. Hopefully, I can get to Villa Malfitano and leave before Angelo della Morte gets to Sicily. After all, I had made great time.

Chapter Twenty-Five

Luigi Servietto strode out of the police station in Rome. His eyes were now blackening, and his nose was visibly swollen. His lawyer was struggling to catch up to him from behind. When Luigi got to the top of the steps outside the door he saw him. You couldn't miss him. It was Piedro Carini. His nickname was 'Il Toro,' which means 'the bull.' He stood every bit of six-foot-four and had shoulders that were about three feet wide. He was standing at the bottom of the steps. He had dark hair and dark eyes and looked every bit the part of a Sicilian hit man. He had the pinky rings, he had the gold bracelet, and he had the gold chain with gold cross around his neck. He had a big gold wristwatch, and he was wearing silk clothes.

He and Luigi had known each other their whole lives. They grew up together in Palermo. Their careers in the Sicilian Mafia mirrored each others. They always had a bit of a rivalry that made each of them work harder. It helped both of them get ahead. The difference was that Luigi used cunning, assassination, and nepotism while Piedro used brute force, intelligence, and intimidation to rise through the hierarchy.

Luigi worked in the prostitution and money laundering side of the family. Definitely more white-collar criminal. Piedro, on the other hand, was in the debt collection and the union shipping and trucking side of the family. He was much more blue-collar. They were never in the same crew, so they didn't work directly together coming up through the ranks.

There was only one time in their whole careers when they worked together. It was when one of Piedro's soldiers tried to stiff one of Luigi's prostitutes. The two captains at the time went to confront Piedro's capo. The capo mouthed off to Luigi. Piedro didn't like the tone or the smug sarcasm the capo was speaking to Luigi. So he broke the man's jaw with one massive blow to side of his chin. Piedro was so enraged and embarrassed with his crew member's attitude and lack of respect that he picked the man up and threw him head first into a brick wall. The impact killed the man on the spot. Luigi told his uncle about the incident. From that day forward, Piedro was the top boss's bodyguard.

Being placed as the boss of boss's bodyguard is one of the highest honors inside the family. It is not supposed to work that way, but because the boss is in hiding, Piedro is more respected than even the underboss. As the boss's bodyguard, Piedro's primary function was making rounds for Luigi's Uncle Vito, the boss.

The fact that Piedro was standing outside the police station in Rome, meant only one thing. It meant that Luigi's uncle was sending him a message. It meant that the boss was not happy. It meant that Luigi better have something good to tell Piedro to tell his uncle Vito, or Piedro would kill him. Piedro was the only person who knew where the boss was hiding. His fierce loyalty and intimidating presence suited him perfectly as the boss's right hand man. That and the fact that everyone knew he had killed a man by smashing his head on a brick wall made him very respected and feared.

This was certainly not the normal protocol. It was a big deal for Piedro to be in Rome. Normally, Piedro would not be very far from the boss. Normally, Luigi would have to get word to the underboss that he needed to get a message to the boss.

If the underboss thought it was worth contacting the boss, he would tell Piedro that Luigi would like to meet the boss. Then Piedro would ask the boss if he wanted the meeting. If he did, Piedro would tell the underboss and it would be arranged. Technically, Luigi wasn't even allowed to ask for a meeting with the boss. There were only three people in Sicily who could ask for a meeting with the boss, and two of them were now looking at each other outside a police station in Rome. The only other person who could ask Piedro to see the boss is the underboss. Only for the fact that the boss was his uncle, was Luigi allowed to ask to speak to the boss. Otherwise, like everyone else, they would have to ask the underboss for permission for whatever he needed.

After making eye contact, Piedro turned back to the curb, climbed onto a motorcycle, pulled on his helmet, and drove quickly away. Luigi stopped and turned back to his lawyer.

"You have something for me," he stated in Italian.

"I was asked to give you this," he said as he pulled an envelope out of his briefcase.

The envelope contained a piece of paper with the name of a small private airport just outside of Rome. Luigi hailed a taxi and told the driver to take him to the airport. When the driver looked over the seat to make sure he heard the beat up man in the back seat, Luigi threw a fifty-euro note in his face.

The taxi pulled up in front of a dirty little private airport in the northeast suburb of Rome. The runway was a short one so the airport got little use. It was used mainly by single engine planes, ultra lights, and hot air balloon enthusiasts. Luigi got out of the cab and spoke sharply to the cabbie.

"Wait here for me." On his ride to the outskirts of Rome, Luigi had planned to tell Piedro that all was under control, and he had gotten what he and his men had gone to America to acquire. He would apologize for the trouble and explain that the American had a lot of guns and friends, and the trip was costly but still successful. It was no big deal to meet at a remote airport, as his uncle was hiding from the Italian police.

They often met in strange places to keep authorities from tracking the boss. They always left in separate directions in separate vehicles. When Luigi went inside the small building that had once served as the terminal, there was no one inside. He then walked out through the back door. When he saw Piedro standing next to the stair steps of the twin engine Beechcraft King Air out on the runway, he knew this was not a normal meeting.

As Luigi approached the plane, he realized there were pilots in the cockpit. The boss was here. His uncle had flown to Rome to speak with Luigi personally. This was bad news. This was very bad news. This was not to be a typical meeting.

"Peter the bull" Luigi said to Piedro in Italian, "It has been too long my friend." He smiled and shook Piedro's massive hand as he kissed both of his cheeks. It is the customary Sicilian Mafia greeting.

"Angel of Death," Piedro stated smugly, "Our friend is inside waiting for you. It is good to see you were able to make it back in one piece. Your plastic surgery is healing quite nicely. You finally got that nose job." He smiled and pointed to Luigi's broken nose chuckling.

"Fucking America cowboys," Luigi replied. The two men turned and climbed the stairs as the twin turbo prop engines fired to life. Piedro pulled the folding stairs up into the plane and secured the door. Luigi turned toward the back of the plane and climbed between the first four seats to the back four where his uncle was rising to greet him.

The boss of bosses was seventy-eight years old and walked with a cane. Not because he had to; he just did. He was dressed casually in a green golf shirt that had a pocket on the front, black slacks, and a black cloth hat. He removed his reading glasses and set them on the newspaper he had been reading as Luigi climbed between the three sets of two seats.

"You look like you have had a difficult journey, Luigi," he said in a low friendly voice. Luigi looked back to see that Piedro was sitting in the front seat facing them and fastening his seatbelt. Luigi turned his attention back to his uncle and kissed his hand and both of his cheeks.

"Come sit with me," the boss said as he pointed to the seat in front of his so they could face each other as they spoke. Luigi sat and fastened his seat belt as the plane began to taxi.

"Can you believe the prices of gasoline these days?" the boss asked.

"They are an outrage, aren't they?" Luigi responded.

"Between their oil and their fucking illegal immigrants in our country, we should kill all the fucking Arabs."

"They just don't shower," replied Luigi.

"They are all going to hell for having a false god anyhow."

Luigi was choosing his words carefully. What Luigi knew was that he was here to convince his uncle not to kill him. The mess in America had brought way too much attention to the family and its business. Normally he was much less formal when he was around the boss of bosses. Normally they spoke as friends, like a normal family. Today Luigi was intimidated. Today he was on his best behavior. You do not speak to the boss. You dare not ask him a direct question. You shut your mouth and listen very carefully to everything he says. He asks you questions, and you answer directly and politely. For the first time in his life Luigi wasn't being protected by his uncle. His uncle hadn't come to scold or threaten him. He was here simply to decide if Luigi was live or to die.

"I don't travel much anymore," he said. "The last time was to New York City. It was hot in July, and I had to thank an old friend." The boss opened a bottle of water and took a sip while looking out the window. The plane was just lifting off the ground.

"You left quite a mess for our old friends." He now stared coldly at Luigi. He was looking right through Luigi's eyes and piercing the back of his skull with his fierce gaze. "This will be the last mess you make?" he asked.

"Yes, it will," Luigi said humbly.

"You look as though you had difficulty arriving. Has that problem at the airport been resolved?"

"No, the problem I had over there has returned home with me," Luigi said angrily.

"You are usually not so sloppy when you work. Piedro will be working with you to make sure these messes don't keep occurring."

"I appreciate the help, but I don't need it." The boss swung his cane at Luigi's head. Luigi was quick to move to the side. The air made a swooshing sound as the cane smacked Luigi on the shoulder. He was stunned. The boss never showed any emotion. It was what made him so powerful.

"Five of our friends. Look at your face in a mirror. You tell me you don't need help." The boss's voice never rose, but his tone had turned much more sinister. "I sent you to be discrete. I set you up with all that help. You have messed this job up beyond repair. You should be one of the five. I can't believe how terrible you have done. You will explain to me what happened."

"We found him where you had said he would be," Luigi explained. "We knocked him out and started searching for the box. I left Antonio and Paulo with him, and we began searching his houses. Somehow he got free and shot Antonio. We took the box and left. As we were leaving he got in front of us and shot Franco, Alberto, and Bruno. He must have found their hotel keys because he showed up there and shot Lorenzo. When we landed in Rome, he was sitting behind me on the plane and attacked me."

"How could he sit behind you on the plane?" the boss asked.

"That is what I found most troubling. I don't know how he did that. We bought our tickets back to Rome at the last possible minute."

"What was inside of the box?"

"It said 'Villa Malfitano, Nero d'Avola, 10-23-41'."

"When we land, you and Piedro will go to Villa Malfitano and find the Nero d'Avola we are looking for." The boss waved

Piedro back to join them and said, "Villa Malfitano, Nero d'Avola. Write those numbers down," he ordered Luigi. He then looked directly into Luigi's eyes. "You will not make any more mistakes."

Chapter Twenty-Six

I pulled the black brain bucket onto my head and stepped onto my rental scooter. It fired right up, and I swung into traffic. This is a very nice scooter. It accelerates quickly, and I am immediately into the flow of traffic. There is another scooter about twenty yards ahead of me, and I decide to follow his lead. As we approach our first red traffic light, I weave in between cars slowly getting to the front of the traffic pattern. The scooter rental guy had drawn my route on a small paper map he had given me at his shop. I had to pull over three times to check my map on my way back to the hotel. I have only been in this city for thirty minutes, and I'm already blasting around its crowded streets at fifty kilometers per hour. I'd guess that's about thirty-five miles per hour.

I find it difficult to find street signs. Some streets even appear to change names from one block to the next. My hotel is located in the older part of the city, and the streets are not laid out in the grid pattern of American cities. It takes me about twice as long to get back to my hotel as it did to get to the rental office. I park on the sidewalk next to one of the round columns in front of the hotel and ring the buzzer for the hotel clerk to let me back inside. The courtyard still smells like cat piss, and I head back up to my room after locking and chaining the scooter. My scooter even has a push button alarm on the keychain just like a car.

I need a shave and shower. Those two flights have me feeling frazzled. Most importantly, I need my gun before I head out to find Villa Malfitano. Inside my grandfather's ammo box was a carved message. It read,

> *Villa Malfitano*
> *Nero d'Avola*
> *10-23-41*

I read in my guidebook that Villa Malfitano is some sort of museum today. It used to be a palace. Judging by the state of the former palace my hotel is located in, that might not be saying much. According to my guidebook, it was the temporary headquarters for General Patton after the army had liberated Palermo. My grandfather must have left something there having to do with the other parts of the carving. Whatever he left there is important enough for the Sicilian Mafia to fly halfway around the world and kill me for. I'm both nervous and excited about going over to see what is there. Being of Sicilian descent, and a raging alcoholic, I know that Nero d'Avola is a variety of Sicilian wine. It is a very good Sicilian wine and one of my personal favorites. The last part of the inscription is my father's birthday. I have no idea why this inscription is so important, but it is what the mob was looking for.

I need a few minutes to think and plan. I have been operating far outside of my comfort level for several days. I decide the best place for me to think is in the shower. Lord knows I could use a nice hot shower and shave. I tried not to linger in the shower for long. I guessed that my one hour head start on the Angel of Death was over. I finished toweling off and walked out into my enormous room. There is a fresco painted on my ceiling, and my balcony is right next to the one Mussolini must have spoken from. I don't think the hotel is proud of the fact that Mussolini once spoke here. I don't believe he was all that popular in Sicily. Sicilians and Italians don't like each other much. Sicilians especially dislike Northern Italians, which is where Mussolini's hometown is located.

The best plan I can come up with is to simply go and see what is at Villa Malfitano. Brilliant plan, Jim. You must be some sort of genius. It would have taken most people an agonizingly long time to come up with that. I walk back inside and look over my street map of Palermo. Villa Malfitano looks like it encompasses about six city blocks. I think I'll just drive a lap of the adjoining streets around its edges to case the villa before I go charging in. The last time I was on a scooter and went charging in was back in Port Huron. I had at least four near fatal misses back there. Charging straight in is not part of today's plan.

I decide to empty my backpack of everything except some of the cash and my raincoat. I check the loads in my gun and place it and the extra ammunition in the backpack. Hopefully whatever is hidden at the villa will fit inside my small pack. As I give one last look around the room I notice a cross above my bed. I decide this is probably as good a time as any to try and make some peace with God. I kneel down at the foot of my bed and say a little prayer. I remember to mention Brad and ask for forgiveness for my transgressions.

I dropped my key off at the front desk and headed for my scooter. It is about a fifteen minute ride before I can find Via Dante, the street that borders the villa. I drive north until I spot the last major cross street before coming to the villa. I decide to pull over and look over my map one last time. I want to be sure I know where all the main roads are in the area in case I have to make a getaway on my scooter. As I sit idling on the corner I glance around the intersection. I wonder if there is a body armor store nearby. I could use some Kevlar right about now. If I run into serious trouble, I will be at a major disadvantage. After all, Angelo della Morte grew up in this town. He will have the same advantage I had back at The Muskee. That disadvantage allowed Brad and me to kill three of his friends. I don't want that to happen to me.

I put the map away and pull into traffic. I speed north toward the villa. As I get close I realize it is surrounded by a large pale yellow wall. I zoom past a black wrought iron gate and keep on riding. There was a small gatehouse just inside the wall. I turn right at the end of the wall into a dead end alley that appears to be some sort of old support building for the villa. At the end of the alley is another gate that leads to a house that looks as though it was part of the estate at one time. The wall that surrounds the villa separates it from this house.

As I turn around and head out of the alley I notice the large shards of glass standing atop the wall. That seems like a good deterrent to would-be thieves to keep them from scaling over it. I head to the next street and turn right and pass another gate. This gate has a steel panel behind the wrought iron and doesn't look to be passable. The road now goes away from the wall, and I need to do a large loop to return to the villa. There seem to be only two streets that touch the villa's property, and only one of them has an operational entry gate.

That's just wonderful—one way in, one way out. With the glass on top of the wall, I can't even go over it if I needed to. I hope I don't need to. If I run into trouble inside, I'm in a bad place. I pull carefully up to the closed front gate and see what I can. I stop the scooter next to a couple of the tiny cars parallel parked on the street in front of the wall by the gate. I don't bother to lock up the scooter or even take off my helmet. I walk cautiously to the large gate and look inside. There is a sign just inside the gate saying that the villa is closed and will re-open the next morning at 9:00. The sign is in Italian, but I'm pretty confident in my reading of it. That makes perfect sense. It's two o'clock on Wednesday afternoon. Why would anyplace be open at such a strange and convenient time? That's Italy for you.

My scooter is supposed to be back at nine o'clock tomorrow morning. I decide to drive back to the rental office, which also rents cars, to arrange to have a car for tomorrow instead of this scooter. If I get into trouble, my testicles will appreciate the fact that I'll be wearing a seat belt. As I wander through the streets of Palermo heading back toward the sea, I pass through a district with a lot of small shops and restaurants. I decide to stop and buy some clothes that look less American. It seems that doctor's comment about me looking like an American is true. I don't look Sicilian. I look like an American trying to look Italian to an American. I park and buy a soccer jersey and some new green, white and red sneakers. That's Italian.

It takes me another half an hour to find the little rental office where I picked up the scooter. The streets are not clearly marked, and sometimes entire words are replaced with single letters. Sometimes the same street will change names three times in about six blocks. A business that is closed during business hours and streets that change names—what's with this place? When I arrive at the scooter shop, I make arrangements to get a car for tomorrow. I ask for a Mercedes Benz. What the hell, I'm not paying for it anyway. The manager explains that will not be a problem. The car is at his parking lot across town, but it will be waiting for me here tomorrow morning at 7:30. That will work fine. I head back to my hotel to sleep. I am fading fast.

Chapter Twenty-Seven

The next morning I wake to a light rain. I feel as though I slept like Rip Van Winkle. My new shirt and shoes fit great. The rain is more of a mist, and the sun is trying to break through. I'm happy to get to the scooter rental and get a car. Rain drops hurt when you're moving 50km/h. I finish the paperwork with the manager, and he hands me the car key with a Mercedes Benz symbol on it. I turn and follow him out and begin laughing hysterically. It seems that the Mercedes he has rented me looks nothing like any Mercedes Benz I have ever seen in the United States. It is a Mercedes A140. It has two seats and three doors. It looks exactly like a SmartCar. It is a boxy sort of wedge-shaped car that looks like it has been cut in half. The manager looks at me puzzled and asks,

"Is something the matter?"

"No, this will be fine," I laugh. "I will see you tomorrow morning before nine o'clock." I climb into the tiny car and drive away.

Again I drive to Villa Malfitano and pull in the front gate. You cannot see the villa as you pull in the gated entry and past the gatehouse. It is located in the center of the property behind some gardens and large pine trees. I park just inside the wall with the nose of my car headed toward the gate. I am very afraid of running into Angelo della Morte or some of his friends. I take two deep breaths and look cautiously around the gardens and see no one. I can see, through the foliage, other cars and scooters and motorcycles parked at what appears to be the front of the villa. I step out of the car and close the door quietly. There is nobody at the gatehouse just across the gravel and sand drive from where I have parked. I double strap my backpack and walk cautiously toward the cover of a nearby pine tree. Peering through the needles I can make out the figure of a very large dark haired man wearing sunglasses. He is smoking a cigarette and leaning on the hood of a car.

The gardens of the villa are in shambles. Like the palace my hotel is located in, this once magnificent estate has fallen into disrepair. Sixty-five years ago when General Patton and my grandfather were here, it must have been spectacular. Today, it is rather sad. I decide to see if I can enter through the back side of the villa. I don't know who the man smoking out front is, but I would rather no one notice me at all.

The side of the villa closest to me is an old greenhouse. It runs the length of the palace along the entire first floor. The palace is two stories tall and a beige color. It is made of stone with a flat roof. A large stone staircase is guarded by statues of sleeping lions on either side around the back of the villa. A row of windows on the lower level have dirty screens covered with steel bars making it impossible to see in, or out for that matter. The twelve-foot-tall wooden doors along the back porch have long clear windows in them, and one of the three sets of doors is open. I don't see anyone inside and decide to have a look at the far side of the house. I want to know what's around in case somebody shoots at me. I round the far corner of the palace and it is just more gardens. There is a hexagonal glass room on the far side of the building with stained glass windows. Inside of which is a spiral metal staircase leading down into the lower level of the house. Next to the glass room is another stone staircase leading into the palace. Its doors are also open.

I step cautiously into the palace from this side entrance. As I do a little old Italian lady steps out of one of the rooms off of the main hallway that stretches through the entire length of the villa. For being so small, she certainly scared me. She smiles and waves and grabs my hand to say hello. She is wearing a long skirt that hangs all the way to the floor. She places her hand over her chest and says,

"Daniela,"

I place my hand over my chest and say,

"James Salvatore."

"Ah bambino. Salvatore. Bambino. Bambino Salvatore," the old lady said as she patted my hand and smiled. It was as if a light bulb had just turned on above her head. She was speaking in Italian now and pulling at my hand to follow her. I have no idea what she is doing or who she is, but she is obviously trying to tell me something. She leads me down the center hallway past some security guards. We walk all the way to the opposite side of the ornate old villa. She looks as if she is hovering as she shuffles along in her long skirt. I never see her feet under her hemline. She seems to be drifting like a puck on an air hockey table.

She leads me into a large ballroom where a platform with a baby grand piano and about one hundred or so chairs are set up for a piano recital. She is still speaking Italian and seems to be gesturing for me to have a seat. I sit down, and she hovers across the room to a door on the left front side of the platform. She disappears through the door and I now sit alone in silence. The security guards I passed didn't seem so secure. They looked like they only had walkie-talkies and blue sport coats.

I look to my left and begin admiring the large tapestry hanging on the left side of the wall. There is a magnificent crystal chandelier, and the floor is a wood herringbone pattern with an inlaid wooden border around perimeter of the floor. Unfortunately, the floor looks as though it has been stripped and not re-finished. It is a shame to see such a beautiful palace in such a state of distress. Just then Daniela floated back into the room and handed me an envelope. Its address reads,

Michael Salvatore
Villa Malfitano
Via Dante 167
Palermo, Sicily

Inside the envelope is a letter with the corporate logo Credit Suisse Group. The letter read: "Dear Mr. Salvatore. There has not been any activity in your account in the last fifty years. As is Credit Suisse policy, your account has been placed in hold. The standard hold time is fifteen years at which time if you have not contacted Credit Suisse Group, your funds will be automatically transferred into our general fund, and you shall forfeit all right to these funds. This is the third and final attempt to contact you at the only known address we have on this account. The account transfer date is November 21, 2010 @ 17:00 GMT + 2:00."

Holy shit! My grandfather has a fifty-year-old Swiss bank account. That means he must have opened it just after World War II ended in Europe. It all made sense now. The Mafia had to have learned about the account and came looking for the account number. That's why they wanted my grandfather's ammo box. That is what is valuable enough to kill for. Holy shit, that really is valuable enough to kill for. Sixty-five years worth of compounded interest on whatever money was in the account in 1945. Holy shit, I'm in big trouble. The Mafia is going to kill me. They want the money in that account. I feel like I want to throw up. I think it might have been better for me not to know how much danger I'm really in. I think I just turned six different shades of green. Daniela is looking at me like I'm ill. She may be correct. I believe I might throw up.

Okay, the first thing I have to do is to find that bottle of wine. I need to find Nero d'Avola. I turn to Daniela and ask, "Nero d'Avola?"

She laughed aloud and said, "No. No vino."

"Si vino. Vino Nero d'Avola?" I asked again staring intently at her.

"Il cantina per vini," she said pointing toward the floor.

"Grazie," I say rising to look for a staircase to the wine cellar. I give Daniela a big hug and kiss on the cheek as I say, "Grazie, Mama bella." I headed into the hallway. I walked toward the spiral staircase in the glass atrium I passed on my way in. There must be something in or on a bottle of Nero d'Avola in the cellar. I can hardly contain my excitement. I'm going to be filthy rich. Even if it were only a hundred dollars in 1943, the interest will make it at least a couple of thousand by now. I don't think the mob would come after me for a few thousand dollars. It has to be millions. I'm now practically running down the hall inside the palace. I can't contain my excitement. I can feel my face stretching as I smile and think about the truckload of money I'm about to go claim.

I have to cut through another room to get to the atrium. I step quickly through the room into the hexagonal glass room with the round iron staircase in the center. My heart is beginning to well with excitement. I step carefully down the narrow metal stairs to the basement. My backpack and I fill the entire stairs as I slip cautiously into the cellar. As I got to the landing, the smell of dust and stale air hit me. I step to the wall next to the arched passageway leading into the next room. I look down and just catch sight of a shadow moving through the next room. I stop and listen silently for a moment. I can hear someone moving about in the next room.

My palms begin to sweat as a terrible feeling of discomfort takes over the elation I had been feeling only a few seconds earlier. I quietly slip my backpack off of my shoulders and try to silently unzip the top compartment. I can still hear someone in the next room clanking glass wine bottles. It sounds as if they are pulling bottles out of a rack and setting them onto the concrete floor. I slide my hand inside my pack and retrieve my pistol. I set my pack gingerly on the floor and begin peeking around the corner. It seems almost unbelievable that he is here. I'm sure he's going to feel the same way. I cocked the hammer back and it made a very distinct and audible 'click,' as I rounded the corner pointing my gun at the back of the Angel of Death.

Chapter Twenty-Eight

"Angelo della Morte," I say sticking the barrel of the gun into the back of his neck. "Don't fucking move. I should kill you right now."

"James, I am going to kill you. I don't know how you keep showing up," said Luigi rather calmly in his thick accent as he raised his hands. "Tell me, James, how did you arrange to sit behind me on the airplane? I must know. I must use this trick myself one day. It was wonderful."

"Shut up," I said as I eased the hammer back into the safety position. I then cracked him in the back of the head with the butt end of the gun. He fell to his knees. Without hesitation I cracked him in the same spot a second time, and he fell to the floor in a heap. "Now you know how I felt in Wisconsin." I then began a series of swift and unmerciful kicks to his ribs and stomach. After four kicks I decided he must be unconscious. He hadn't moved or even groaned. There was just the dull thud of my shoe hitting his midsection. He was either out cold, or one hell of a great actor who didn't feel pain. Those last two kicks had to hurt, as I squared up and let him have it.

The Angel of Death had been busy taking bottles of Nero d'Avola out of their racks. He was then looking them over and setting them on the floor. This was a daunting task as there was an entire large cabinet full of that particular wine. I removed my raincoat from my backpack and tied Luigi's hands behind his back with the sleeves. I knew he would eventually be able to free himself, but not before making enough noise for me to notice. I walked around to the front of him and delivered one more swift kick to his stomach.

I then set about continuing the work he had started. I grabbed a bottle of wine off the shelf and examined it for any signs of a message or bank account number or anything else that might look amiss. The date on the first bottle I looked at was 1967. Luigi was an idiot. I was only looking for bottles dated 1943 or earlier. Then I remembered the carving in the ammo box. It said, *10-23-41*. I must be looking for a 1941 vintage. Hopefully one marked, *10-23-41*. I quickly scoured all the various wine racks for any bottles with heavy dust collected on them or anything labeled Nero d'Avola. After a quick scan of the entire cellar, I realized there was only one rack that had Nero d'Avola bottles in it. It was the set of bottles the Angel of Death was searching through. I guess he's not such an idiot.

The bottles on the bottom had collected more dust over the years. I un-stacked the bottles and set them on the floor beside Luigi's body. The dust began to cloud the area. After about six loads, I stepped back to get a breath of fresh air. I kicked Luigi in his stomach once more hoping to burst his appendix or rupture his spleen. He groaned in pain and opened his eyes just in time to see me kick him again in the stomach.

"Don't make another sound, or I'll kill you," I say pointing at his face with the most menacing face I can possibly make.

"I'm going to…" He didn't get the last words out before I kicked him once more in the stomach.

"If you don't shut up, I'm going to have a very sore foot." Luigi was obviously in a great deal of discomfort. I kicked his face with the sole of my shoe and pointed to him again saying, "Shut up." After rolling his eyes and coughing, he complied.

I continued taking bottles out of the rack and setting them on the floor. The age of the bottles continued to get older and older. As I got into the 1954 vintage I noticed something carved into the inside of the wine rack. I removed the bottles along that side and wiped away the years of dust. It was carved just like the bottom of the ammo box. It read,

CSG

Zurich

08-01-42

This was my uncle's birthday. He was born after my grandfather had shipped out to fight the war. I couldn't leave the carving for Luigi or whoever followed me. I needed a knife or something to scratch and shave the carving to make it unreadable. I picked a bottle off the cellar floor and smashed it. The pop and shattering sound that the bottle made were quite a bit louder than I would have liked. I began chipping away at the wooden rack with a piece of the broken glass. The carving was deep and my piece of broken glass was merely scratching at the surface. This was going to take some time. I pressed harder on the piece of broken green bottle trying to speed things up. This only caused the sharp end of the glass to splinter off and stick into the wood.

I looked down at the pool of spilled wine and broken pieces of bottle to see if there might be a better piece to use. I was using a piece of the stem and neck of the bottle and the only other large piece that might work was the bottom of the bottle. The rest was fragmented and held together by its label. As I reached down to change pieces, Daniela floated around the corner. This time I could see the tips of her shoes kicking at her skirt. About the time our eyes met she let out an ear piercing shriek. For such a tiny little old lady, she had one hell of a set of lungs. She was screaming and took off around the corner. Her shriek was unbelievably loud.

"No," I shouted, "You don't understand." It didn't matter. She was racing up the steps at the far end of the palace. I could hear footsteps running upstairs in the palace. Daniela was still screaming, only now she was saying something in Italian.

"Now you are in trouble, James," said Luigi while wincing in pain.

I reached down and grabbed my backpack. I grabbed a bottle of wine and hit Luigi over the head with it. He was out cold again. I quickly admired my new bottle of wine, and stuffed it into my pack. I spun around and ran for the metal stairs I had come down. I could hear footsteps rushing down the staircase Daniela had run up. I stumbled up the round metal staircase and dashed out the side door. I ran around the back of the palace and headed directly to my rental car. As I climbed into the driver's side I saw the large spooky man who had been smoking a cigarette on his car earlier, running from the palace across the sandy gravel parking lot to his car. I wasn't sticking around to see what he was up to. I started the car and mashed the gas pedal in my little Mercedes. The engine wound up before I even had it in gear.

The way the little engine whined, you would think I would have zoomed right out of the gate throwing gravel all over the place. To say this little car didn't have much pick up was an understatement. I sped like a tortoise out of the gates and cut right into Palermo traffic. Two cars screeched to a stop and honked at me. As I raced down the street I turned left and saw a large silver Mercedes bouncing down the curb and tearing out of the villa's gate. It was the dark haired man. He was chasing me. There were tires screeching and horns honking behind me. I could just hear those weird European sirens in the distance.

Although traffic was heavy, I hit the spot between all the scooters at the front of a traffic pattern and the automobiles following behind. I was now racing to turn right onto Via Noce and hopefully get there before the silver Mercedes made its first left. I locked up the brakes and made a hard right. My backpack with the stolen bottle of wine slid across the floorboard and made a loud thud as I screeched around the turn. It was now rolling around on the floor by my feet somewhere. I stomped back on the gas pedal and began speeding toward a stop sign where the narrow alley merged into Via Noce.

I was really working the steering wheel to keep control of the car. I had chosen this as my quick getaway route because it was the fastest way to the highway. The second exit to the south of the highway entrance would take me back to my hotel or the train station. As I looked in my rear view mirror I saw the silver Mercedes pass by the alley I had turned down. He had missed the turn to follow me. I merged into traffic and sped toward the highway. I slowed to blend into traffic. I smiled widely and tried to breathe normally. As I slowed and turned onto the highway I sighed in relief. There was no one following me.

When I entered the highway, I saw the large silver sedan with the dark haired man inside speeding on the street below me to the highway entrance. He had to have seen me going up the ramp. I tried to reach down and grab my backpack to retrieve my gun. As I leaned forward my seatbelt caught me. I unbuckled it as I accelerated up the ramp. There was no way I was going to take my foot off of the gas pedal. I was struggling to reach the bag when I got onto the freeway at the top of the ramp. I pulled it up onto the seat and checked in my rearview mirror. The dark haired man had a much faster car. He had already merged in front of a car and was racing up the freeway ramp. His car was quickly getting larger in my mirror as it approached. I grabbed frantically at my backpack trying to unzip the top and retrieve my gun.

There was a large dump truck traveling in one of the two center lanes. All I could do was to try to put the truck between his car and mine. My plan was to try to play ring-around-the-rosy while keeping the dump truck between our cars until I could get off on an exit. Before I could get my gun out of the backpack, I had to cut hard to the left to get in front of the truck. The man in the silver sedan pulled alongside of me. Man, was his car faster and more agile than mine! He was driving the Mercedes that I had wanted to rent.

I looked over at him and smiled and waved. His window slid down, and he raised a gun at me.

"Fuck!" I yelled as I ducked my head as low as I could. It was just in time to hear both windows on either side of my head shatter. Maybe the wave wasn't such a good idea. It really seemed to piss him off. The shattered glass rained over my head and down my left arm. I swerved violently to my left and tapped the brakes. The nose of my car dove, and I fishtailed a little before regaining control. The dump truck passed between my car and the dark-haired man's. The truck was now to my right, and I had no idea where the silver sedan had disappeared to. I looked through my newly-spidered windshield and noticed the two bullet holes. One was directly below the rearview mirror just above the dashboard. The other was dead center of the passenger's side of the windshield. The man following me had shot more than once.

The driver of the dump truck had stepped on his brakes either when I swerved or when he saw the man in the Mercedes shooting at me. He was now slowing fast. It didn't matter because he was no longer hiding my car from the sedan. My car had now overtaken the truck by at least two car lengths. I looked to my right and saw that the sedan was once again to my right. There was the guy with dark hair pointing a gun at me. I smashed the brake pedal, and my chest hit the steering wheel as all four of my tires screeched. The dump truck shot past me on my right, and my windshield cracked into a million little pieces but managed somehow to hold its original shape. Other drivers were now honking their horns and screeching to a stop behind me and the truck.

The truck had now slid to a stop about fifty yards ahead of me. The silver sedan had slid sideways locking up its brakes. It was in front of the truck and was now smoking its rear wheels as it spun to face my car head on.

"Holy shit!" I shouted. That guy with dark hair is going to kill me. I turned the wheel hard to the right and stepped down on the gas pedal trying to steer behind the truck. His sedan was heading right at my little car. Pieces of glass began spraying out of my windshield, and my back window now shattered as well. He was still shooting at me. My car sped to the right but it was going to be close. He was trying to run head-on into my little car. Keeping my head down, I could see him getting closer through my driver's side window.

As I sped around the back side of the truck I saw his car skidding sideways to a stop behind my car and the truck. All I could do was make a run for it. I could not press any harder on the gas pedal as my little Mercedes began fleeing from his big Mercedes. I was slouching as low as I could to still see through the cracks of the windshield. There is an exit sign and a ramp that I can see a little way up the freeway. The highway is simply a four-lane road with concrete walls on either side. There is absolutely nowhere to go. As I look ahead to my right at the exit, a scooter shoots by my car. I am totally dumbfounded and amazed at the same time. This guy is shooting at me in a traffic snarl, and the guy on the scooter just doesn't seem to care. He must really be in a hurry. I look up to my mirror just in time to see the pissed off dark-haired man. I could tell he was pissed off because he was that close.

Suddenly, the whole rear end of my car was lifted off the ground as the sedan rammed into the back of me. There is more shattering glass and the crunching sound of metal. The sudden blast of air to my face has blown all the water from my eyes. My car has no windshield at all any more. That little bit of bumper-tag sent it sliding off to the left side of the car and then shattering onto the pavement. My car bounced down onto the road, and it is all I can do to hold on to the wheel. At this point I'm not sure if the sedan hit my car again or I just lost control. It all happened very fast. I spun completely three-hundred-and-sixty degrees. I saw the concrete wall to my right, a Mercedes grill with the angry dark-haired man driving, the other concrete wall on my left, the dump truck, and then the road and an exit. About the time I saw the yellow barrels, the car with the dark-haired man and I both collided very hard.

Chapter Twenty-Nine

The impact knocked the wind out of me. I was soaking wet, and there was this sort of talcum powder floating around the inside of my car. There was a rather attractive woman saying something in Italian to me through the driver's side window. My door was open, and she was speaking Italian into her cell phone. It took me a moment to realize what was going on. I reached over the center console and grasped my backpack with my right hand. There was a large pain in my left shoulder, and I was dazed. The air bag was hanging out of my steering wheel. I rolled to my left and fell to my knees out of my open car door. I was collapsed in a big wet heap. The woman standing there put her hand on my back and was saying something in Italian.

I had lost my backpack when I fell onto the wet pavement. I placed one hand on the car door and one on the driver's seat and pressed myself back up to my feet. There was a lot of pain in my chest as well as most of my left side. I turned back away from my car to see the silver sedan was on its side about thirty yards away in one of the traffic lanes. All I could see was the black undercarriage of the car. There was a man running over to aid the driver that had just tried to kill me. I reached into the front seat and picked up my backpack. I wasn't going to wait for the authorities.

I staggered toward the rear of my destroyed car. As I got to the back of my rental car, the passenger side front door of the Mercedes sedan lifted open skyward. I turned back to see the dark-haired man staring at me. He looked pissed off. While holding the door open with his left hand, he raised his pistol at me and began firing. The woman who had been aiding me screamed and took off running toward the front of my car. I crouched and ran. I ran right to the concrete wall on the other side of my car. I put my left hand on top of the wall and jumped over.

Now had that man not been shooting at me, or had I taken a moment to look over that wall, I never would have jumped.

Chapter Thirty

Over that wall was the steepest mountainside I have ever seen. I fell a good six- or eight feet. My free fall was high enough that I could feel the acceleration of gravity. When my feet hit the loose rocky and sandy soil over the wall, they both sunk in about a half an inch. As my backside hit the loose soil at the back of my ankles, it created a massive landslide. My entire body began sliding as I struggled to my feet and began running sideways. I had dislodged a massive slab of earth. The entire football field-sized slab of earth was sliding down a slope that was as steep as anything I had ever seen. In reality, it was probably much steeper.

All I kept thinking was keep your feet moving. If you stop moving your feet, you will tumble all the way down the side of this mountain—this very tall and very steep mountain. I was staring at my feet and churning them as hard as I could. The slab that had broken loose now began to pick up speed. It was terrifying. My heart and lungs were pounding. The muscles in my legs and stomach were starting to burn. I was coughing up dust and dirt and gravel as I stepped as fast and light as I could. I was flailing my arms about trying to stay balanced. I fixed my gaze at the tops of my now wet and dirty new shoes. Run, Jim, run, was all I could think as I plummeted down the side of the mountain. I was looking straight down at my feet—before it was too late. I saw the passing green plant just as I realized what it was. At that moment of realization, I felt the cactus needles stab into my left arm and stomach.

"Ouch!" I screamed while trying not to loose my balance. Holy shit, that hurts. I was now chugging away with a big piece of a cactus stuck into my left forearm. I could see my own red blood under the large green cactus stuck to me. Worse yet, I could finally see the bottom of the hill I was now sliding and stomping down uncontrollably. I was going to end up directly in front of a tunnel that had cars and scooters shooting out of it at about fifty miles an hour. Whatever came out of that tunnel would have no chance of seeing me at all. They would simply plow right over me.

I had to keep running sideways or risk falling over the top of the tunnel and dropping directly into the path of an oncoming car. I began leaping sideways as I kept my feet moving. I cleared the top side of the tunnel just in time to see the van coming out of it. The driver was looking totally in the opposite direction. He never saw me. I hit square against the side of the van just behind the door and spun a full three-hundred-and-sixty degrees. The rotational force of the impact was unbelievable. That truck ripped me around like a rag doll. I spun helplessly onto the pavement directly into the path of another vehicle. I landed on the pavement with an audible smack. The vehicle, which was a small green car, skidded and swerved just in time to miss me. I quickly rolled over onto my butt. As I slid pushing myself backward over to the hillside on my butt, my backpack fell, hitting me directly in the back of the head.

"Ouch," I said aloud as I rubbed the back of my head with my right hand. That bottle of wine nailed me. Now I know what the Angel of Death felt like ten minutes ago. I looked down at my bloody left forearm. There was still a very large chunk of cactus sticking out of my arm. It was about the size of my tennis shoe and had maybe thirty, three-inch-long needles sticking out of it. Man! did it fucking hurt. I guessed it would be a lot like removing a band-aid or maybe even an eyebrow waxing—Yes, I've had one; I'm Italian—I gripped the cactus as tight as I could and gave it one fierce jerk.

"OUCH!! FUCK!! Holy shit!" I yelled before falling over backward in pain and screaming curse words at the sky. That was by far the most painful thing I have ever felt. Oh, my God, was that painful. I still had at least twenty-five needles in my bloody forearm and probably five more in my stomach. Just then another car screeched its brakes and swerved to avoid me. It scared me back into reality and completely terrified the driver of the car.

Pain or not, I was leaving.

I reached down and picked up my backpack. I had to get out of here. I looked up but couldn't see the top of the hill or the concrete wall I had jumped over to get here. I felt confident that the dark-haired man wouldn't be stupid enough to follow me down that hill. Had I seen that hill before jumping, I wouldn't have jumped that wall. The dark-haired man wouldn't follow me, but he would find his way here very shortly. I ran across the street to the sidewalk and limped painfully into the tunnel.

As I cleared the darkness of the tunnel I heard those weird European sirens approaching. I carefully slid my bloody needle-punctured arm through the loop of my backpack and repeated the process with my right so I was double strapped. I headed south back toward my hotel. I ran to the first alley and turned into it. I began walking briskly to get a few streets over so I would be harder to find if the man with dark hair was looking for me. I guessed it was about a three- to five-mile walk back to my hotel. That wasn't going to work. I had to get to a pharmacy right away to get something for my arm. I would then have to catch a taxi or take a bus or something. The police would be looking for me by now, and so would the mob.

Chapter Thirty-One

Piedro was pissed off. He was hanging from his seat belt in Luigi's destroyed Mercedes Benz without Luigi. Luigi had somehow messed it up again. This fucking American had gotten past both of them at the Villa Malfitano. Now this American had caused a major accident on the only freeway in his hometown. Piedro released his seatbelt and fell onto the driver's side door. His airbag had deployed and there was white powder and smoke inside the car.

He bumped around looking for his gun and trying to untangle his large frame from the steering wheel and the foot pedals. His gun was lying on the door beneath him as he struggled to twist around and stand upright across the now vertical front seats. As he tried the passenger side door, he realized it was locked. He found the automatic lock and pressed it and the locks released. He immediately pulled the door handle and pressed the heavy door skyward. As he lifted the door he peered over the wreckage of the car.

The American was standing behind his car looking right at Piedro. This enraged him. He raised his pistol and began shooting. After the first shot his clip was empty. Piedro dropped the door, and it slammed shut over his head. He began kicking and punching at the windshield of the car as hard as he could. He was going to kill that fucking American. It took several kicks and about a minute and a half before the windshield finally yielded and fell to the street. When he got free of the giant coffin of a car, Piedro was panting and furious. He ran over to where the American had been and saw someone down the freeway point to the concrete wall. Piedro ran over to the wall and looked over.

Piedro looked back to his right and his left down the side of the highway, but there was no trace of the man he had been shooting at. Can this American fly? He thought to himself. As he looked back over the wall, he saw dust and a few loose pieces of gravel and stone coming to rest. His eyes widened with disbelief. This American had just committed suicide. Piedro had to go see the body below. No one could have survived a fall down the side of that hill. He ran toward the exit ramp as the sirens in the distance began approaching.

As he got to the bottom of the exit, Piedro saw something. He wasn't sure, but he might have seen the American just turn down an alley about three blocks away from where his body should be lying. He thought the American had a blue shirt and black backpack, and he was pretty convinced that was what he saw as he got to the bottom of the freeway ramp.

Piedro decided to begin walking casually to the next street in the direction the man in the alley was headed. The casual walk was because the policia had just arrived and were passing him. As Piedro got to the next street he leaned against a storefront and watched and waited. There he was. The American was hustling across the street and heading into the next alley. Piedro began smiling. Now he had him.

He decided to mirror the American's movements one block to the north. He should be able to stay right on top of the American without the American knowing. After all, he had grown up pick-pocketing American tourists all over Palermo in the early 1970s. As a child thief in Sicily, Americans were better than piggy banks. He tried to call Luigi on his cell phone, but there was no answer. Next he did something he had never even thought of until now.

The underboss's cell phone rang as he was sitting at a little café table having some fresh pineapple.

"Well, the job must be finished," he said very excitedly as he answered the call. "I can't wait to tell our friend."

"No" came Piedro's response. "The man from the new land is between the highway and the university. I don't know about the Angel. I will be his shadow and call back." Then Piedro hung up. The underboss looked across the table at the boss with a look of disbelief; the boss was reading the paper and having his morning espresso and pastry.

"So, it is done?" asked the boss.

"No," responded the underboss. The boss looked over his paper puzzled.

"Piedro is following the American and doesn't know about Luigi."

"Where are they?" asked the boss.

"West of the university inside the highway."

"Call everyone," the boss had emphasized the word *everyone*, "and tell them I will pay 10,000 euros to the man that kills this American. I want all of our friends to go to Old Town and the university and wait for Piedro's call."

The underboss sat in disbelief, trying to take in what was happening. The most feared man in Palermo had just called for help. The boss said to send everyone they knew. Nothing like this had ever happened before. Who was this American who has caused so much trouble?

"Now!" The boss shouted and slammed his fist on the table, rattling his espresso cup.

Chapter Thirty-Two

Luigi woke up as soon as the EMT put the smelling salts under his nose. He had a terrible headache, and his shirt was wet with red wine. The EMTs were asking him questions and trying to place a neck brace on him. Luigi swatted their hands away and snatched the neck brace. He threw it across the basement and cursed in Italian. A police officer walked over and asked what was going on.

"Nothing. A crazy American attacked me with a wine bottle," he said. Luigi stood and looked into the wine rack. He immediately saw the carving and turned and walked away from the EMTs and the cop. He saw Daniela speaking to another officer, and she pointed at him. The other officer was looking at him as well. Scratching his sore head he dashed up the stairs and out of the palace.

There was no sign of the American or Piedro. His car was missing. He pulled his cell phone from his pocket and dialed the number. It began ringing as he walked to the front gate of the palace grounds.

"What the fuck happened to you?" asked the underboss.

"Where is he?" asked Luigi.

"You fucking call me to ask where he is?" the underboss was shouting. "Weren't you supposed to have already taken care of this problem in America? Just get your dumb ass back here now." He then hung up.

The Angel of Death was enraged. This fucking American had messed up his life again. This fucking American was going to die a slow and painful death. Luigi hailed a cab.

When he arrived at the café where the boss and underboss were sitting at the table, he had calmed down somewhat. He was still absolutely furious, but he was calm. The boss and the underboss both stood.

"Come with us," the boss said. Luigi immediately feared for his life. He said nothing. He was wondering where they were going, and if they were going to have him killed. The three men got into a waiting car with a driver. The bosses sat in back, and Luigi rode in the front passenger seat. As the car pulled away, the boss spoke.

"We're going to Rome. If this American is going to the bank in Zurich, he will be headed to Rome eventually. You will wait for him there. You will be ready for him this time. You will take care of your unfinished business when he arrives. We have arranged help for you with our friends up north. We will wait for you in Milan. When you have finished, we will meet you in Domodossola. From there, we will cross the border together."

The fact that the bosses were not staying with him made Luigi fearful. If they were going to kill him, this would be the perfect way. Just have their associates in Rome kill him and dump his body. It would be totally clean for the bosses.

"You didn't lose your gun, did you?" the underboss asked Luigi.

"No, the police didn't search me at the villa."

"I guess that means you're not a total fuck up."

"Stop," said the boss. "You will fix this mess, Luigi, and we will see you in Domodossola. If the American gets by you in Rome, you will call us. We will have our Milano friends ready to make sure he doesn't cross the border."

Chapter Thirty-Three

I walked out of the alley and saw the green and red cross, and the sign read 'farmacia.' The man in the 'farmacia' took one look at me and walked to the back of the tiny store. The aisles were so narrow that I had to walk sideways or risk brushing my arm into the stacks of items for sale. He had a little section of the store set aside for this sort of emergency. There were ointments and tweezers and gauze and bandages and rubbing alcohol.

"Do you speak English?" I asked.

"A little," he responded.

"So you have seen this before?"

"The university is not far, and a lot of students come in with needles stuck in worse places than this," he smiled as he responded.

"I can only imagine," I said. "So you think I will live?"

"You need to get all the needles out and clean the area very well. If you break a needle and don't get it out, you will have to see a doctor because of infection. You will be in quite a bit of pain. Just keep it clean, and you should be fine. I recommend Jack Daniels after you finish of course,"

"Since I am in Italy, I would have thought Lemoncello," I replied.

"You are in Sicily, not in Naples," he said sharply. It was obviously some sort of insult to mention Lemoncello to a Sicilian. He headed to the cash register. I paid and thanked him again and asked where I should catch a taxi. He directed me down the street about three blocks and one block to the left to the taxi stand.

I got back to my hotel room and began the arduous and painful task of cleaning my arm. The bleeding had stopped. My sweat had made little tracks in the dirt and blood around the needles sticking out of my arm. I never had to remove cactus needles from my skin, so I didn't understand how painful some could be. Cactus needles have little barbs on the end like fishing hooks. When I pulled them out they stretched and ripped the skin. They also had some sort of film or venom or poison on them that irritated the whole area. The entire experience was very unpleasant and hurt a lot. I started with the six needles in my stomach and then worked on my arm. It took about twenty minutes to remove all the needles and another fifteen to shower. When I was finished I applied a generous portion of ointment and wrapped the whole thing in gauze and then an ace bandage. My arm was swollen and sore but seemed like it would be okay. My entire body felt swollen and sore, and I hoped it would be okay as well.

As I dressed all I could think about was getting to Switzerland and getting whatever was in that bank account. It might not be an account at all. It might be some sort of safety deposit box. I wonder what could be in that bank. I hope it's not some famous piece of stolen art work or something that will get me into more trouble. It can't be something that would get me into more trouble. I really couldn't be in more trouble. Besides, the Mafia wants it. It has to be valuable and easily converted into cash.

Looking down at my watch sitting on the sink, I realized it was just eleven o'clock. That meant that I would still be able to get that money grubbing surgeon to fly me back to Rome. From Rome I would need to get to Zurich. It should be reasonably easy to get from one major city to another, I hoped. I opened my balcony door, and before I could step out, something strange grabbed my attention.

There was a group of men inside a large sedan across the street. I was on a very busy street so it was possible I was imagining things. However, it looked to me like those four men were watching my hotel. I walked out of my room and around the corner to the main salon of the hotel and looked out another balcony window. It was the balcony Mussolini had spoken from some seventy years ago.

Sure enough, the men in that car were watching my hotel. Just then another man walked over to their car and lit a cigarette and began speaking to the men in the car. He pointed at the hotel and continued speaking to the men inside the car who were now laughing. I turned to look the other direction down the street and saw another car at the end of the block with other men watching my hotel.

The sickening feeling that came over me was absolute terror. They had found me. They must have followed me or somehow found out where I was staying. It didn't matter how or when because they were here. It was only a matter of time before they would all come in to kill me. I rushed quickly back to my room.

"How do you get out of a hotel without being seen?" I asked myself aloud. I quickly gathered my things and shoved them into my backpack. It didn't take long. My entire list of possessions was something like: a stolen 1953 bottle of Nero d'Avola, a letter from a Swiss bank, a gun with ammunition, some money, some bandages and a tube of ointment, a guidebook, underwear, socks, and some torn-up dirty clothes. I think the clothes can stay behind.

I walked quickly down the hall and around to the front desk. The clerk was sitting in a chair watching the news in the lobby. I greeted him with a nervous, "Ciao."

"Ciao," he responded looking up but not moving from his chair.

"Coache, car, automobile?" I asked.

"Si," he responded. He stood and walked over and picked up the scooter rental brochure.

"No, no," I responded. "Paper, pen?" I asked while making writing gestures with my hands.

"Si," he said with a puzzled look on his face. He slowly walked behind the desk and handed me a piece of paper and a pen. I drew a car with a man inside and pointed to the clerk and said,

"You." I made car motor noises and pointed to him and did an impression of a man driving an invisible steering wheel. Again he responded,

"Si." I then pointed to myself and drew myself inside the trunk of the car and said, "Me. Okay?" and like before he said,

"Si."

"I'll pay you euros, okay?" I asked.

"Si," came his response. With that he turned around and walked over to the large padded chair he had been sitting in, before I had disturbed him. He then stretched and sat back down to watch television. It was obvious that he did not comprehend what I was saying. He didn't get it at all.

"Shit," I said aloud. I stared at the clerk who was watching television for another moment. I realized that trying to get him to understand and cooperate was futile. He really didn't give a shit. He had spent enough time humoring me and just wanted to be left alone. I started laughing. I don't know why; I just found the entire situation totally ridiculous. Here I was in a foreign country begging for my life and for this guy's help— and he just went back to watching television. Well, Jim, you're just going to have to find another way.

I ran down the stairs into the center courtyard. I needed to find a way out other than the front door. The smell of cat urine was particularly strong today. I ran to the back of the old palace into another courtyard that was smaller and appeared to be a different building. It was like a sloppy new addition to the palace. It had large back doors just like the front wooden doors with a little door inset into one of the larger doors.

I pulled the small paper map out of my back pocket that I had been using to drive around town. It showed several smaller streets and alleys behind my hotel. My guidebook had said my hotel was located right in the middle of the market district. The whole area was full of dozens of storefronts and shops and little carts peddling anything from women's shoes to duct tape to fresh butchered chickens and fruit. Lots of people and lots of distractions. It was a perfect place for me to get lost. More importantly, it was a perfect place for me to lose the men watching my hotel.

Once again my haphazardly thought out plan would have to do. I would need to get all the men watching my hotel to come to the front doors. I would then shut the door and run through the two courtyards and out the back door to safety. I could either lose them in the market or head straight to the train station and catch a train to the airport. Of course, that is assuming there is a train to the airport. Maybe I could simply jump in a taxi if I saw one along the way. First things first, I need to get those men to try and follow me into the front door of the hotel. I walked back through the courtyard and stood behind the massive wooden entry doors at the front of the palace. I took my gun out of my backpack and checked to make sure of the loads.

"You only have six shots, Jim," I said aloud to myself. I took one last deep breath and opened the little entry door. I stepped through and propped it open with my backpack. I took two strides out to the curb and looked to the right, down the street at the car and the men standing outside of it. They all stopped and stared right at me. The men outside the car began trotting toward me, and the four men inside stepped out and followed quickly. I then looked across the street at the four men inside the car who were intently watching my every move. The man standing outside the car waved at another two cars parked on the curb about thirty yards to my left. Their doors flung open and that group of men came toward me. Some of the men were dialing their cell phones.

I raised my gun and shot at the car directly across the street. The first shot shattered its windshield. My second shot I'm just not sure. I turned and jumped back through the door pulling my pack out of the way. The first shot startled the men coming toward me. The second shot had them scrambling for cover. I slammed the door behind me and started running across the courtyard. As I got to the far side I could hear them pounding on the doors and screaming in Italian. They would not be far behind me.

As I got to the entrance between the old and new additions, the bright sunlight and smell of cat piss was shattered by some sort of tank on wheels blasting through the back castle doors. The doors exploded with a flash of light and quite a bit of smoke. The power of the shockwave from the explosion was amazing. It was like being hit in the chest during a pillow fight. I'm deaf...

I can't hear...

I only saw the smoke and vapor trail off the back of it before the impact. It took my breath away. The impact to my stomach is indescribable. A guy in a helmet on the back of that tank just shot a smoking three-pound canister into the second to the last fold of my large intestine. You can feel the imprint of the canister just to the left and a little lower than my naval to this day.

I still can't hear ...

I fell over backward, and my head hit one of the large stone slabs that make the floor of this courtyard. When you get hit with something that has been shot from a cannon, you fall very hard and very fast. As I opened my now watering eyes, I noticed a helicopter full of commandos sliding down ropes. I think I spit up blood. My first gasp of air was not really air at all. It was tear gas that was now spraying out of the canister that almost went through my stomach.

There is still no sound...

I can't hear myself cough. I can sure as hell feel it. If the booze-in-the-eyes at The Muskee were a 7 on the scale of burning sensations, the tear gas was about a 249. I now saw nothing but smoke. I was writhing in pain and coughing. The impact to my lower stomach from the canister was the most painful thing I have ever felt. I might piss blood for days.

Just then some guy in black riot gear that said 'POLICIA' and an Uzi type weapon slung over his shoulder, grabbed me by the collar and poured about half a gallon of water on my face and eyes. I was gasping and choking and trying not to piss myself. I was in torturous pain. As I coughed and flailed at my eyes, he dropped me back to the stone courtyard, and I saw the muzzle flashes. I was in the middle of World War Three. The men in riot gear that followed the big tank, as well as the guys from that helicopter right there over my head, were shooting at the guys that just followed me into the hotel because I shot their car.

None of that really matters. I'm going to asphyxiate right in the middle of this courtyard. The entire act of breathing is extra ordinarily painful. It burns; it really burns. I begin rolling away from the smoke. I can't hear. I can't breath. After about three full turns, I bump into that nice black little pregnant cat. It turns quickly and claws the shit out of the back of my hands, which are covering my face because of the gas. I jump to my feet and start running. I might be screaming. I don't know because I still can't hear anything. Fucking cat. I run all of three steps before hitting the first of twenty-five marble steps leading to the first landing in the back of the palace.

It was more of a stumble. I managed to land by cracking my left bandaged forearm on one of the marble steps. It plowed the heel of my hand into my cheekbone and twisted my head all the way around like an owl. Had I been looking over my right shoulder, I'm quite sure that I would have seen my left heel. That was right before the back of my right, bleeding, cat scratched, hand hit the marble riser. I eventually landed on my chest and this made it more difficult to breathe normally.

Aside from still having no hearing, I couldn't open my eyes because of the gas. I stumbled to my feet, up the steps and just kept running. I had to get away from the gas. That's just a ringing in my ears. It's not really sound. That was when I hit glass and felt a cool rush of air. The split second that fresh air hit my lungs was delicious. I opened my eyes just in time to see a giant swordfish fish head slap my face like some sort of frozen meat bat.

I had broken through a second story window and fallen into a fish cart. I had exploded some sort of ice stacked on top of crates of not so fresh fish. Those would be oyster shells that dug into the tops of my thighs. I rolled onto my back and drank in the air. There was still ice shrapnel and various types of shellfish and squid and water raining onto me. I lay in the ice rubbing my eyes and trying to breath without dry heaving and coughing violently. My lungs are still burning, but the fresh air is helping. Holy shit, what just happened? My stomach really hurts. I struggle once again to my feet and begin to sort of half run and half hobble away from the tank and helicopter.

It seemed my plan had drastically changed. My new plan was to run away from the helicopters and tanks and gunfire that I can't hear. I'm struggling to open my watering eyes and see a shop owner pulling a steel garage door over the front of his shop. All his goods for sale are still sitting out front. I can't believe they didn't even get these people out of the street before the war started. I guess that would technically be the war that I started.

I see a bottle of water in a fridge right outside the next storefront. I still cannot hear. I open the fridge and pour an entire bottle of water into my eyes. This made the burning stop getting more intense. Right now, it just burns a lot. The pain in my stomach is unimaginable. I might have internal damage. As I kind of half sit and half lay in a heap next to the refrigerator, I begin to get my bearings. I am beginning to breathe normally. By that I mean I'm not coughing my lungs up. I hope my hearing returns. I pull my map out of my back pocket and realize I have to go the other way. The train station is the other way. Shit.

I need another new plan. I could run away and try to find a taxi to the airport. Somehow I'm pretty sure that every taxi in Palermo left the area when that big tank arrived. If I was anywhere and a tank arrived with riot police, I'd leave. That surgeon might have already left with his plane and my money. I don't think I'll make it to the airport by one o'clock anyway. Forget the airport, Jim. You have to get out of this war zone now. You need to get to the train station right now. Just get out of Palermo. I don't want to get caught up in this war between the riot cops and the Mafia. It looks like I have to go all the way back around the hotel building to the train station.

Of course, the train station was directly through the middle of the hotel that was being demolished because I shot at some people that I didn't know. There was a lot more going on than I had realized. Not only did the Mafia find my hotel, the authorities had found the Mafia at my hotel. I had to get moving. I did not want to be here when the smoke from the teargas cleared.

The fact that all the shop owners hadn't had time to clean up was a good thing. It meant that there would be people running everywhere. I had to run right back through the policia who were now attacking the hotel. It just might be possible if all the cops were still inside shooting.

When I got to my feet the fridge behind me exploded with a powerful water blast. The fridge flew about two feet when the water hit it. I fell over. It seems my left leg is not working very well. I'm sure that has something to do with the canon that shot me. It might have something to do with the fall from that window. Come to think of it, my bleeding hands, my thighs, my neck, and my poor left forearm really hurt.

I looked down the street and saw more 'POLICIA' in full riot gear beating black batons on Plexiglas shields. They were marching toward me. As I rolled onto my back I realized there were several helicopters in the sky. Being deaf might be a hindrance. There was now water raining over me off of the car I was sitting beside. It seems those riot cops are shooting the water cannon at me. Why not? I seem to make a pretty good cannon target today. I pressed my hand against my badly bruised abdomen and started to scurry back toward the tank and gas and battlefield. I crawled to the front of the car beside me and managed to get to my feet.

I ran, or hobbled, through about a dozen policia cars and a couple of busses that seem to be wearing steel straps and a chain link fence. I cover my face as I run through the remnants of the gas. The street is now completely empty. Anyone with any sense is running as hard away from here as they can.

It took me two whole blocks before I passed another human being. It was a little old lady shuffling as fast as she could. Not bad, Jim, I think to myself. You can give an old lady a head start and pass her in less than two city blocks even while limping. The pain in my stomach is getting worse. I pass another older gentleman with a cane and decide to begin walking. I'm holding my stomach and now crossing into the piazza where the busses converge in front of the train station. The policia have forgotten to block off the other end of the alley. I guess they figured no one would get through the tank. Aside from the unusual number of busses in front of the station, and the street in front of my hotel being blocked and empty, it is business as usual in Palermo.

I limp into the train station and look at the departures television in the middle of about ten railroad tracks. It looks like the first train leaving the station is going to Messina. It will be leaving in seven minutes. I look to my left and see the ticket desk behind bulletproof glass. I stagger over and say nothing. There is no one else in line, and this is the only desk open. The teller says something in Italian through a speaker. At least he looks like he is speaking into the microphone. I hold up one finger and say,

"Messina." I might have yelled it at him. I really have no idea. The teller says something else in Italian through the loudspeaker. I cannot hear him, but his mouth was moving, and I can't read his lips. That's probably due to the fact that my vision is blurry, and he's speaking a foreign language. The digital read out says twenty-six euros. I slide fifty under the glass. He slides me a light blue twenty and two brass coins along with a ticket the size of two 3 x 5 note cards. He points to the train over my right shoulder. I turn to the train and begin limping in its direction as fast as I can.

Chapter Thirty-Four

It was a nice new train car. The train was shiny and white and very aerodynamically streamlined. I sat in the first set of four seats by the door. No one else was in the train. As I walked through the train station there was no one there either. Just then the door closes shut, and the train begins to roll away slowly. I took off my backpack and saw that my hands were badly scratched but not terribly bleeding. Fucking pregnant cat. I pulled some bandages out of my pack to redress my left arm when a man wearing a green hat and coat approaches me. I saw his shoe and followed his black pant leg up to his green coat. He had a little man purse and a computer. He was hovering over me and scowling rather rudely, I thought. Of course, I was a real mess. I'm sure my eyes are red. I'm bleeding. I smell like a fish wagon. I'm soaking wet with sweat and water and God only knows what else. I hand him my ticket, and he eyed me with a look of absolute hatred. He was holding a paper punch and looked carefully at my ticket, holding it close to his face. I think he said something. I pointed at my ear, and I know I yelled at him.

"I just got shot with teargas and can't hear." His head jerked back before regaining his composure. He was now trying to mouth something to me in Italian. I continue pointing to my ears. He held up five fingers and motioned like I was to give him money. I gave him my blue twenty, and he looked pissed. He went through his man bag and then pulled out his wallet. It appears that he doesn't have correct change. I have no idea why I am getting shaken down at this moment, but I just don't care.

It's not like I don't deserve to get ripped off. If some wet fish smelling fucked-up foreigner dude got on my train, I'd sure try and shake him down. The conductor walked away. I still don't care. I retrieved my paper map, and it only shows Palermo. My ears are now ringing. I think they may be starting to work. I hope so anyway. The conductor comes back with my change. He handed it to me and walked away before I even really saw him.

All I want to do is wrap myself in some sort of giant ice pack. My entire body hurts a whole lot. I realize that the only thing I have for pain is a bottle of wine and I have no corkscrew. Nice. I should just shoot myself and end all of my pain. I manage to get to my feet and see that there is no one on my half of the train. I decide to yell as loud as I can to see if my hearing has started to return. I take a deep breath and yell as loud as I can. That was totally inconclusive. There was a sort of ringing in my ears the whole time. I'm not sure if I heard anything or just felt pressure in my ears from my vocal chords. I guess that sort of answers my question.

I take my backpack into the restroom to finish redressing my left arm and cat-scratched hands. I hate fucking cats. Or in this case, I hate cats that have been fucked. I take the bandages away from my arm, and they peel the now dry blood and scabs away from my swollen forearm. I slather ointment on my arm and the back side of my hands. This time I bandage my entire left arm including my hand. It figures that the water in this train is not potable. It's not like I could use a drink right now.

I stumble back through the now speeding train and collapse in my seat. Man does my stomach hurt. You can cross getting shot by a cannon and mauled by a pregnant cat off your 'to do' list now, Jim, I think to myself. I stare out the window of the train looking out over the Mediterranean Sea to my left and the mountains to my right. I close my very heavy eyes. Six hours to Messina will give me time to think.

Chapter Thirty-Five

I opened my eyes just in time to see Angelo della Morte raise his pistol and shoot me in the chest. My eyes pop open and I knocked my backpack onto the floor of the train. The bottle of wine and my pistol land with a thud and then a clank. The Angel of Death was gone, and I was sweating. What a horrible dream. My heart was racing. At that moment, I realized how stressful the last four days had been. I lifted my backpack, and as I raised it to about seat height, I dropped it on purpose. It hit with the same thud and clank.

I could hear again. I was excited and thankful. I was grinning so wide my face hurt. My ears are ringing, but I definitely heard the backpack hit the floor. What a relief. I picked it up and slammed it to the ground once more laughing. This time it hit with a much louder thud and clank. Nice, Jim, you can hear but now you have a broken bottle of wine in your pack. Fortunately, the wine bottle hadn't broken. I looked down at the Rolex that used to belong to Brad and became very sad. I thought about Brad for a moment. I had been asleep, probably more unconscious, for over three hours. I licked my thumb and wiped a little dirt off the crystal watch face. I was thinking of my old friend the whole time.

There was a digital scrolling screen beside the bathroom that indicated the next stop was Capo d'Orlando. As the train slowed to a stop, I could see the blue sign on the station reading Capo d'Orlando. That makes sense, I thought. We were arriving. The train slowed to a stop, and the doors opened. I didn't hear much noise when the doors opened, so it is no wonder I was able to sleep so long. Not being able to hear does have its advantages. The conductor who had fined me five euros stepped through the doors and lit a cigarette. I figured if he had time to smoke, I probably had time to find a bottle opener. I need a drink.

I jumped up and pulled my pack over my right shoulder. That little nap rejuvenated me. I was still slightly limping and in a whole lot of pain, but I felt better than I did when I left Palermo. That might have had something to do with the shooting and gassing and falling. My entire experience in Palermo was somewhat less than pleasurable. I was also beginning to get used to feeling pain every time I moved my body. I had, after all, been in pain for the past few days.

I walked in through a glass door where there was a glass counter in the shape of a horse shoe. It stretched around the room. Along one side was a stand-up counter with a cash register and espresso machine. The counter was full of various pastries and sandwiches. The counter that crosses in front of me has a large cooler with cold drinks and perishable items. Several tables and chairs were in front of the coolers as well as filling the side of the room opposite the register. Along the far wall appeared to be the area where I might find a corkscrew. I walked over to the various hanging items along the wall and began searching for one.

Just then something caught my eye. I saw a reflection in one of the sets of sunglasses. Several men ran through the restaurant. I didn't get a good look at them, but they ran straight out to the platform. I turned just in time to see the train I had just departed rolling away.

"Fuck." I must have said that aloud because at that moment one of the men turned and looked at me. He grabbed the sleeve of the dark haired man who had smashed my car back in Palermo. We made eye contact. Instinctively, I was reaching for my gun, and so was he. I got my pack off my arm and saw the flash of dark blue steel inside my pack. I squatted down just as glass and plastic began raining down on me. They were shooting. People seated at the tables were diving to the floor, flipping tables and chairs as they tumbled to relative safety. I pulled up my pistol and actually saw the red dot on the sight of the front of my gun before squeezing the trigger. I hit the man from the car chase square in the chest. I saw his shirt dent into his sternum through a cloud of blue and black smoke. He dropped on to the concrete platform. His two friends looked down at him and then back at me. I now had the bead of my gun sight on the man to his left. Again, I squeezed off a shot. This one hit the man in his right bicep and he fell over to his side. The impact gave off the look of red dust blowing out of his arm.

He fell back away from the side of the door he was shooting through. The third man began running. He disappeared from my sight. I looked across the bar and saw a policia officer was reaching for his gun and speaking into his radio. I wasn't thinking. I grabbed my backpack and ran for another door leading onto the train platform. I was running back toward the railroad tracks. As I passed through the door, I saw the last of the three men who were shooting at me run around the side of the station. He was in a hurry to leave. He never looked back, he was out of there. I don't know if the policia man was shooting at me or not. I assumed he was and kept running.

I looked over my shoulder and saw the bodies of the two men I had shot bleeding on the train platform; beyond them I saw a train coming toward me on the far set of tracks, and beyond that was a hill that fell down toward the town and waterfront. The train was approaching much faster than the one I had ridden to get here. At first it appeared that I would easily have time to cross in front of it and then get down the hillside before the cop could follow me.

I jumped down the couple of feet to the first set of railroad tracks and stumbled as I cleared the second rail. The train was nearly on top of me. I throw my pack forward and jumped as hard as I can, flinging both my arms and legs forward. The hole that the fast moving train punched in the air was like a slap in the face. The air washed over and engulfed my entire body. It propelled me several feet away from the train on the other side of the tracks and down the hill. For what felt like the six thousandth time, my head smacked the rocky ground first, followed immediately by my face and right arm before I plowed with my chest to a stop in the gravel. It seems every bit of exposed skin on my body is now cut or scraped or generally fucked up somehow.

The train that almost crushed me is a freight train. It is long but blowing past me rapidly. My hearing has gotten much better. I definitely heard that train's horn blasting at me. I saw the look of horror on the engineer's face as he drove the train. He probably looked as terrified as I did as I flew past his windshield. I staggered to my feet and reached for my pack. Throwing it over my shoulders, I grabbed the flowering bush attached to the brick and iron fence behind the train tracks. Of course, it has small thorns. Why is everything about Italy so painful?

I flung myself over the wall and began running down hill and toward a piazza. The train station is in the heart of town. I dashed across the piazza and onto a city street. I ran into the first alley and crossed onto the next block. There were an awful lot of people in the piazza who saw me climb over that wall. I need to hide and I need to hide fast. I continue walking briskly and turn back toward the waterfront when I pass a man rolling up the steel garage door that protects his store. It is a men's clothing shop. Perfect.

I stop and follow the man inside as a policia car goes roaring by me with its sirens blaring. It is headed toward the station. My hearing is getting better, but the ringing is still making things difficult. The deafening blast from the train horn certainly didn't help my hearing problem. My head must have passed less than a foot in front of the horn as I leapt in front of that freight train. I began to chuckle thinking about that poor engineer driving the freight train. I think he might have shit himself instead of me this time. I was now chuckling uncontrollably.

The man working in the store looks at me with a scowl. It is all I can do to keep from laughing in his face. I'm sure most of his customers aren't as dirty and bloody looking as I am. I can't tell if I still smell like fish. I'm pretty sure that I do. He has obviously just returned from lunch and a nap. He has a toothpick in his mouth and isn't in any kind of hurry. I should take up siesta time at The Muskee. I reach into my pants pocket and pull out the wad of euros I have been carrying. The man smiles and begins chuckling along with me. He motions with his hand showing me his entire store.

"Grazie!" I say with a smile. I grab two t-shirts and look around. I then slow down and begin to shop. It seems to me this store is as good a place to hide as anywhere. I put the shirts back on the shelf and walk over to the more formal section of the shop. I think I'll replace my whole wardrobe. I grab a pair of black dress pants and an orange golf shirt. The store owner sets me up with socks and shoes as I try on the pants and the shirt.

I leave my backpack in the dressing room and walk out. As I exit the dressing room two police look into the store at me. I stare frozen and motionless. I am looking right into the cop on the left's eyes. He is studying me. My mind is racing. What do I do? Suddenly that kid who drove me to the airport in Rome flashed through my brain. He said,

"Policia kill man a with a gun. Nobody care. You a dead." I can hear my heart pounding through the ringing in my ears. The store owner says,

"Buona sera." The police say nothing. They simply stare at me. I can now hear sirens racing toward the store. I'm caught.

Just quit, I think to myself. Just get into the back of the squad car and relax. There is nothing left to do but get a lawyer. A police car suddenly screams past the door of the shop. It sped by directly in front of the store and continued down the street. The two police men turn and head in the direction of the sirens. They trot off following the police car.

Apparently, my disguise is working. I look at the store owner who shrugs his shoulders and shows me a pair of black leather shoes. I take the shoes into my cut and bandaged hands and hope I'm starting to look less American. I sit in a chair beside the dressing room glad the guy is there to dress me because I'm so frazzled I can barely move. My nerves are all on high alert, and my stomach is wound up tighter than I have ever felt. The shop owner smiles and takes the shoes from my hands and places them beside my feet. They are too small. He stands and walks into the back room.

I sit frozen, staring at a rack of multicolored pants hanging in front of me. I just killed two more men. I know the dark-haired man is dead. He collapsed when the bullet struck him. He didn't fall backward, and he didn't fall toward me. His lifeless body just dropped where he had been standing. I'm pretty sure the bullet that hit the other guy in the arm went right through his arm and into his chest. The way he was turned, the bullet would have had to have hit his torso. He fell over. He didn't drop like the man from the car chase. It looked more like he got knocked down. There is enough black powder behind those hollow-point bullets to push them through a frozen tree stump back in Wisconsin. I'm sure he has a big hole in his arm. I'm sure he has an even bigger hole in his body. The way those bullets mushroom on impact, he must be dead. Or at least he soon will be.

Wisconsin sure feels far away right now. It feels like I'm on another planet. If I weren't in so much pain, I'd know I was dreaming. I don't like the new reality that has become my life. I just want to go home. I want to eat one of Brad's undercooked burgers and listen to Barnacle Bill and Sam tell the moose story.

The store owner emerged from the back room with another pair of shoes for me to try on. I continued to shop with the help of the store owner and ended up with two whole dress casual outfits and a beach outfit. I also get a black sport coat, underwear, socks, and shoes. I hadn't planned on buying that much, but I was having difficulty functioning. My mind was stuck thinking about the murderer I had become. That put me at five. Mr. stand on my hand with your fancy fucking shoes was number one. The man I shot in the neck with my hunting rifle was number two. The guy in Port Huron was number three. Two more at the train station made five. I was a full blown mass murderer. I was in a daze. How did I get myself into this shit? How was I going to get out of this shit?

I spent a half an hour just nodding and trying to smile. The store owner kept finding and bringing clothes for me to try. I was now completely head-to-toe Italian. From my sunglasses to my loafers, I was a genuine Sicilian Guido. My big gold watch didn't look so out of place anymore. I would have been happy with my purchases had I not just shot two men to death. Had I not seen those two cops, this might have been one of the nicest shopping experiences of my life.

I walked out the front of the store with three large shopping bags and headed for the waterfront. I looked like a rich Italian. I felt like a walking zombie. The total damage was seven hundred and sixty-five euros. I didn't care. The fact that the cop looked right at me and thought I was a local was enough. I made that store owner's week. The sudden sound of a set of sirens caused me to jump into an alley. Maybe I'm not as local as I thought. I better find a place to hide and re-group. I might have a heart attack at any given moment. I need a strong drink, or maybe seventeen.

I walked two more blocks to the waterfront and found a busy street with dozens of boutiques, shops and restaurants lining the sidewalk. Across the street was a concrete walkway and the beach. I walked to my right and headed into the first nice looking hotel I saw.

It was a three-star hotel with a large revolving door. At least I'll have nice accommodations before they arrest me, I thought. I walked to the front desk and asked if the clerk spoke English. He said he did and helped me get a room with a "view good sea." He asked for my passport, and I hesitated. I asked if he would accept my driver's license instead. He said that was fine, and made a photocopy of it and stuck the copy in the mailbox behind my room key.

Why that matters I don't know. If the authorities were looking for me, my driver's license had the same name and photo as my passport so I wasn't sure why I felt better about giving the clerk my license. The bellhop came along and placed my shopping bags on his cart and showed me to my room. Before leaving the desk I changed another two thousand dollars for twelve hundred euros. Man does the exchange rate suck.

Chapter Thirty-Six

It was getting to be early evening as I stepped out onto the tiny balcony at my hotel room overlooking the sea. The sun was setting and my room had come equipped with a bottle opener. As I prepared to remove the cork from my stolen bottle of Nero d'Avola, I had second thoughts. My last stay in a hotel hadn't worked out so well. It didn't work out for me or the hotel itself. The train idea hadn't worked out so well either. Maybe I should figure out a plan for getting the hell off this island and finding a way to Zurich. The last time I stood still for thirty minutes in a hotel, a war broke out in the courtyard.

I have no idea where I am on this island. I know I'm on the north shore of Sicily, three hours from Palermo and probably about the same distance from Messina. I know I can't go back to the train station. I know every cop in town is looking for me. I know every hired Mafia killer in Sicily is converging on this town. Where am I going to go? I look out over the sea. Well, I suppose that's my move. I guess I'll have to take a boat of some kind. I had seen several small wooden fishing boats along the coast. They are all painted light blue and white and red.

That's what I'll use. I'll go buy food and a couple of dry scuba diving bags and steal a boat after it gets dark. Hell, I've hot-wired more boats back home than anyone I know. We did it in high school to our buddies. We'd steal their boats when they weren't home and call them once we had used all their gas. They'd have to come fill it up at the marina, or we would just leave it there. One way or another they had to come and put gas in their boats. Usually their parents were pissed off, but we were just kids messing around. It's not like we tried to sell their boat. We were just too broke to pay for gas. Except for Brad, he always had money from selling pot. He also always had pot. I could use some pot right now.

I put my gun in the pocket of my new black sport coat not wanting to carry my backpack dressed the way I was. I checked my loads and realized I only had four rounds left. I reloaded and headed out to find a grocer, a bread store, a butcher, and a scuba shop. The hotel concierge was very accommodating. He told me to hurry because all of the stores closed at 7:00 p.m. It was 6:15 p.m. when I left the hotel.

I decided to try hiding in plain sight instead of sneaking through the alleys. I strolled casually looking everyone I saw directly in the eyes and nodding. I was one of them. At least I looked like one of the locals. The fact that I looked like they did still didn't make me feel better. I began sweating every time I saw a cop or heard a loud noise. A barking dog in a store doorway made my heart completely stop at one point. It was a little wiener dog in some dress shop I passed. I turned away from every cop I saw. I tried to keep my eyes focused about fifty-to-sixty-yards ahead of me down the street. If I saw a cop or cop car I made a detour.

I didn't feel comfortable at all. Paranoia had taken over my normal thoughts. Everyone seemed to be staring at me. I saw everyone as a cop or mob hit man. Even the women appeared to be reaching into their purses to retrieve guns. I actually thought I saw a woman with an M-16. When I looked again, she was carrying an umbrella. I must get off this island. I'm going to lose it.

I went to the dive shop first and had no trouble getting two dry bags. The food was simple as well. I wish I had a grill. The fresh sea food, and especially the meat in the butcher shop, looked delicious. It seemed as if every cut of meat was rolled or wrapped with onion or basil or rosemary. Each roast had goat cheese or garlic and was tied up ready to be grilled. I wish Brad was still alive to see this. I would send him here to learn how to cook.

When I returned to the hotel, I carefully packed all my new clothes and half of my ammunition in one of the dry bags. I put the food and the other half of my ammo in the other dry bag. If something bad was to happen to me at sea, and I could only get one dry bag, at least my gun would stay loaded. I took one last look around the room and headed down to the lobby.

"Are you leaving senor?" the hotel clerk asked.

"No, I'm going on a night dive," I responded with a large grin as I carried my bags to the door.

"Taxi?" he asked pointing to the white cab out front.

"Grazie," I responded with a nod and smile. The cab dropped me off in front of the marina on the other side of a mountain from my hotel. As I had hoped, all the fishing boats were just sitting on the sandy and rocky shore inside the breakwater of the marina. I walked cautiously over to the fleet and saw no one around. There were a couple of lights on inside a few of the larger boats, but otherwise the harbor looked empty.

I walked over to the group of small wooden fishing boats. They were all about fifteen- to twenty feet long. Some of the larger ones had in-board motors. I just realized the first of many flaws in my plan. How the hell was I going to drag one of these boats across the sand and into the water? I looked for the smallest boat that was closest to the water. The closest small boat was still about three boat lengths from the water and I guessed I would have to drag it at least another boat length into the sea before it would be able to float. Oh that's going to be a real fun task, I thought.

After selecting the boat closest to the water, I tossed my dry bags into the wooden vessel and climbed in after them. There was a wooden bench seat in the back of the boat right in front of the small outboard motor. There also was a small storage cutty in the front which could be used for a seat or platform for standing atop. Two small wooden doors with louvered vents allowed the objects inside the cutty to dry. The doors had a small rusty padlock securing them. I braced myself against the bench seat and kicked through the door on the right. I was surprised that it only took one swift sharp kick.

The door made a loud crack which startled me as I broke through it. I lay low in the boat to see if there might be anyone I hadn't seen while walking over to the boats. I sat silently looking cautiously around the marina to see if there was anyone who might have heard the noise. I saw no one. The night was cooling rapidly, and I was happy to have some extra new clothes. I looked to the sky and saw no stars or even the moon. That didn't bother me at the time. It should make the shore lights easier to see, I thought.

I sat forward and pushed the broken louvers aside and began removing some that hadn't broken all the way through. There was a surprisingly large amount of fishing gear as well as the gas tank and tool box inside. I lifted the gas tank to find it was close to being full. That's great, I thought. I hopped out to steal another tank from one of the other boats. As I jumped over the side of my boat, the toe of my new shoe got caught in the dry bag handle. I plummeted, face first, into the sand before the bag with the bottle of wine hit me in the center of the small of my back. Very smooth, Jim. It's really a shame no one was around to see that. You idiot!

I brushed the sand off my new clothes, and I began searching for a second tank in one of the larger boats. I hoped they would have larger tanks with more gas. After all, I have no idea how far it is to Italy. I don't know if this boat is even seaworthy enough to make it there. I decided right then that I would be wearing a life vest for the entire voyage. I mean I'd much rather get shot in the face or spend the rest of my life in jail, than drown in the sea off the coast of Italy.

I only had to break into one other boat to find the gas tank I needed. I did have to cut through the fuel supply line with a pair of pliers I found in that boat's toolbox. There's going to be a couple of pissed off fishermen on this beach tomorrow. I know I'd be mad as hell if someone cut my fuel line and stole my gas tank. Just add them to the growing list of people looking to find and kill you, Jim. After wrestling the heavy red tank into my boat, I dragged that motherfucker across the sand and into the water. It was a terrible pain in the ass, but the boat wasn't nearly as heavy as it looked. I jerked and heaved and drug it backward until the water was up to my thighs and the boat began to float. That was almost as hard as dragging the dead bodies into the weeds back in Wisconsin.

I was sweating and panting as I jumped in to remove the tarp that was covering the motor. I pulled the tank from my boat out and set it behind the bench seat. Connecting the gas lines together, I found the key hanging conveniently in the cutty beside a very giant spool of fishing line. The spool was the size of a small car tire and hooked up to a little electric winch. I imagined if they hooked one of those really large swordfish I saw in the market today, they would need a bigger winch. Of course, the fish might just drag this little boat and its fisherman all the way to North Africa or Israel or God only knows where.

The motor started on the second pull of the ripcord. I was off like a turtle. It was going to be a long journey. I estimated that this boat had a top end of fifteen- to twenty-miles an hour, probably a lot closer to fifteen. I had to be careful of the anchored boats in the harbor. There was a large dock with many bigger boats tied up to my left. All the smaller boats were moored in a chaotic mess in front of me. As a fellow marina owner, this guy needs to get his shit together. Someone should tell these idiots how to park.

I assume that I am still on the north shore of Sicily. That means I just have to turn right and I should run into Italy at some point. The wind and waves picked up force as I passed between the red and green lights on either side of the entrance to the harbor. I glanced down at my gold watch. It is 9:10 p.m. I wonder how long it takes to get to Italy? I brought enough food for three meals. I brought six liters of water and the bottle of wine, of course. I certainly hope it doesn't take that long. I can't wait to get into that bottle of wine.

As I pass the breakwater I felt the spray of the sea against my right cheek. I quickly realize that isn't sea spray—it's rain. It has begun raining heavily, and the wind and waves are getting large. This could be the beginning of the worst night of my life. That would be par for the course. My clothes quickly become saturated. It is absolutely pouring. It is raining so hard that water is beginning to pool around my new shoes and I'm getting very cold. I may have to start bailing water soon.

"Fuck! Fuck! Fuck You!" I scream at the rain and the clouds while flipping the bird to all the clouds and rain pelting my entire body. This is just my luck.

"Can I just get a little help for once?" I scream to the sky. I spit rain water out of my mouth and focus on navigation. I am concentrating on the shoreline. If I stay about a hundred yards off the coast, I figure I will be okay. I will be soaking wet and pissed off and sore and cold and tired, but otherwise I'll be just fine. I'll follow the coastline all the way to Messina and hopefully I'll be able to see the lights of Italy from there. Or I'll just keep sailing away from the lights of Messina and pray I run into Italy. If the Greeks could make this voyage three thousand years ago, surely I could tonight; on this cold, awful, shitty, rainy, miserable, God-forsaken night.

A loud crash brought my boat to a dead stop and I slammed onto the floor and into the broken doors of the cutty. I had hit something. Everything in the boat had been thrown forward including me. The next wave lifted the boat and smashed it back down on top of whatever I had hit. Water poured into the boat and tipped it onto its side, as another wave picked it up and slammed it onto its other side. This bounced me, and my dry bags, into a pile on the bottom of the boat.

That was when the motor died. There was water everywhere. Had I not already been drenched, I would have been soaked. I was up to my chest in liquid. I don't know if it was rain or sea water or my own urine. That initial hit scared the piss out of me. I could see water pouring in through the cutty. There must be a hole in the bow.

"Shit! Shit! Fuck!" I yelled at the top of my lungs. The frustration I felt at that moment was unimaginable. I grabbed my dry bags and abandoned ship. I was now very cold and wearing ten pounds of soaking wet new clothes. The other half of my new clothes were floating very nicely in their dry bag. I was bobbing on my back in the life vest. I'm happy that I decided to wear the life vest. Between the life vest and the bags I am totally buoyant. The dry bags act like giant bobbers. I am totally cold, but floating quite nicely. The waves and rain really suck. It is taking all of my self control to stay positive at this moment. I really want to shoot myself.

Thankfully, my gun has stayed in my pocket like a miniature three pound anchor. I kick my way up the front of the wave and coast a little on the back side of the wave before another one washes over my face. Then I spit salty water out of my mouth. Then I repeat the process on the next wave. And I repeat. And I repeat. And I repeat…

I kicked backward toward shore until my butt touched the sandy bottom. I stood up and dragged the dry bags onto the beach. It was now raining less severe, but it would still be considered heavy. The rain was now that sort of 'soak you to the bone' shower that would absolutely ruin your afternoon barbecue. I collapsed onto my dry bags trying to catch my breath. I needed to take a break before returning to the boats and starting over. I was freezing. Man is it going to be a long night. I wish I had brought an umbrella. Good thing I bought those sunglasses today. They've come in handy.

As I walked back toward the marina, I began admiring some of the larger boats and began thinking how nice it would be to have a boat with a covered cockpit. I might even find one with a heater. I continued walking to the marina with my bags and talked myself out of stealing a larger vessel. A small wooden fishing boat would be easier to hide. I would just have to find a port with more little fishing boats. There seemed to be little wooden boats all over the coastline and in every town bordering the sea.

Aside from that, a large boat would attract attention and be difficult to tie up without help once I reached Italy. Yeah, I was thinking about stealing a big boat. That sixty-foot yacht right there might be nice. It looked more like a ship really. It also had a waverunner and a kayak. The dingy wasn't much longer than my Jon boat back home. Of course my Jon boat doesn't have two, 150-horsepower outboard motors hanging off the back. That's a very nice tender.

I don't think that will work; plus, the fact that it wouldn't have a full gas tank. It probably has twin diesels. It may burn fifty gallons an hour. It just won't work. It's not practical. I will have to stick with a shitty little wooden boat, and remain cold and wet. I kept slogging along toward the marina in my squishy socks and wet new shoes.

By the time I found extra fuel, and tugged, and heaved, my crappy little boat into the water, it was 11:00 p.m. Fortunately, the rain had subsided. The wind was still gusting, and the sea was still churning, but it wasn't raining anymore. There was a stiff crosswind as I passed the breakwater from the harbor to the sea. I decided to take an immediate left and put more distance between my little boat and the shore. I did not want to hit whatever I had hit earlier.

That is the most dangerous harbor I have ever seen. There was no marker. No bell. No light. Something straight out of the harbor, one hundred yards off shore, just ate my boat. You'd think they might have a sign. Just a sign with an arrow perhaps? Any kind of warning at all. If you go straight, you'll wreck your boat.

It took three cold, wet, and stress filled hours to reach the Straits of Messina. At least it seems to be the Straits of Messina. The sandwich I had eaten had warmed me up a little. The bottle of wine relaxed me and took away some of my many aches and pains. I had changed into my other dry outfit once the rain had stopped for a half an hour. I was still cold, but no longer hypothermic. The hum of the small motor had caused me to doze off more than once. Each time, I was startled awake by some strange splashing, a large wave, or a nightmare about my own death.

When I reached the center of the Straits of Messina, I followed the coast north. I needed to go north to Switzerland anyway. It would be obvious for the authorities to begin searching for me directly across the straits. It was really picturesque staring back at Italy on my left and Sicily on my right. I stared back for five minutes before turning and resuming my task of driving the boat. I can't imagine I'll ever be here again. If the rain hadn't started, this would have been a nice little journey.

I began staring at the Italian coast looking for a town to beach my boat near. I wanted to find one large enough to have a train station, but small enough not to have a large police force. Between the mess in my Palermo hotel, and the mess I left in the train station in Capo d'Orlando, the whole of Europe should be looking for me.

After ten minutes of listening to my outboard motor and staring at Italy, something caught my eye to my left. I didn't have time to turn my head before it was past me. I rotated my head upward straining to see the top of it. It was a freight ship. I never heard or even saw it before it was over me. I mean literally over me. It was like looking up at a ten-story building. Its bow had passed me about ten feet to my left. My boat was now rocking quite violently. I have no idea if they had seen my boat and avoided me, or I just got lucky enough not to be in their way. I don't think they would have stopped to look for me. I don't even know if they would have known they had run over my little boat.

They must be moving very fast because I never saw them in the strait. It had only been about ten minutes since I looked behind my boat. They were already past me and growing smaller as they put more distance between us. Chalk up one more near death experience, Jim. I didn't even want to think about how many near death experiences I had lived through in the past few days. I wasn't even sure what day today was. Right then I decided it was better to be operating on dry land than churned up like some sort of human fish chum by the propellers of a several-hundred-ton freight liner. I turned the engine and pointed the bow of my little boat at the lights of some town along the shore.

Chapter Thirty-Seven

It was five minutes past three a.m. when my boat ran onto the sandy shore of what I thought was Italy. I hope I got my navigation correct. Knowing myself, it was entirely possible I was not where I was supposed to be. I left my wet clothes in the boat and began consolidating everything I had into one dry bag. I gathered what I needed and turned to see that I had landed on the side of a mountain.

I was on a little sliver of beach that appeared to have fallen off the side of a cliff. The city lights were to my left so I headed up to the street ahead of me and followed it into town. The railroad tracks ran right alongside the road, so I would find the station soon enough. It was eerily quiet as I walked along the road. There were no cars or scooters or trains rushing by. The smell of fresh flowers was a nice sort of soothing aromatherapy as I hiked. I could hear the sea lapping against the shore.

I walked for about forty-five minutes and found the train station. I was in a place called Palmi. I couldn't find any maps but Palmi sounded Italian to me. At least I'm in the right country, I think. I found a television that said the first train would be departing at 6:15 a.m. and was going to a place called Lamezia. I looked down at my watch and had two hours. Nothing was open so I tossed my dry bag onto a bench inside the station. Using it as a pillow, I fell asleep almost immediately.

I woke up when I heard some noises inside the station. I looked down at my watch, and it was 6:00 a.m. People were having espressos at the café that was now open. I walked to the ticket counter and was second in line. There was a man in front of me who took his ticket and walked away. Looking at the grumpy man inside the ticket booth I asked,

"Do you speak English?"

"A little," he replied.

"Rome, I need to get to Rome." He typed into his computer and pointed to the digital screen. It said thirty-five euros. I slid fifty euros through the slot and said, "Which track?"

He pointed and held up one finger. "Train a come now," he said with a nod.

"Grazie!" I said with a smile as I took my change and ticket. I walked out to the platform where I could see the train approaching. The man who had just purchased his ticket in front of me was sliding it into some sort of yellow time clock. I grabbed his arm and said, "Scusa, do I need to do that?" He nodded and took my ticket. He shoved it into the machine, which printed the time and date onto my ticket. He handed it back to me and smiled.

"Grazie!" I said smiling back. That must be why that conductor in Palermo fined me five euros. It wasn't a shakedown after all. We both climbed onto the train, and he walked up the car and sat down. I took a set of four seats by the doors. I placed my dry bag up onto the overhead rack and kicked my feet up into the chair that was facing me. I wasn't sure how far I was from Rome, but I guessed this was going to be a long ride. It took about an hour and a half to fly from Rome to Palermo so it had to be some four hundred miles I guessed. I laid my head back and once again dosed off immediately.

This time my nightmare was about Brad and the man I shot in Wisconsin. Once again I woke up sweating with my heart pounding. By now the sun was up and shining brightly into my train car. That figures. It couldn't be beautiful last night when I was at sea, it had to ugly then. Now that I'm in a comfortable air conditioned train, it's sunny and beautiful. My watch said it was 7:00 a.m.

Since my time in the boat, I had been trying to figure out the best way to cross the border into Switzerland. I was pretty sure that the Italian Police would be looking for me. Killing two men in a train station in front of a cop made that a safe bet. It had been two days since I pulled that fire alarm in the hospital. That had to be some sort of crime. The ink on my right hand was fading into a lighter shade of purple. Then there was the obvious list of multiple felonies I had committed in Sicily. I wonder how bad 'grand theft boat' is in this country? Since the first boat sank, I think they can only get me on one count.

The point is the cops are looking for me. I can't simply get on a plane in Rome. I probably can't take a train, as I'm sure they will be checking passports at the border. The policia in riot gear that raided my hotel in Palermo had been bothering me. They were at my hotel way too fast. It had only been an hour or so since I'd crashed my rental car. I went directly to the hotel with just the stop in the drug store. I pulled all those fucking needles out of my arm and took a shower. That's when the war started. How did the riot cops get there so fast? How did the mob guys find my hotel so fast? How the hell did they find me in Capo d'Orlando?

They must have had someone at the train station in Palermo. They had to see me get onto that train. I barely made it onto that train. It makes sense that someone saw me get on the train to Messina. I was a dirty, wet, bloody, fish smelling, deaf tourist at that point. I was walking with a limp and coughing a lot, as I recall. I think I yelled at the ticket agent. That still didn't explain the hotel in Palermo. I just didn't have an answer for the hotel in Palermo.

I remembered the guidebook I had purchased back in Toronto. Maybe it would have a suggestion about smuggling myself into Switzerland. Doesn't every good guidebook tell you the best way to smuggle criminals across the border? I flipped to the map in the front of the book and began looking at the Italian border with Switzerland. The first city that stood out was Macugnaga. I heard that doctor's voice once more.

"They had to dig him out of the ice and he had only been dead for a couple of hours." I'll be eliminating Macugnaga from my list of possible border crossings. I wonder if I can rent another car. I did pay for the insurance on my last rental. I should have been fully covered. I'm sure that the Mercedes was a total loss. That car was destroyed. I mean it was wasted. I don't think I could have done any more damage to that miniature Mercedes if I tried. I'm quite sure the deductible will show up on my next American Express bill. The hell with it! When I get to Rome, I'll just go buy a motorcycle. I'll charge it. Chances are pretty good that I'll be dead or in jail and never have to pay for it anyway. Why not? I'll just ride north and see what happens. I'll figure something out when I get to Northern Italy. Great plan, Jim. I wish I had some booze.

The train I was riding to Rome stopped at every station along the coast. People got on, people got off. Sometimes the train stopped and people got on and off where there was no station at all. You know you live in the middle of nowhere when you don't even have a train station in your town. They just stood next to the tracks and waited for the train on the side of the road. The conductor came through every hour or so to check tickets. The first three or so hours I slept and had nightmares on and off. I'd wake up sweaty with my neck all sore from slouching over. When the train stopped in a town called Sapri, there would be no more sleeping. My entire car was suddenly filled with some sort of school field trip. There were grade school age kids everywhere. They were all seated and well behaved, but they were loud. They were singing and yelling and talking over the backs of the seats.

I figured this to be a good thing. I guessed that the mob wouldn't start shooting in a train car full of kids. At least I hoped no one would start shooting. I would like just one day where no one shot at me. Hell, six or eight hours of no shooting would be nice. The noisy remainder of the trip was kind of pleasant. I managed to sleep through the mayhem of children almost all the way to Rome. When I stepped off the train at the station in Rome, I was feeling refreshed. I had a bit of a stiff neck and a sore shoulder, but compared to the rest of my injuries, I could live with the neck and shoulder ache.

I followed the school kids down the platform toward the exit. I had the strange feeling I was being followed. I glanced over my shoulder frequently but never saw anyone tailing me. I sure had my suspicions. The mob had managed to find me everywhere I had been. I walked right out of the station and climbed into the front seat of the first cab I saw.

"Ducati. Ducati dealership. Okay?" I said and handed the driver twenty euros.

"Okay" he replied, taking the money. We drove for a whole three minutes before he stopped and pointed out his window at the Ducati dealership. I could have walked this far had I known it was so close to the station. It didn't matter. I got out and crossed the street into the dealership.

How cool is this, I thought as I looked over the shiny new motorcycles in the showroom. A man in a white Ducati golf shirt approached me and said, "Bueno sera."

"Bueno sera," I replied. "Do you speak English?" He motioned to another man behind a desk who hurried over to us.

"Do you speak English?"

"Yes, I do."

"Good. I want this motorcycle right here." I pointed to the gorgeous red and white Desmosedici RR standing on its kickstand in front of me.

"You know this is the finest motorcycle in the world? Signore, it is very expensive."

"That's why I'm here, pal. I subscribe to the *Robb Report*," I said handing him my Platinum American Express card and passport.

"I'll be needing full leathers as well. Do you have the factory racing team leathers?"

"Yes, sir, right this way. Will you need boots and a helmet as well?"

"Yes, I will. I expect to be on my way as soon as I can change into my new leathers. I hope you have my size."

"If we do not have your size, signore, I can have others here in one hour."

"Let's hope you have it. I want to be riding north in thirty minutes," I explained with a smile. He grinned and led me to a wall of helmets resting on shelves. It is so nice dealing with a guy who gets it. He knows how much fun I'm about to have when I ride away on my new 1000cc, 200 horsepower street rocket. Just thinking about it makes my smile get larger.

"If you would like to find a helmet that fits, signore, I'll have someone begin the paperwork."

"I'll need some bungee cords to attach my luggage as well."

"We have everything you need, signore. Would you like a bottle of water or a Coke?"

"A bottle of water would be great."

Chapter Thirty-Eight

Exactly forty-two minutes later I was firing up my new motorcycle. It sounded awesome.

"Ciao," I said to the salesman and then snapped the tinted visor on my helmet down. I shook the salesman's bare hand with my leather-gloved hand and nodded. I had taken all my belongings out of the dry bag and transferred them to my backpack. It was secured to the bike just behind my seat. I revved the engine and blasted down the street. This bike rules! They had given me a street map of Rome and a map of Italy as well.

The total bill came to fifty-two-thousand, three-hundred-sixty euros. Yeah, I had to speak with my American Express service representative over the phone from the dealership. They know me pretty well. I'm always buying boats and guns and scooters and hundreds of pounds of airplane fuel on my card. I never pay for plane tickets when I travel. They do have a great rewards program.

The sticker shock was harsh, but what the hell. I don't think I could afford the gas in a Ferrari. Three euros for one liter of gas. I don't know how many liters are in a gallon, but it has to be more than one. I figured I'd take a quick spin around the city and see the Vatican and the Coliseum. I think the best way to see anything is from the back of a ridiculously expensive motorcycle. I would also be able to lose anyone following me. The traffic and narrow streets would make it impossible for anyone to tail me. Or so I thought.

The motorcycle was awesome. It had great throttle response but the rear shock seemed a little stiff on the bumpy streets of Rome. That's to be expected on a racing motorcycle. The fact that I can be going from a standstill to eighty miles per hour in like three seconds or less says a lot about this bike. Weaving through traffic and riding around cars, scooters, and buses just isn't what this bike is designed to do. I need to get out of the city and into the mountains. I'll have to go sight seeing some other time. Right now, I want to ride.

I find my way to a main street and follow it to the next larger street I pass. It appears to be a main road through the city. I follow the busy street riding in the middle of a pack of scooters looking for a gas station. Apparently, 52,000 euros didn't include a full tank of gas. According to the digital screen on the handlebars, I only have a quarter of a tank. I pulled into a gas station and topped off the tank. My bike and leathers are attracting more attention than I'd expected. Because everyone in Italy rides a scooter, they appreciate my motorcycle that costs more than most of their cars. I have to reach into my backpack to get the money to pay. My leathers don't have pockets. I paid the attendant, who seems to like my bike.

"Bella," I say to him as he doesn't stop staring at my bike.

"Perfecto," he says with a smile.

As I start the engine, a large black Mercedes and a Range Rover screech into the parking lot. There he is. Angelo della Morte is riding in the front passenger seat of the car. I twist the throttle and shoot over a curb and some grass, across the sidewalk, onto the busy street. The car I almost hit swerved and honked at me. The highway on-ramp is only a block away. The Angel follows me across the sidewalk and hits the car that I missed. This isn't even going to be a contest, I think to myself.

I reach the ramp and roll the throttle back. The front wheel pulls away from the pavement as I begin to climb the freeway entrance ramp. A motorcycle with two hundred horsepower is awesome! I shift up through the gears and pull to the right of the bus in front of me. Each time I shift gears, the front tire rises about an inch off the ground. I blow past the bus like I am shooting out of a cannon, the pressure of speed wanting to pull me off the back of the motorcycle as I accelerate. It is a good thing the rear suspension is so stiff, or it would seem like I was riding a marshmallow. I have ridden dirt bikes with this much pull, but never a street bike like this. I shift up three times in about two seconds. When I get to the top of the ramp, the entire bike gets airborne.

The landing is much smoother than I would have thought. I immediately have to swerve again to miss a car pulling into traffic. I lean left, and the bike flows into the far left of four lanes, as I continue to accelerate. One more up shift and I'm traveling faster than I ever wanted to go on two wheels.

I have no idea how fast I'm now moving. To say I'm passing cars like they are standing still is a gross understatement. I'm passing cars like they're going backward at eighty miles an hour. I don't dare move. My eyes are locked on the road and traffic in front of me. There are a lot of buses. I am straining to scan the horizon in front of me. As soon as I see the back of a car or bus on the horizon, I have to lean gently to one side or the other. Any sudden movement would send the bike shooting off in another direction. I can feel the pressure of the wind on my entire body.

As I lean the bike glides to the left or to the right. Then I blast past the car or truck I had just been straining to see on the horizon. There is no metaphor I can use to describe the feeling of absolute horror I am experiencing. I know that if anything goes wrong, I will be sliding to a painful, burning, road rash and abrupt death. The engine is screaming. I can't stop, and I dare not slow down. I don't know what the top speed of a Mercedes is, but I'm going to do my very best to outrun them all.

I feel a breeze cutting across the highway. I don't feel it on my skin per se; I feel the pressure of the bike beginning to drift to my left. It is scary. I lean slightly to my right to counteract the breeze but it doesn't seem to be working. Something is pulling my new motorcycle toward my left. The white dashes on the road between lanes have become a solid white line. The speed is too much. The whole bike, with me holding on for dear life, has now blown all the way onto the far edge of the left lane of the highway. I am now riding on the solid yellow lane marker. I can feel pure adrenalin being shot into my blood stream from my adrenal gland. I am almost in the gravelly, trash-and-shredded-tire strewn unused roadbed. There is a car approaching directly in my path. This is insane! Holy shit, I'm going to die. I'm now fighting with all my might to lean into the wind and not fall off of the motorcycle.

The bike responds quickly, and I clear the right side of the car by inches. I'm sure I made the lady in the front passenger seat jump as I tore by her car. I can't believe how fast that car was on top of me. I can't believe the wind could blow me off course. I can't believe this sensation of pure speed. It's too fast; I am moving way too fast.

There are now more cars in front of me. I don't believe my heart could be pounding any harder. I just catch sight of the sign for Highway A1. It looks like the exit is just up ahead and approaching rapidly. I don't dare blink or even move my eyes to look in my mirrors and see if they are still chasing me. If I were to look over my shoulder, by the time I turned back around, I would be right into the trunk of the car on the horizon. I am moving so fast.

I have to slow for the turn. I let off on the throttle and raise my chest to act as a parachute to slow the bike. The front of the bike dives as I let off the gas. I would not even dream of touching the front brake as I don't want to flip the bike. The last thing I need is a bobble at this speed. I step gently on the rear brake lever. The back end of the bike slides out to the left a little and I take my foot off the lever. The back end recovers and is back under me. That was scary. I always thought that those professional motorcycle racers were crazy to hang off of a bike pressing their knee into the ground. Obviously at this point I have lost my mind.

Right at this moment I am literally pulling on the bike as hard as I can, trying to lay it over on its side. I am leaning as far off the bike as I can without letting go with my left hand. My whole butt is off the seat and I am trying to counteract the g-forces pulling against me. My knee might be touching the concrete. I just can't tell. This is one hell of a workout. I now know for a fact just how out of their minds those professional motorcycle racers are.

I can hear the tires of the motorcycle screeching across the pavement as I complete the turn. Once again I begin scanning the horizon for traffic. I shoot past a truck and begin to slow. My hands are beginning to cramp up from the tightness of my grip. I'm quite sure there will be imprints from my hands on the handlebars. I slow to a relaxing 160 km/h. I don't know how fast that is, but it is certainly more manageable. I can begin to breathe and look around. I check both of my mirrors and do not see the car with the Angel of Death any longer.

This is the highway that leads directly north out of Rome straight up to Florence. It was my original plan to go from Florence to Bologna and then ride northeast through the mountain plateau of Tuscany to Milan. Having the Angel of Death following me makes me want to re-think my plan. How the hell did he find me? The traffic thins out as I get further from Rome. I decide to roll the throttle back and accelerate. I have to stay ahead of the Angel. When I reach 210km/h I decide to stay there. This is really fast but not totally insane. At least at 210km/h I have a little time to check my mirrors before I will plow into the back of traffic.

I need to stop and look at my map. I wish I hadn't bought leathers that make me stand out like an anorexic Santa Claus. This red suit and motorcycle can be seen for miles. I might as well be wearing a bull's eye. I should have bought a less conspicuous black bike and black leathers. I blast by another car and smile. This motorcycle is worth every penny. I totally dusted that Mercedes. They had to be pissed off watching me get smaller in the distance and then disappear over the horizon.

I'm now torn in my strategy. Should I stay on the main highway and move as fast as I can to the north, or should I move through the less obvious back roads and hide in the nameless towns of the countryside. The nameless towns would take longer, but I would be harder to find. This is the most direct route to Switzerland. I won't have to decide until I need gas or get to Florence. Keep checking your mirrors, Jim.

I guessed that it was best to keep moving north as fast as possible. It took a little over an hour to get to Florence and another twenty minutes to get to Bologna. I pulled to the side of the freeway for about two minutes just to check my map. I quickly decided to drive straight through Milan and up to some place named Lago Maggiore. On my map, it looked as though the lake crossed into Switzerland. I will go to the lake and find a way across the border when I get there. I didn't think I would need to stop for gas.

I guess I really was being followed at the train station. That wasn't just a creepy feeling. The Angel of Death is quite good. Nothing could possibly surprise me at this point, but seeing him try to run over me at a gas station in Rome was rather unexpected. That guy tracks better than a bloodhound. I really wish these leathers had a place where I could carry my pistol. I wonder how far behind me he is?

Chapter Thirty-Nine

The Angel of Death had been busy while Jim was sailing to Italy. He and the bosses had left Palermo at roughly the same time as Jim. They had gotten word that several men had been arrested or killed at the hotel. The police were now looking for and rounding up anyone associated with the Mafia in Sicily. The police were also looking for an American named James Salvatore.

After landing at the small airfield outside of Rome, Luigi went about setting a trap for the American. He had people watching the airports, the train stations, and the bus stations. He even had people watching the guided tourist busses coming in from Naples. Anyone who saw the American was to follow him and call Luigi. He had gotten photos of Jim off The Muskee's website.

He also guessed that if the American didn't come through Rome, he would have to stop in one of three cities to the north. He would have to go through Livorno on the west coast, or try and run through Florence or Bologna to get north. Luigi sent men to these cities to watch the train stations. As soon as Jim got out of sight on the motorcycle, Luigi was calling his friends to the north. Jim didn't know they had seen him speeding over the horizon on Highway A1. He would be easy to see and track on the red Ducati wearing racing leathers.

"He is on a motorcycle heading north to Florence," Luigi told the underboss on the phone. "We are behind him on the highway."

"Why is he not lying cold in Rome?" the underboss asked.

"He was able to outrun us on a Ducati."

"He could outrun your dumb ass on foot," the underboss hung up on Luigi.

"I am going to kill this fucking guy," Luigi shouted and pounded the dashboard three times with an open hand. "Drive faster," he shouted at his driver. He called his associates in the three cities and told them to get to the highways and watch for the factory racer on the Ducati. They would easily spot Jim and tail him north. Once they spotted him, they would keep in constant contact with each other and begin speeding to rendezvous.

While Luigi and his men were trying to get the exact location of Jim, the bosses were amassing an army in Milan. They had fifteen men including themselves waiting next to four cars. Each man carried two guns and had orders to shoot any American, in any town they were called to. If a man looked anything like an American, he was to be shot. The new bounty on Jim was twenty-five thousand Euros. That's about forty-two thousand dollars. The Mafia hit men couldn't wait to find out what city this American was hiding in. They were busy making wagers on the side about who would kill the American.

Luigi would be dealt with swiftly after the American was dead. Angelo della Morte had become a liability. By letting Jim get away in Rome, he had sealed his fate. The bosses would not give him another chance to mess things up.

Chapter Forty

It was nearly five o'clock when I decided to stop for good. I had been driving around the west side of the lake and decided to stop in a town called Arona. It was picturesque. The Italian Alps plunged down into the steel blue lake. There was a castle across the lake overlooking the whole region. I rode along the lake looking for a bed and breakfast. The caturine hotel where I stayed in Palermo was sort of known. The place appeared in my travel guidebook and on multiple lists of hotels. I wanted something small and not so mainstream. I needed a little place to hide. I needed a little boutique hotel or just a room for rent.

I spent ten minutes riding along the shore of Lago Maggiore before finding the hotel. It was a house. It wasn't a hotel at all. I parked my motorcycle and walked into the house with my backpack. There was an elderly lady who spoke no English but smiled when she greeted me. She indicated the room would cost forty euros for one night and that included breakfast. Perfect, I thought. I paid her and asked if there was a place to hide my motorcycle. She pointed out the back window to the open garage. This really is perfect.

I pulled on my helmet and shoved my gloves into my pack. I headed out the front door. I wanted to hide my bike fast. When I walked out the front door, there was a car parked next to my Ducati. Three men were standing next to it. One was on the phone. I saw them just before they saw me. The man on the phone was the first to see me. He dropped the phone onto the pavement as he shouted and reached into his coat pockets. All three men pulled out guns and each man started shooting and walking toward me.

The visor on my helmet spider-webbed in front of my left eye and something had made a loud popping sound on my helmet. I had been shot. That was at the same time that I fell over backward. I already had my pack in my hand and I felt the steel of my pistol. I didn't waste time pulling it out before I felt the trigger and was shooting. I hit the man closest to me twice before he fell. The first shot hit his left shoulder and turned him sideways. The second shot dropped him.

He was the only man I could see after I fell backward. I was now sitting on the front porch behind a two-foot high wall of wrought iron fencing and bushes covered with red and purple flowers. I couldn't see the other two men, but they were still shooting in my direction. I could tell because those flowers were exploding and showering me with petals. I could also hear a lot of gun fire. The front of the house was being peppered with bullets.

I rolled over twice and hit a small metal chair next to a glass top table. There were other chairs and some large flower pots on the patio as well. The two men continued to shoot through the bushes where they had seen me fall. I quickly crawled to the edge of the bushes. The two men stopped shooting. I could hear the old lady in the house screaming and crying. Sucks to be you, lady. Welcome to my life.

I heard the sound of a shoe scuff the sidewalk over the hedge directly next to me. I could see one man's silhouette through the bushes. I stood up and shot him in his ear. I saw the opposite side of his head blow apart. He dropped behind the bushes. The other man was standing next to him and he started to run away from me. I dropped behind the hedge and continued shooting at him. As he was running he was still shooting in my direction without even looking at me.

My gun was now empty. I took careful aim at the man and pulled the trigger. The gun made a loud click. That was when I realized that I had fired all six shots. The last bad guy now threw his gun as he ran down the narrow back street. He disappeared around a corner. He must be out of bullets as well. I stepped over the body of the first man I had shot and picked up both of his guns. I ran around the Ducati and jumped into the front seat of their car.

As I stepped into their car, I smacked my helmet on the roof. I have never climbed into a small car wearing a motorcycle helmet. When my helmet hit the roof, my half shattered visor popped out of my helmet and fell to pieces. I now had half of a tinted visor covering my right eye. I threw the guns onto the passenger seat and dropped the car into gear. I mashed the gas pedal and the car doors which had been open, now slammed shut. I turned the corner and caught the running man in no time. I drove right into him.

I hit him directly in front of me. As soon as I hit him he fell down and disappeared under the car. I felt the front and rear left side tires bounce over his body right under my seat. He made an awful yelp as he passed beneath the car. I screeched to a stop and got out to look at him. His legs were obviously broken and twisted around on the pavement. He had large gashes on his face and he was crying and clutching at his legs.

I reached in and pulled one of the guns off the front seat and walked directly to him. He was now sobbing and praying and making the sign of the cross while lying in the street.

"How are you tracking me?" I yelled through my helmet. I pointed the gun right into his face and screamed in anger again, "How the fuck did you find me?"

The man was blubbering hysterically and muttering something in Italian. It was obvious he had no idea what I was saying. This guy didn't speak English.

I was torn. I was absolutely pissed off. I wanted to kill him. I was completely enraged. At the same time I had just destroyed this man's body. He was twisted and bleeding and his legs were useless. I couldn't do it. I couldn't shoot that bleeding and crying man lying helplessly in the street. I began running.

People were coming out to see what all the noise was about. I ran back to the front of the house and grabbed my backpack. I had shot a really big hole in the bottom of it. I picked up my revolver. I didn't even realize that I had left it sitting on the ground. I don't remember setting it down. I stuck the gun in my backpack and strapped it to the motorcycle. I pulled my gloves out and shoved them inside my leathers.

I started my bike and raced away. I headed back south. I didn't think it would be good to try and cross the border in this area after that gunfight. Surely the police would begin scouring the area soon. I turned off the road that I had ridden in on and headed west. Maybe I would have to drive into France and then head north into Switzerland. How the hell did they find me? Those guys were right on top of me. I had only stopped for about three minutes before they started shooting. I won't be stopping again.

Chapter Forty-One

The Angel of Death had been on the phone with the man in Arona when all the shooting started. They had just pulled up to the red Ducati in front of a bed and breakfast. Before Luigi had a chance to tell his men to wait for help he heard the shooting. He was still twenty miles away when he heard the gunshots over the phone and then lost contact.

He was furious. The increased bounty on the American meant everyone was out for themselves. No one would be waiting for help to arrive. Every American tourist in Northern Italy better be wearing a bulletproof vest. He wished he had a bulletproof vest. The army of shooters the bosses had amassed meant that there would be bullets flying at anyone on a Ducati motorcycle.

His phone rang. It was his men who had been racing north out of Livorno. They were the second group to arrive in Arona. Police were at the bed and breakfast investigating two bodies in the street. Luigi's men didn't get to look at either of them. The motorcycle was nowhere to be seen and it was difficult to hear over the ambulance sirens. Someone was injured and on their way to the hospital. That was when Luigi saw him.

That was when Luigi saw a man in factory red leathers on
a Ducati RR blow by him exiting on to a freeway headed west.
That fucking American had gotten away again. Luigi shouted
at the driver and pointed at the motorcycle. He told the men
to leave Arona and head west. They were all going to tail Jim.
Luigi dialed the underboss and let him know what was going
on. They would have to start heading west as well.

Chapter Forty-Two

I was racing to get away from Arona. I had no idea of what to do or where I was supposed to go. I couldn't figure out how I was being tracked. I had only stopped for a moment to check my map while driving north. I really didn't drive—I raced north out of Rome. I had been blasting through traffic my whole ride to Arona. How can they keep finding me?

I obviously cannot outrun these guys. I have been running since I arrived and they have caught me each time. I am going to have to hide and evade them. How do you hide on a bright red motorcycle? How do you hide in a red leather suit? I guess I'll either have to go to a Santa Claus convention or change clothes. I know I'm close to Milan. I think they have something to do with fashion there. However, I would be back tracking if I go south to Milan. I'm not going there.

The road I am driving on is beautiful. The Alps rise like a wall to my right all the way through the clouds. That's where I'll hide. Brilliant, Jim. You'll probably be the only American tourist ever killed by a Yeti in Italy. Go hide up in the mountains, you fool. That's probably just what that witness the doctor in Rome told me about thought, the one that had the skiing accident in Macugnaga. The good news is that the Sicilian Mafia probably doesn't have a lot of hunting, camping, skiing, or mountain climbing experience. They don't seem to be the back to nature, granola-munching type of guys. They seem a whole lot more like the "beat you death and shoot you in the face" kind of people.

I need to pull over and look at a map. I need to put on my new sunglasses. It's hard to see with only one eye open because of my broken visor. I hope there isn't a bullet lodged in my brain. They did shoot me in the head after all. I haven't had a chance to look at my helmet. I seem to be feeling all kinds of aches and pains everywhere on my battered body. I think I'd know if I had been shot in the head, or would I?

Before I had any idea where I was, I reached a town called Biella. I decided to find a dark alley to pull into and hide. I had to look at my map. When I stopped, I pulled out my sunglasses case and saw a nice round bullet hole through the right side. I wonder if I shot through my sunglasses, or if they shot through my glasses. Opening the case I noticed that my new sunglasses had become a sunglass. The right lens was shattered inside the case. Perfect. At least it would work. I would wear the sunglasses and keep half of my visor down. That way, at least each eye would have some sort of wind protection. I would look ridiculous, but it should keep the wind out of my eyes.

Looking at my map revealed that the closest town to the border was Monte Cervino. Monte Cervino is located at the end of a box canyon. There is only one road in. It looked like it was less than two miles into Switzerland if I walked due north out of town. I'm sure it looked much easier on the map. Walking two miles through the Alps in September would surely be no joke. The mountains I had seen so far looked more like the mountains of Tennessee than the mountains of Colorado. I guess I haven't yet seen the real Alps. I had always heard that the Alps were larger than the Rocky Mountains. I would soon find out.

I removed my helmet and saw a bullet hole through the left side just above my visor. You are one lucky man, Jim, I thought. Another inch or two and I wouldn't be alive. I shoved my map down the front of my leather jacket. I re-loaded my gun while I had a moment. I strapped my backpack down again and was on my way. Next stop, Monte Cervino.

The ride through the mountains to Monte Cervino was magical. It was by far one of the most beautiful places I have ever laid eyes on. The steep slopes of the Alps rose almost straight up on either side of the road. There was a rushing river right alongside the highway. The grassy and rocky mountains were snowcapped and gorgeous. The farther up into the mountains I got, the larger the mountains got. The Alps are much larger than the Rockies.

The town of Cervino sits at the base of the Matterhorn. To say it is beautiful is like saying steak and lobster tail is good. You have trouble quantifying how good it really is. Cervino is at least as good as steak and lobster. It is amazingly beautiful. It is getting late in the day and the shadow of the mountain has overtaken most of the valley. The late afternoon sun has made the purple rock of the Matterhorn turn pink. I will not be walking into Switzerland. I might just ride my motorcycle right up the mountain. Not really. I could do it with a snowmobile. I could even camp on the mountain. The sheer size and scale of these mountains is daunting. They rise quite a bit higher than the Rocky Mountains in the lower forty-eight states.

The city of Cervino is small, barely spanning six blocks. It's just a little ski village really. The place looks a lot more Swiss than Italian. I drove around town looking for a winter sports outfitter. That took all of two seconds. When I find the one that has what I need, I pull around back and hide the motorcycle. I'll be needing to change out of these leathers as quickly as possible.

I'm feeling drained. I still can't figure out how they are tracking me. I've changed everything I have at least twice. Clothes, hotels, cities, method of transportation, nothing seems to throw these guys off my trail. I haven't stopped moving for a week. They just keep coming. They just keep shooting at me. The shooting is the awful part.

Chapter Forty-Three

I parked the motorcycle one street over in an alley behind the store. I would have parked farther away, but this red suit and the general lack of pedestrian traffic in this town make me stand out. There aren't a lot of tourists riding motorcycles through the Alps this late in September. It looks as though snow might be moving in on the top of the mountains. There were frozen piles of snow on some of the streets in town.

I make my way to the winter sports outfitter and go inside. The nice young man clerking inside looks at me with a smile. This is a nice change of pace. I was growing tired of the scowls, frowns, and gun shots that usually greet me.

"Hello, do you speak English?" I ask.

"Yes, you will find everyone in the border towns speaks at least four languages quite fluently. We tend to get better tips that way," he said.

"What four languages?"

"The most common are English, French, Italian, and German. Most people speak Spanish as well. So really I guess that would be five. However, my Spanish isn't very good. We seem to be getting more Russians too, but they speak broken English pretty well. What can I do for you?"

"I need to go skiing."

"Are you going to join the flare procession tonight?"

"What is that?"

"It costs twenty euros, and you ski without poles holding a red or blue flare in one hand. They do it on the Italian side first, and then everyone rides back to the top and they repeat the procession on the Swiss side. It looks like a giant red and blue snake slithering down the mountain. The whole thing takes about two hours. They are already gathering at the restaurant at the top of the first cable car. It is a big party. You'll have to take two high-speed quads to get up to the first cable car platform. Be careful not to drink too much champagne, it hits you harder at altitude. You don't even want to know about the headache you will have tomorrow."

"Set me up. I wear a size eleven ski boot. I like an intermediate level shaped ski and I weigh one hundred ninety pounds. I'll want to take ski poles up with me, just in case I chicken out. I'm going to need all new clothes, so I'll be over here. Okay?"

"No problem, you better hurry."

This will be perfect. I hated to just ditch my eighty thousand dollar motorcycle, but I could simply drink champagne and slide right on into Switzerland. How cool is that? No hiking, no camping, no hassle. I'll just ride the ski lift up and party on down the other side of the mountain. I'll be needing a lot of champagne.

Let's see what the latest European ski wear looks like. Grey pants with black knee patches and a white coat. Hat, gloves, sweater, and silk long johns complete my look. I'll look just like the rest of the snake party ski people. While I was gathering my new clothes, the salesman came over and asked for my credit card.

"I'll need a card for the rental deposit on the skis and boots. I'll set your boots right here in the dressing room so you won't have to walk all the way back up to the counter in your socks."

"Thanks a lot."

I handed him my card and took the clothes and my pack into the dressing room. It took me several minutes to change out of my leathers and into my new ski clothes. I was sweating by the time I got my shoes back on. I left the leathers out of my backpack. I decided to wear my still wet Italian loafers until I got to the top of the mountain. I really hate stomping around in ski boots. I velcro'd the boot straps together so I could sling them over my shoulder.

"I have your skis and poles finished," said the salesman through the dressing room door. "I'll put them out the back door in the rack. You will need to hurry. It's a long ride up to the top."

"I'll be right out," I replied.

He startled me when he shouted through the door. I was checking my gun and putting the two leftover bullets in my coat pocket. I couldn't believe I only had a total of eight shots left. I had left home with twenty shells. I stuck my gun into my pocket and slung my backpack and ski boots over my shoulder. The ski boots were heavy, and they slammed into the small of my back with a thud.

That hurt much worse than it should have. My entire body ached. As I bent to pick up my motorcycle boots and leathers, my bones made horrible popping and cracking noises. It hurt to bend down. Of course my backpack slid off my shoulder and bounced into my right elbow. I now had to jump and swing my pack back over my shoulder. Again it smacked onto my lower back. I was in rough shape.

I pushed the dressing room door open, and the salesman was speaking to two police officers in the front of the store. The salesman pointed directly at me and shouted,

"Mr. Salvatore, these officers want to talk to you." He turned and rushed toward the front door. The officers began walking toward me so I dropped my boots and my leathers and my backpack fell to the floor with a thud. It was over. I was in a world of shit. They were here to arrest me. I took one big deep breath and exhaled. I wonder what jail in Italy is like? I hope they feed me. I could use a bite to eat.

As the salesman approached the front door, it flew open. The Angel of Death had arrived followed by three men. The Angel plowed over the poor salesman and raised his guns. I don't know if he even saw the police. I don't think he cared. The second police officer turned and looked back just in time to see the smoke and hear the shot.

I was already diving to the floor behind a wooden bench and the many clothes racks between myself and the front of the store. After the first shot I could no longer tell who or where the shooting was coming from. There were a lot of guns firing a lot of lead in my general direction. The wall behind me was splintering, and the wood pieces were raining over me.

Those poor fucking cops had no idea what they were dealing with. I'm sure there isn't much action in this sleepy little resort town. An occasional bar fight, maybe a tourist's lost kid or wallet, a ski accident, whatever. But to have four men burst into a store and just start blasting was clearly not what they had been used to. As I crawled across the floor, I saw the one in front covering his head looking down into the carpet.

I can't blame him. If the gunmen weren't walking toward me shooting, I would be making myself as small as possible on the floor as well. As it was, they were walking toward me shooting. I was getting the fuck out of there!

I was sliding as fast as I could to the door dragging my backpack. I had grabbed my gun the moment I saw the Angel of Death. I slammed against the door and rolled out onto a small wooden deck. There was more gunfire. Not only were there bullets blasting through the door coming from inside the winter sports outfitter, somebody outside was shooting at me as well. I kept rolling—down three steps and into a frozen pile of snow.

Between the snow drift and a parked car I finally had some real cover. I looked in the direction I had heard the shots.

I could see under the parked car a couple of sets of men's shoes. Just then a carload of men with guns sped down the street and screeched to a stop right next to me. I shot the passenger through the door twice before he had the chance to shoot me.

The rear door was opening and someone was shooting back there as well. I put one shot through the back door. I then jumped as hard, high, and fast as I could over a pile of ice at the back corner of the building. As I crested the top of the pile in the air I felt a sharp stabbing pain in my left shoulder blade. I had been shot.

The worst part was that on the other side of the pile of snow was a large drop. The winter sports outfitter is located on a second floor. The first floor was behind the building. The first floor was a drive-in garage. I fell about seven feet and landed on my chest with a splat because the large ice pile had been melting into a shallow puddle in front of the garage door.

I forgot about the sharp pain in my shoulder blade when I hit the pavement. The pain in my chest was much worse. The free fall had knocked the wind out of me. I rolled to my right and struggled to my feet. My left arm seemed to be functional, but it hurt to move it. I got to the triangular shaped wall on the far side of the garage and gasped for air. I was in terrible pain and couldn't breathe.

All the shooting had stopped, and there was a split second of silence. The silence was quickly shattered by car tires screeching to a stop at the top of the ramp to the garage. A small Mercedes like I had rented in Palermo slid to a stop to my right. The driver was struggling to park and get out and aim his gun at me, when I shot.

I was running up the ramp as the car was slowing to a stop. I shot the driver almost point blank in the forehead. I blew the entire top of his head off. His head snapped backward as his body rolled forward onto the ramp. His passenger was struggling to round the back of the car and get his gun pointed at me when I shot him. I put a round through the back of his head. I think I saw his eyeball fly out of the front of his skull.

My only thought was, 'My God, what a horrible way to die.' I didn't stop moving. I jumped over the body of the man who had been driving, and into the front seat of the car. I pulled the shift lever on the column down and stepped on the gas. I lay sideways across the seats as the car sped away. I had absolutely no idea what direction the car was pointing.

I should be passing in front of that other car, with those other guys trying to kill me. I was staring up at the illuminated dome light of the car. Someone had forgotten to close their door. The engine was winding up, and I could feel the car accelerating. I could feel that, and the pain in my shoulder and chest. I was moving rather fast. This certainly is not going to end well, I thought.

I pulled myself up by the steering wheel. I peeked over the dashboard just in time to see the Swiss-looking chalet. I nailed it. I have never been in a car accident that forceful. There was a massive pop at impact. There was shattered glass and more talcum powder everywhere. My chest and left shoulder hit the airbag and I bounced back into the seat. I punched a hole through the dashboard with my gun. How I managed to hold on to it, I can't even imagine.

When my body came to rest, I was lying face down in the street. I was looking back into the headlights of the other car that was now accelerating toward me. I mean right at me. I got to my feet and jumped as high as I could once again. I rolled over in the air when my right knee hit the hood of their car. My back hit the windshield, and the entire car went through the wall of the chalet. The back of my head hit the windshield, and I bit my tongue.

The car smashed completely through the outside wall of what had been a hotel dining room. It came to a dead stop when it hit the inside wall across the dining room. I slid off the side of the hood of the car and onto the carpet. There was blood pouring out of my mouth. It was all I could taste.

"Holy fuck me," I mumbled as I crawled away from the car bleeding from my mouth. I stood and fell immediately onto the staircase leading up and away from the car. My tongue, knee, and shoulder were really hurting. I was in awful pain and trying to spit the taste of blood out of my mouth. I stumbled up the stairs and turned to my right.

The reason I turned to the right was because I ran out of wall. I was leaning against the wall and using it to prop myself up because my right knee was not working. I stopped. I didn't want to be going to my right. That would lead me back toward the people shooting at me. I spun around and limped off in the other direction. I was hoping for another stairwell at the end of the hallway. There wasn't one.

I limped to the end of the hall and heard sirens. The door had a number four on it, and it was not locked. I closed the door behind me and walked to the curtains. The room had a balcony. I walked out and looked over the railing. Normally, it wouldn't have been a long drop. If I hadn't been shot and in simultaneous car wrecks the eight or so feet wouldn't have been a problem. If my knee were in working order, I wouldn't have hesitated. Fortunately, there was another pile of snow off to the side of the chalet.

I sat on the railing and kicked my feet over. I pushed off and dropped right onto the pile of snow. It was the first semi-soft landing I had made. I was relieved. As I was falling I just knew it was going to be solid ice covering a bed of nails or something like that. I was about thirty yards from the first high-speed quad I needed to take into Switzerland. I rolled out of the snow and hobbled over to the ski lift.

The kid working the lift looked at me and my gun and said something in Italian before he got a good look at my condition. I tried to smile, but I had to look sinister. I'm sure my blood covered teeth and crazy eyes scared him. I was in pain. I was a mess. I didn't even know what I was doing. The chair swung around, and the kid working at the lift guided it into the back of my knees. I flopped back and hit the chair with a thud. I was off. The chair accelerated, and I bobbed up into the Alps. I guessed that any second they were going to stop the lift and just leave me stranded on top of the lift. There was no possible way down. I was a good five stories in the air.

The Italian police would probably send some cops up to shoot me several times until my lifeless body fell to the ground. —Unless the Mafia catch and kill me first. They'd call it another skiing accident like the doctor in Rome talked about. The only difference would be that I was outfitted in ski wear.

Chapter Forty-Four

Luigi and the other three hit men had caught Jim in the winding mountain roads not long after he rushed out of Arona. They had hung back and waited patiently while Jim looked over his map and decided on Monte Cervino. When Jim made the turn north into the box canyon with no way out, Luigi called everyone. A car waited at the base of the mountain just in case Jim got past them again.

The instructions from the boss had been to wait for all the hit men to arrive. Luigi wasn't going to wait long. As soon as the first two cars of men showed up, he was going up the mountain. There would be no place to hide. This road only led to one place. It led to Cervino. The Angel of Death would kill the American there. He would do it himself and collect the bounty. If he did that, he would be fine. At least that's what he thought.

It took another ten minutes for more men to arrive. That was all the patience Luigi could muster. He told the other cars to follow him and they raced up the mountain. It didn't take long to spot the motorcycle. This American was an idiot. No one rides a motorcycle into the Alps in late September. They pulled up next to the bike, and Luigi got out.

He leaned down and found the engine still warm. They had made good time up the mountain pass. A man walked by and said,

"Nice bike, isn't it?"

"It belongs to a friend of mine," Luigi said. "He didn't tell me where he would be staying. He's wearing red leathers. Have you seen him?"

"Yes, he went to the ski shop one block over. I couldn't believe someone would be riding up here this time of year. Your friend should be careful to make sure he doesn't get caught in a snow storm." The man said pointing in the direction of the outfitter.

"Right down this street?"

"Yes, it is two doors from the corner."

"Grazie!"

Now The Angel of Death had Jim. He wasn't going to take any chances. He sent the two men in the small Mercedes to the back of the building.

"Stay in your car. Don't let him get away. Wait for me if he comes out the back door." He next sent the other car to the far side of the building.

"Stay in your car. If you see the American, follow him. Do not allow him to see you. He is very clever. He has evaded us since Palermo. He has killed at least seven men. He does not look dangerous, but believe me he is." He told the other three men to check their guns and come with him. He would kill this American as soon as he saw him.

The four left their car and walked down the street. When they got to the door of the ski shop, Luigi led the way. The sight of the American in the back of the store enraged Luigi. He didn't even notice the two police inside the store. He simply started shooting. He saw Jim drop, and he began walking toward him still shooting with both guns.

When he got to the first cop, he removed the cop's cuffs, and handcuffed the police officer. He did the same to the second. The men behind him were still shooting. They saw the American drop, but didn't see where he went. When Luigi reached the back door, one of the other men was already checking the dressing room.

"He ran out this way," Luigi shouted. When he pushed the door open, the men outside were shooting at that side of the building. Luigi was furious. He turned and pointed toward the front door of the store.

"Tell them to stop shooting at the store," he shouted. One of the men ran for the front door. Luigi waited for the shots to stop before heading out. He pushed the door open just in time to see the small Mercedes race down the street with Jim lying across the seats. He waved for the car to pursue him.

Luigi ran down the wooden stairs and saw the two bodies bleeding in the street. As he turned back, he saw the Mercedes with Jim inside plow into the side of the hotel down the alley, then Jim climb out. He watched as the large sedan smashed into Jim and through the wall of the hotel. He was taken back. What just happened? The American got out of the building, killed two men, and destroyed a hotel. He was going to go view the body of the American and then get the hell out of town.

He ran down the street to survey the damage. There was no body. He couldn't believe it. He stepped into the hotel aiming his guns ahead of himself. The old dining room was destroyed. Tables and chairs were overturned and a car stuck against the far wall. A woman stood crying in the entryway to the room. His men were unconscious inside the car. The windshield was bloody and lying across the men in the front seats. The men in the back seats were slouched over moaning.

That was when he saw the blood and heard something upstairs. There was a blood trail leading up the staircase and to the right and left. When he got to the top of the steps, he saw the door down the hall to the left was open. He was aiming his guns in either direction down the hall. Swinging his head back and forth, he approached the open door. When he saw the balcony doors opened and the curtains blowing in, he knew Jim was still alive.

He rushed over to the balcony and saw Jim getting onto the ski lift. He ducked quickly inside and ran down the stairs. The woman who had been crying was now screaming at him. Luigi knocked her down as he rushed out the front door. The other hit men were surveying the damage to the hotel. Luigi rushed to the ski lift, but Jim had already disappeared over the crest of the first mountain.

Luigi pointed his gun at the lift operator and motioned for him to get into a closet with the kid who was helping people climb onto the lift. He shoved a snow shovel up against the door handle and shouted,

"If you make a noise, I will shoot you both through this door." He rushed over and hopped on the next chair headed up the mountain. He could not see Jim, but he would not be far behind.

Chapter Forty-Five

It grew colder as I rode up the lift. The kid at the ski outfitter had said I would need to take two ski lifts and two cable cars to get to the top of the mountain. There is a glacier at the base of the Matterhorn that is open all year for skiing. I could see the blue and red flares from the skiers sliding down the glacier. They looked like a giant red and blue snake slithering down its side.

I was concerned about my tongue. It was still bleeding and I needed some way of stopping it. I pulled open my now red and white coat and ripped the bottom of my shirt. I tore a much larger piece off my shirt than I had intended. Not having a pair of scissors made the task pretty tough. I folded the piece over and shoved it onto my tongue. I wrapped my tongue as much as I could and closed my mouth. I was struggling to breathe through my nose.

I didn't know what I was going to do next. I had no boots, no gloves, and no skis. On top of that, I had lost my backpack. It was left sitting down in the outfitters shop. Luckily, I still had my passport and money in the money belt I had purchased in Toronto. I also still had my wallet and credit cards, my gun, of course. I looked back down the mountain and couldn't see the town from my vantage point. I would have to wait until I got over the next hill. I just knew the lift was going to stop at any moment.

As I crested the next hill I looked back down the mountain. Turning and twisting my body was difficult and painful. My knee was also getting sore. I could now see flashing blue and red lights moving through the town. There seemed to be an awful lot of emergency vehicles for such a small village. I struggled to see if I was being followed on the lift, but could only see back about ten or twelve chairs. It appeared no one was behind me.

Stepping off the lift was a difficult task. Usually, I am wearing skis when I dismount a chair lift. It makes standing and sliding away much easier. This time I had to get running as soon as I got to the dismount area. I wasn't running very well at the moment. My bum knee made me hop and limp, not really run. The wet Italian loafers I was wearing didn't help anything either. When I got away from the lift I removed my coat and flipped it inside out. No sense showing the bloodstains to anyone else, I thought.

It took nearly half an hour to get to the top of the second lift. I face planted in the snow when I got off the second time. It seemed my knee had just decided it didn't want to work anymore. It was painful to bend at all. I couldn't see it through my ski pants, but I knew it was badly swollen. The lift operator helped me up after stopping the lift. He looked at me rather leery. After all, I did have a bloody piece of cloth hanging out of my mouth and no ski equipment.

I limped the last twenty yards up through the snow to the cable car platform. Walking on a glacier at night in wet Italian loafers is difficult with a bum knee. I gimped and hopped and one-legged it, up the steel mesh steps. I was the only person around. I passed the guys running the cable car as I hobbled onto it.

The cable car was probably fifteen feet wide and at least twice as long. The operator walked on behind me sliding the metal gate shut behind him. He closed the doors and locked and latched the safety mechanism allowing the ride to the top to begin. I limped across the car to the back and watched as the car slowly swung away from the platform.

There he was. The Angel of Death came running toward the cable car. I pulled my gun out of my pants pocket and fired. The echo inside the cable car was louder than any shot I had ever heard. I fired at him again. The first shot spider-webbed the window panel. The second shot completely shattered the glass panel at the rear of the car.

The Angel placed one foot on the steel fence and leapt from its top. I couldn't believe it. He jumped off the platform right at the cable car. That was insane. It was at least thirty feet down to the ice below the car. He hit the back of the car where the inside handrail runs around the perimeter of the car. He was dangling off the back of the car struggling to pull himself inside.

"I'm going to kill you," he shouted as he struggled to hold on. I flipped my gun cylinder open and pushed the rod, causing all six spent shell casings to fall to the floor. The cable car was now rocking back and forth and picking up speed. Luigi was struggling to hold on. He had no foothold and would need quite a bit of upper body strength to pull himself inside the car.

"Maybe we will see if the Angelo della Morte can fly," I said as I fumbled about with my coat. I finally got my inside-out pocket open and pulled out the last two bullets I had with me. I slid them into the cylinder and snapped it closed. Luigi had gotten his foot to the bottom of the window sill and was hoisting himself up to his feet as I got to him. As he pulled himself upright he saw that I was directly in front of him pointing my pistol at his chest.

"Fucking American!" he shouted as I squeezed the trigger. Again the pop of the gun echoed around the inside of the cable car. Luigi spit saliva and blood at my face and tried to hang on. I raised the gun to his face and said,

"This is for Brad." I heard the pop as Luigi fell. There was silence and smoke swirling out of the back of the cable car. I stood staring down at the lights of the town far below. I looked out the back of the car hearing the cold mountain air blow for a good thirty seconds before I heard the whimper of the kid operating the doors of the cable car. I limped and turned to face him.

He was obviously distraught. He had just witnessed a murder. He was huddled in the front corner with his hands raised. I tossed the gun to his feet. It bounced once and slid to a stop in front of him. He didn't know what to do. He looked down at the gun and back to me.

"No more," was all I could say. He seemed to understand. I collapsed. We both sat on the floor in what had to be the most awkward silence the world has ever known. We just sat on the floor staring at each other listening to the thin, cold, mountain air blowing around the car. When we reached the top, he opened the doors and ran from the cable car. I struggled to my feet and hobbled around the deck of the restaurant that overlooked both countries. I needed transportation down the mountain into Switzerland.

I limped across the large wooden deck over to the door with the red cross and opened it. Two ski mountain rescue workers were sitting at a table with their radios in front of them.

"Do ou spheak Engish?" I asked with a swollen and bandaged tongue.

"Yes." They both responded.

"I need a wide do Zer-matt." I struggled to sound coherent. "I will pay ou fibe hun-wreb euros." They both paused to look me over. I sounded like a moron. I had a bloody face, wet loafers, and a bloody inside-out ski coat. Not to mention the fact that my tongue was now so swollen it didn't work at all.

"I am Swiss, so I could do it. It will cost me my job. I will need more money."

"I will pay ou ba wrest of ba ye-yas sa-la-wy."

"Do you have that much cash on you?"

"No. I hab ate teen hun-wreb euros."

"I'll take all the money you have. I never want to see you again after we reach the bottom."

"Okay, wet's go," I said with as much of a smile as I could muster. We walked over to a snowmobile, and he asked for the money. I gave him all the euros I had and climbed on the back of the sled.

The ride down the mountain took about ten minutes, and my ears popped twice. He dropped me at the gondola just below the cable car station on the Swiss side of the mountain.

"You are now in Switzerland. Take both gondolas down, and you will be in Zermatt. I suggest you leave on the first train tomorrow. It is called the Glacier Express, and it will take you to Bern at eight o'clock in the morning. Do not miss it."

"I will be bear. Tan koo." He nodded and sped back up the mountain.

Chapter Forty-Six

I managed to get checked into a hotel before I collapsed onto the bed. I laid there for several minutes. It took me a while to run a hot bath and get ice for my knee. Of course, the hotel had no elevator and there were no guest rooms on the first floor. The ice machine was down there as well. I told the attractive blonde woman at the desk I would give her double the room rate if she would bring me a bottle of booze. She brought me three airplane bottles of Jack Daniels and a Pepsi. I thanked her.

How pathetic, I thought. Sixty euros for three little bottles of Jack. She apparently doesn't understand that I have the alcohol tolerance of a five-hundred-pound man. I was a physical wreck. The good news was that the bullet I had taken in the shoulder blade had simply grazed me. It only ripped open the flesh on my back. Ya that's all it did, Jim. It was just a small flesh wound. I soaked in a hot bath with my knee iced and enjoyed my cocktail. I had a warm wet washcloth over my eyes. The first sip of my Jack and Pepsi burned my tongue. It reminded me of the unbelievable journey I had just undertaken.

The burn reminded me of the Everclear that the blonde-haired dude poured into my eyes. I recalled two scooter crashes in Port Huron that crushed my manhood. I felt the pain in my neck from the fist fight on a commercial plane. I thought about the car crash on a Palermo freeway. My arm had some thirty holes from that cactus. My hands were cut from that smelly pregnant cat in my hotel. I probably still smelled like the fish cart I fell through a window to find. I could feel the cold waters of the Mediterranean Sea and see the cargo ship that nearly ran me over. Only three hours ago I had been shot and smashed through a wall after being hit by a car. I then remembered my dead friend. Mostly I sat and thought about my dead friend, Brad.

I woke up a couple of hours later shivering in a cold bathtub. I had fallen asleep in my warm bath. I pulled the plug and stepped out to watch the water drain. I was freezing. I must have been asleep for quite some time. My fingers were pruned up nicely, and the water was cold. I waited outside the tub as long as I could before turning on a hot shower. I stepped back into the pink-tinted, bloody water up to my shin and let the hot water of the shower warm my body. I dried off and left a wake up call for seven o'clock.

The call startled me, and I woke up feeling very stiff. I got dressed and hopped down the stairs one tread at a time. My knee wasn't working at all this morning. I had a train to catch. I was going to Zurich. I struggled to stay awake the whole ride on the Glacier Express. Riding the train through the Swiss Alps was scenic to say the least. Just the ride down out of Zermatt would be worth an overseas plane ticket and *Europass* to see. It was some of the most beautiful, mountainous terrain I had ever seen.

It was three o'clock when I finally entered the building marked *Credit Suisse Group*. I had made it all the way to Zurich. It was an impressive bank. It sits right on the shore of a giant lake surrounded by snowcapped mountains. The entire city is clean and beautiful. I didn't know what to expect from the bank tellers.

I was about to ask someone to give me the contents of an account that had been opened when my parents were infants some sixty-three years ago. Until three days ago, I didn't even know it existed. I walked to the center of the lobby and spoke to the young woman receptionist.

"My name is James Salvatore, and I have an account here."

"Just one moment Mr. Salvatore; I'll call someone to help you."

About a minute later a man in a suit came over to me and introduced himself.

"I am Hans Friedlanden," he said shaking my hand. "What can I do for you, Mr. Salvatore?"

"I have an account here. I received a letter about it and came as soon as I could. I'd like to know the balance in the account, please."

"Right this way, please. We'll go to my office and begin the paperwork. Would you like something to drink?"

"Yes, I would. I'd like a large glass filled with scotch and a bottle of water please."

"We typically don't keep scotch inside this office, but I'm sure we can find a bottle of water."

I followed Hans up the marble stairwell to a glass office overlooking the bank. He asked his secretary to bring me my water, and we sat at his desk.

"Now you said you were notified by post?" he asked.

"Yes, I received a letter at Villa Malfitano in Palermo. It was addressed to my grandfather as he opened the account for me years ago."

"Do you have the letter with you?"

"No, I didn't bring it with me."

"May I see your passport or some form of identification? Obviously, we do not just give money to people who show up and say they have an account with us."

"That's perfectly understandable."

His secretary brought in my bottle of water with a little Credit Suisse Group cocktail napkin. I drank my water and waited patiently while Hans was busy entering information in his computer. He asked me for my social security number, and all my contact information that wasn't already on my passport. He then had his secretary photocopy my passport. I finished my bottle of water by the time he finished.

"The only thing I need from you is the account number, Mr. Salvatore."

"You mean you do not have it?"

"Of course, I have it. In numbered accounts of this age, you simply need the account number. They didn't use passwords or codes back then. The only real form of security we have is the guarded account number. If you do not have the account number, I cannot help you. You may either tell it to me, or you could enter into my computer yourself."

It occurred to me just at that moment. I did know the account number.

"How many numbers are in the account number?" I asked.

"It is typically a twelve-digit number."

"I have two sets of six numbers. I don't recall which set goes first, and which set goes second."

"That's alright; I can try both sets differently."

"Go ahead and try 10-23-41 followed by 08-01-43."

"That is the correct number sequence, Mr. Salvatore. The current balance of your account is 32,643,197.52 euros."

I was in shock. That's worth flying around the world and killing someone over. I figured it had to be a lot of money, but I didn't think it would be fifty million plus dollars. I stared at Hans grinning.

"Would it be possible for me to get a line of credit?" I asked.

"Certainly. Might I suggest we issue you a credit or debit card? That way you do not have to carry any cash. You wouldn't even have to make a withdrawal. If you needed cash, you could simply walk into any bank in the world and ask for a cash advance and hand them your card. You could also call me directly, and I could wire you funds."

Just then Hans' secretary re-entered the room. She whispered something to Hans, and he looked at me rather puzzled. He then asked his secretary something in a language I didn't understand. She was now speaking aloud in what I guessed to be German. Their conversation continued for a moment or two before Hans turned back toward me.

"It seems there is a representative of the Italian government downstairs. He would like to speak to you. He asked for you by name, and he is insisting to see you. He has no jurisdiction in this country, and he is not armed. Would you care to speak to him? I would leave you alone, of course."

"Do you think I should?" I asked.

"I don't see what it could hurt. You are very safe inside this building. This man is not here to harm you. He is an Italian police officer. He is actually the head of the Italian police and has come here from Rome."

"I might need a lawyer or some legal advice."

"Like I said, Mr. Salvatore, he has no authority in this country. You cannot get into trouble as long as you do not cross over the border back into Italy. If it were me, I would see what he has to say. He did travel quite a distance just to speak to you."

"Alright. I'll see him."

"Would you like me to stay in the room with you?"

"No. I don't think that will be necessary."

"I'll send him right in, and I will wait just outside. Call me if you require assistance."

A man in a navy blue uniform entered the room a couple of minutes later. His pants had a red stripe running down the side of each leg. He was clearly a police officer and his jacket was decorated with numerous medals. He smiled and introduced himself.

"I am Santonio Valducci. I am the Comandante Generale of the Carabinieri, the Italian military police forces."

"It is a pleasure to meet you," I said shaking his hand.

He laughed and said,

"You left quite a mess in my country, Mr. Salvatore. It seems you have quite a few enemies in both Sicily and Italy. You left a trail of dead bodies all over the country. I both admire and despise you."

"I understand why you despise me. Why did you come to see me?"

"You don't even realize what you have done. Do you realize what you have done?" he asked. "You are solely responsible for bringing down the largest and most dangerous organized crime family on the planet. Because of you, we were able to capture the boss of bosses. He has been a fugitive for many years. We arrested almost one hundred members of the Mafia. There are about twenty of the most dangerous men in the world lying dead all over Italy. You have managed to destroy the largest, oldest and most powerful Mafia family in Italy. We have been trying to catch you since you left the hospital in Rome. You managed to do, in less than one week, what my government has been trying to do for hundreds of years. You have destroyed the Sicilian Mafia."

"So that's why you are here?"

"No. I came to give you this." I hadn't noticed the blue velvet box he had been holding. He opened it and held it up for me to see.

"This is the *Medaglia al valor civile*. It is the highest honor given to Italian civilians. It has never been given to a non-Italian citizen before. On behalf of the entire Italian government, it is with great pleasure I award it to you. Thank you for your help, Mr. Salvatore. My country is in your debt."

"I don't know what to say. Thanks, I guess."

"I am also to tell you to never return to Italy. If you do, you will be arrested and held accountable for the numerous crimes you committed. You will be brought up on multiple murder charges. I can assure you that you will spend the rest of your life in jail."

"Oh, okay. Is that all?" I asked.

"No. Any property you may have left in Italy is to be seized and sold to cover some of the expenses incurred from your pursuit. Tell me Mr. Salvatore, was the Ducati everything you had hoped it would be?"

"It's worth every euro."

"I will personally be taking it back to Rome to be sold at auction."

"Might I suggest taking it through the mountains and then maybe down the coast."

"I will be taking all weekend to get it back to Rome. I might even call in sick a day or two. May I ask you a couple of questions?"

"Certainly."

"How did you get from Rome to Palermo so quickly?"

"I'm a pilot. I flew."

"How did you get out of the hotel in Palermo? My men said they had you, and then you were gone."

"I fell out of a window behind the hotel. How did you get there so quickly?"

"We listen to phone conversations of known Mafia members. After your fight on the airplane in Rome, every Mafia phone we were tapping in Italy started ringing. They told us right where to find you."

"Amazing."

"That is all I have, Mr. Salvatore. I will be busy doing paperwork for another year because of you. Do not ever come back to Italy."

"Believe me, I won't." I couldn't stop grinning.

We shook hands and he turned and walked out the door. Hans appeared before the door swung shut.

"Is everything okay, Mr. Salvatore?" he asked.

"Everything is just fine, Hans. Everything is just fine. I believe you were telling me about my new credit card."

The End